Praise for *Farewell, I'm Bound to Leave You*

"Funny, brooding, romantic and heroic.... A genuine patience distinguishes Chappell from the vast herd of writers—especially Southern writers—who mistake languid melancholy for lyricism. He writes with a feel for emotional timing that is as acute as his sense of style."

—*Publishers Weekly* (starred review)

"Mr. Chappell...draw[s] upon a rich tale-telling skill to bring into merry remembrance the stories of those who themselves stand soberly at the still point of the turning Earth, where time and the timeless intersect."

—James E. Person, *The Washington Times*

"Enchanted and enchanting.... This book deserves to be read, and taught, and loved."

—Beth Gutcheon, *San Jose Mercury News*

"Chappell writes with a poet's love of language.... [H]e remains an industrious chronicler of the changing South, evoking a nostalgia for the past and a recognition of the present with the same keen-eyed clarity."

—Greg Johnson, *The Atlanta Journal/Constitution*

"Chappell is a true poet, and his language has the authentic frisky lilt of fiddles at a barn dance."

—Robert Taylor, *The Boston Globe*

"Busy, satisfying, and wholesome: Chappell casts a sharp eye upon a very rich landscape and gives us a portrait as poignant as it is clear."

—*Kirkus Reviews*

"Chappell's new novel is pure mountain moonshine: an instant and total intoxication.... *Farewell, I'm Bound to Leave You* bears Chappell's inimitable stamp: irresistible homespun stories well stocked with humor, pathos, poetic lyricism, and compassionate wisdom."

—Susan Lynne Harkins, *The Orlando Sentinel*

"More lyrical than didactic, the stories are burnished by the rich art of Mr. Chappell, one of the South's more gifted writers."

—Bob Trimble, *The Dallas Morning News*

"More I cannot wish you than the opportunity to come under the spell of Chappell's stories.... You'll think you've died and gone to storytelling heaven."

—David Finkle, *The Trenton Times*

"Chappell possesses perhaps the finest ear for Southern speech of any writer since Flannery O'Connor. The ten tales recollected here sing with the sort of music that begs to be read aloud."

—Ron Carter, *The Richmond Times Dispatch*

"Fred Chappell has written a novel specific in its Southernisms but universal in its knowledge of the binding cords of family and language."

—William Porter, *The Arizona Republic* (Phoenix)

"This is a novel of sweetness and profundity, written in a style as eloquent as it is gracious."

—William W. Starr, *The State* (Columbia, South Carolina)

"A book of subtle beauty...filled with intriguing characters and beautiful writing. There's something important happening at every level here, and by the end of the story, Chappell's lucent prose, his wit, his generous view of humanity bring deep satisfaction."

—Anne Barnhill, *The Winston-Salem Journal*

"Dazzling.... This novel explores women and their complexities, yes, and in significant ways, but it is also very much about the power of story: how story not only communicates meaning, but makes meaning and investigates meaning. Pleasure yourself; take time to delight in the inventiveness of our most inventive storyteller."

—Sally Buckner, *The Spectator*

FAREWELL, I'M BOUND TO LEAVE YOU

Books by Fred Chappell

NOVELS

It Is Time, Lord
The Inkling
Dagon
The Gaudy Place
I Am One of You Forever
Brighten the Corner Where You Are

SHORT STORIES

Moments of Light
More Shapes Than One

POETRY

The World Between the Eyes
River
The Man Twice Married to Fire
Bloodfire
Awakening to Music
Wind Mountain
Earthsleep
Driftlake: A Lieder Cycle
Midquest
Castle Tzingal
Source
First and Last Words
Spring Garden: New and Selected Poems

ANTHOLOGIES

The Fred Chappell Reader

ESSAYS

Plow Naked

Fred Chappell

FAREWELL, I'M BOUND TO LEAVE YOU

Picador USA New York

Library of Congress Cataloging-in-Publication Data

Chappell, Fred.
Farewell, I'm bound to leave you / by Fred Chappell.—1st Picador USA ed.
p. cm.
ISBN 0-312-16834-9
I. Title
PS3553.H298F37 1996
813'.54—dc20 96-17313
CIP

First Picador USA Paperback Edition: September 1997

10 9 8 7 6 5 4 3 2 1

In memory of
Gay Wilson Allen

Contents

THE CLOCKS

The wind had got into the clocks and blown the hours awry. It was an unsteady wind, rising to a wail at the eaves and corners of this big brick house of my grandparents, then subsiding to insistent whispers that rustled inside the room. My father and I listened to the wind and tried to talk to each other, but it was difficult and we fell silent for long stretches, forced to attend the wind we feared so much.

The room we sat in my grandmother had always referred to as the front room. There was a small black wood heater before us, its flat top handy for coffeepots and soup pans. We sat, my father and I, before this stove, which now held ashes and cinders and no fire, he in a wicker rocking chair and I in a cane-bottom straight chair. A little table where my grandmother took her frugal and often-solitary meals stood by the west wall. On our right-hand side loomed the door we were not going to open. It entered upon the long dark hall that led to the back bedroom.

In that room my grandmother lay dying while my mother kept watch beside her. A doctor had been called for, but long hours had passed since my father had telephoned, choking back his sorrow and speaking in a strained, hoarse voice. Now and then he would rise to go into the kitchen, where the black tulip telephone sat on the oak cabinet, and dial again. Each time he returned, he looked grimmer.

We were not allowed to be with my grandmother. My mother had given orders. "I want to be alone with her," she said. My father nodded and rubbed his eyes with his wrist. When my mother closed the door and walked down that long dark hall to the bedroom, her footsteps made a sound like she was marching for miles through a great deserted midnight warehouse.

Then my father and I sat in our chairs and stared at the clocks on the mantel behind the wood heater. A tall wooden clock stood in the middle; behind gilt-filigreed glass it showed a dingy face with sharp Roman numerals and suspended below that an ornate gilt pendulum. Beside it sat a fancy clock Uncle Luden had brought from Memphis; it had four brass balls that circled below a small face, and the whole was enclosed in a spotless bell jar. There was a little dull electric clock in a black housing; my father had brought it here last week because he didn't trust the other clocks to keep good time. Then there was a large silver watch encased in a velvet box with its face open to display the hour its owner—my grandfather—had died; it always read 12:12.

Only now it didn't. Now it read 2:03 or 11:00 or 6:15. The wind had got into it and blown the hours awry. Under the bell jar the four brass balls of Uncle Luden's clock turned one way and then another, whirling swiftly or barely moving. The pendulum in the gilt clock was as irregular as a cork bobbing on a fishing line. The wind had got into the electricity also and the hands of that clock pointed where they pleased.

When I told my father what was happening, he said, "Yes, time is getting ready to stop."

"Stop?"

"Yes. For our family at least. Time will have to stop for us and it's hard to think how it can start up again."

"I don't understand," I said.

"If we lose your grandmother, if Annie Barbara Sorrells dies, a world dies with her, and you and I and your mother and little sister will have to begin all over. Our time will be new and hard to keep track of. The time your grandmother knew was a steady time that people could trust. But you can see for yourself that we are losing it."

The clocks read 10:21, 3:35, 9:06, 4:06.

"Yes, I see," I said, "but I still don't understand."

He seemed not to hear. "This is a solid house," he said, "as solid as your grandaddy ever built. But can't you feel it trembling in this awesome wind? If the wind that has come upon us can make this house unsteady, it's no wonder what great damage it can do to time. Time is so flimsy, it is invisible."

"Is grandmother going to die?"

"Your mother thinks so."

"What do you think?"

"I can't bear to think."

"Neither can I," I said, "but what are we going to do?"

"We will watch the clocks at their strange antics," my father said. "We will listen to the wind whisper and weep and tell again those stories of women that your mother and grandmother needed for you to hear. We will hope that this house stays rooted to its earth and is not carried away by the wind into the icy spaces beyond the moon."

"Do you think that can happen?"

"I don't know," he said, "but I am going to hang on here as tight as I can."

It was true. When I looked at his hand on the arm of his rocking chair, his knucklebones shone as white as if his skin had been peeled off them.

THE TRAVELING WOMEN

Jesus Jesus O now Jesus, they said or thought, now show Your sweet face.

O daughter, my grandmother said or thought, the hardest is to know that you must come this way, too, sometime.

We must all of us die, my mother said or thought. I cannot bear it you are going away. After you are gone and if I can learn to live with that, it will be easier for me to die.

Nothing will make it easier, my grandmother said. Not even having you by my side right now makes it easier. No matter how much you are with me, I am still alone.

I'm right here.

Yes, but I'm alone. I can't well say how alone I am. Do you remember once when you climbed up into the big poplar in the back pasture and stayed there all day and didn't come down and nobody knew? And then just about dark you showed up in the yard and looked in through the window at us eating supper. You commenced crying then, tears as big as seed corn, and I heard you and came out and you hugged my waist and said you were crying because you thought none of us remembered you. You said it was like you had passed away to another world and was not one of us any longer.

I had forgotten, my mother said or thought, but now when you remind me, I remember. You were still wearing your apron and I pressed my face against the pocket and there was a paring knife in it and a ribbon of apple peel and I stood back and began pulling the apple peel out like I was untying a present and forgot all my sorrow.

Did you, now? I don't remember that part.

There was always something in your pocket. A spool of white thread with the needle slipped down the side. A little ball of string or sea-grass twine. A rusty spoon. Daddy's old hawk-bill knife that wouldn't cut butter, gummed up with tobacco tar. A thimble, that old dented tin thimble you said you hoped you'd lose and never did. Your first pair of eyeglasses that wouldn't see good anymore. Or the black steel case for them, and you'd left the glasses somewhere. One time there was a little mouse in your pocket. It was dead.

Yes. I remember. I took it away from Quadrille. I couldn't stand to watch that cat playing with it and then I forgot it was there. I got busy doing something else, I reckon.

When I ran up to hug you, I put my face on that mouse. It was a frightful thing to me.

Yes, but you didn't cry that time.

"I put my face, I guess, to everything you had in your pocket when I was a little girl," my mother said.

"O Cora," my grandmother said.

Mama, I'm right here, my mother thought or said.

O Cora, you were the skinniest little girl. I speculated sometimes when I saw you hoeing in the fields that it would be a miracle if you ever grew up. Rowe was as spindly as you and just as pale. He was the one I lost. That was before you were born.

I know, Mama.

He was the sweetest child.

You always said.

His eyes were so big in his face, you know, and they looked up at me lonesome and watery. He was looking at me that way when I held him in my arms and he breathed his last.

You told us about that.

It was the gentlest thing. He didn't shiver or pee on me. He just closed his eyes and went away. I couldn't even feel sorry for him; I felt sorry for me. I said to myself, Annie Barbara Sorrells, you have lost the most precious thing that you will ever have. That was August 8, 1911.

That was the day Joe Robert was born. What did he die of?

"Joe Robert?" my grandmother said. "Is Joe Robert all right?"

"Hush, Mama. Lie back," my mother said. "Joe Robert is all right. He's in the front room with Jess." I meant Rowe—what did he die of?

It was nothing they ever gave a name to. These days now the doctors would know what it was and I reckon might could cure him. But that was a long-ago time and we lived over in Hardison County, where the medicine was mostly homemade. Horses and cows and sheep got better doctoring than people did. If it was a different place, Rowe would be alive with us today.

I'd like that. I'd like to have another brother.

He might could have kept Luden in line a little bit. He would be three years older than Luden and might set an example for him.

Luden's all right. He's coming to see you, Mama. He's on his way, flying here from California. Luden's a good son to you.

I wish he'd quit the whiskey.

I know you do, Mama.

Many's the hour I've spent on my knees by the bedside praying for him to leave the whiskey alone.

He doesn't drink as much anymore.

And the trashy women, too. I wish he'd leave off running with them.

He's married again now, Mama. I don't think he fools around. I hear Bessie keeps him on a tight rein.

I would say, Jesus, please help Luden to quit his awful thirst. Send the spirit of Rowe to help him quieten. Send the spirit of his older brother that You took away to succor my son Luden in his troubles. O please . . .

"O Jesus."

"Hush now, Mama. Lie back. It's all right. It will be time to take some more medicine directly."

Cora, the medicine ain't no good anymore. I'm past all help of that kind now. I'm getting ready to see the face of my Maker and to be joined again with Rowe and my mother and daddy and Aunt Tildy and Uncle Lige Goforth and many another soul that belonged to the times of my youth. I'm getting ready to meet . . .

"Jesus."

"Lie back now. Everything's all right. Soon you can take some medicine and the doctor will be here."

I don't put much stock in doctors. Do you remember Holme Barcroft? He said he was the kind of doctor who couldn't even pull a splinter out of your thumb. I really am a doctor, he said, but not a medical doctor. It's just some initials a university tacked onto my name. What does this university think you're a doctor of? I asked him. Music, he said. Is that right? I told him, I hadn't heard that music was sick. He smiled when I said that and it looked like his blue eyes got even bluer. I never saw blue eyes like that again. Well, maybe it's not sick, but then I'm not through doctoring it yet, either, he said, and it pleasured me that he would be so nimble to come back with a remark after I'd said the sassiest thing to him I knew how. Holme Barcroft, there was never another man like him.

I remember Dr. Barcroft, Mama. The second time he came I was eight years old.

He was just smitten with music the way Samantha Barefoot always was. It made him a sweet man, the music did, the way it made Cousin Sam sweet, too. Music will get in your soul, I believe, and dampen down the rage and sorrow to be found there. Some people love horses the way she loves the fiddle and the bow.

I used to have a saddle mare. You-all called her Bella, but I called her Princess. Princess was her secret name. I rode her to school.

We always had a saddle horse or two in those days. That was the only way sometimes to get where you needed to go. People still have saddle horses, I reckon, but you don't see buggies anymore.

I used to simply worship that horse. Time and again I thought Princess was the only friend I had in the world.

Nowadays they have cars and folks tear around in them day and night like they were mad at somebody.

One time, though, I was riding her to school on a warm morning in April and Princess ran away with me. I don't know what got into her. She rared around in a circle and took off back down the road where we came from. I pulled and tugged to no avail. I don't know I've ever been so scared for my own life, and it was all I could do to hang on. All I could think about was Dessie Hawkins and how her horse had run away and pitched her against a fence post and broke her back.

It seems like the world has gone wild sometimes with cars and airplanes. All this killing, too. People killing one another all the time.

And I would have been hurt bad and maybe crippled if it

wasn't for Tim Dollard. He was coming up the road toward me and he just turned that dapple gray of his crossways in the road and Princess had to stop. It took a long time to gentle her down and then we turned and trotted off to school as docile as you please. And I was never afraid of her, not even after that time. I still trusted her and she never ran away with me again. Do you remember what Uncle Dave said one time? You and that horse, he said, you're a matched pair. There couldn't anybody have said anything that would please me more.

They say Uncle Dave Gudger killed a man one time, but it was never proved on him, because he went away. Or something happened. Maybe he died, too, because his wife, Chancy, took to wearing his old hat as black as sin. Her mind went weak at that time and was never strong again. Cousin Samantha I sent to play her music, but what good it did, I never heard. I always hated the sight of that old black hat on Aunt Chancy's head. They say when she died they found a man's cutoff private thing tangled up in her hair, hidden underneath that black hat. I don't know as I believed that talk.

I remember Uncle Dave, my mother said or thought. He frightened me when I was little, his face looked so mean. The way it was when he'd hold a match to light his pipe.

"Light."

"What do you mean, Mama? Do you want the light turned on?"

"Light" in the window there, what was that flash? Is there a storm? But it wasn't like lightning, not sharp. It was a great and sudden glow, all golden, and it washed against the sky like the surge of a flood on the river.

"I don't know what you want, Mama. I don't know what you mean."

What time of day is it? What time of year? I thought I was lying here in the dark of the night with the silence all around me except for my daughter, Cora, doing the best she can to go at least partway with me up this steep and stony path that I am traveling lying down. My body is lying down, but my soul is trying to make it up this rugged Ember Mountain path like the dry bed of a stream with all its rocks bare and jagged in the parched sunlight. She is doing the best she can, Cora is, but there's nothing anybody can do. This lonesome road, you've got to travel it all by yourself. That's what all the preachers said, every last one of them, but things like that don't mean much when they say them. It's only when it happens to you at last that you understand what they were talking about. But how would they know? They have to do it the same way as me and everybody else and I expect they're just as surprised and scared as anybody to find their words have come true.

"Do you want me to turn the light on? I thought it was hurting your eyes."

"No." No light now, the golden light is gone. But there is a wind beyond the window there; I can hear it singing. I've heard it singing sad and fierce time out of mind. My husband, Frank, built this house and many another and pitched them all stout enough to stand till doomsday, but this one has got turned crossways to the wind and there are winter days and days in the springtime and autumn when it hums and moans like a sorrowing widow and won't let up. Sometimes it will get in your mind so sad, you think there's not a smile of hope left anywhere in the world. It's a good stout house, right enough, but the wind that swarms it comes from a place where there are not any human people and the house that a man has built cannot keep the sorrowful feelings out of that sound, him being only a human man.

"All right. I didn't think you really wanted it on. It shines right down in your eyes." This old fixture, just a bare bulb hanging here in the room. It's got a gilt chain that's kind of pretty with the wire twisted through it, but it makes a harsh and ugly light and shines right down in Mama's eyes. I can hardly bear to look at her with that light on. It makes her look like a dead person, with her eyes so dark and sunken now and her cheekbones sticking out and her skin all blotched like a potato peel. Her hair has gone dull, too. I wish I could think of a way to wash it for her. That part maybe hurts the most. Her hair was her glory, dark russet hair that reached down her back to her waist. She always took special care of it, with a balm she knew about and her tortoiseshell combs that held it in place. On a farm, she told me, a woman's hands and face are going to turn rough, but she can still keep her hair pretty if she will look after it and take thought.

There are many things happening outside the window of this room. There is light and music and sobbing and spirits. But I don't know if this dry, rocky creek bed goes all the way up to the window.

I always loved to be here in the room when she was fixing her hair. The way she kept it long and brushed it slow and careful entranced me. One hundred strokes. It was thick and heavy and sweet-smelling when she oiled it with that balm. I could pick it up with my right hand and pour it into my left, pour it back and forth like spilling coins or water. One hundred strokes. I wanted her to show me how, but we fought and struggled with my own hair and it didn't do. She told me at last it was too fine and dry, that I'd have to wear short hair, and I felt like it was a lifetime sentence against me to know I'd never have the hair my mama had.

Trudging up this cruel road with my head bowed down, I see that some of the rocks are silvery and some are burning blue and some are red. There's no water anywhere. I think there's a kind of sky overhead that never has rained since the world began. Yet there are shadows just out of the edge of my eyesight and in these shadows there are spirits—I don't know what kind. Maybe they are some I used to know when I was young. Maybe they are stranger-spirits just as lost as I am. I don't know if I'll meet them to speak to or even see them, but I am not afraid. It's just that the way along is so hot and dry and stony.

Sometimes I would sneak in alone and take the combs out of that box that brother Luden sent and try to put them in my hair. Mama did that so neatly, like slipping a knife into gingerbread. Inserting the combs. But out of my fine dry hair they fell to the floor and clattered. Then I would stare at myself for long and long in the mirror. If I didn't have my mother's hair, would I have any of her looks at all? I thought she was a proud beauty with her cheekbones and her firm chin and the way she carried herself so straight with her shoulders back. As straight as the red line down a sheet of Blue Horse paper. And the way she had of looking at you direct but gentle, too. Never mean, but not easy on anybody, either. I never had good looks, but she taught me not to mind.

Now it does seem like the shadows are crowding to the edge of this path. But they are not cool shadows. They are as hot as the light, or hotter. And nowhere anywhere is there any "water."

"All right. We'll need to raise you up a little so you'll be able to drink. Can you do that? Can you raise your head and I'll put my arm around your shoulder? Here's the glass. Can you see it? Now there. Just a little sip at first. Take your time."

It is not shadows, but a rain cloud. It has started to shower a little in this hot place. The refreshment is so good, I can't tell you. It makes the way easier, a lot easier.

"Easy now. Take your time."

Only a gentle shower is all that is needed here. If it was to rain too hard, it would come a sudden flood in this creek bed. The climb is so steep, the waters would rush down angry and I would sweep away. O Cora, that's enough.

"Is that enough water? Have you had enough to drink?"

"Yes."

"All right. I'll get my arm out from under you and you lie back now. Here, let me set this glass down."

I am wanting to say thank you, but now I feel more tired than ever before. I can tell, too, that this rocky climb before me is going to get worse. Still, I need to say thanks.

"Is there something else you want? What is it, Mama? I can't hear what you're saying."

"Mmm." There. I've said it now, I think.

"That's all right. You don't have to say anything. It won't be long before the doctor is here."

There are spirits in these shadows, but none of them is Jesus. I will know Jesus not in shadow but in light. A light different from the burning kind and not golden, either, not that. Different from any other kind of light, sweeter and deeper.

"Let me smooth out your pillow a little for you."

It seems cooler than it was before. In 1900 they told me it was not the twentieth century yet. That it wouldn't start till 1901. One day in July 1900 I went down by Sugarbush Branch to sit in the shade and cool off and I made up a song about it. *There's a new age a-coming* was how it started and there were a lot of different verses I made up on the spot. Now whenever I feel that same shade of cool I felt that day by Sugarbush, some of the lines of my song come back into my head. I never sang that song to anybody. I thought now and then I would sing it for Holme Barcroft the first time he came here and maybe even let him take down the words the way he was always doing with the old songs, but I didn't. I couldn't figure a way to get him off by himself with me without everybody knowing about it and believing the worst of me. I was never one to sing my songs in front of people, my own songs I made, and I was never one to go off alone with a man, however much I felt about him. It grieved me to give up my music, but Daddy wouldn't have it. *I hung up my fiddle and my bow.* There. That's the line of an old song. The older the song, the more heart's truth in it—that's the way I always felt.

She is resting some easier now. That little sip of water did her good. But I wish we were somewhere else. I wish she would have agreed to go over to Bracecoro to the county hospital. But nothing will suit her except to die here in her own house in her own bed.

My voice was sweet and true but had no ring. When we were girls together, always singing, Samantha Barefoot would make me take the harmony part. Because they'll never hear a note of the melody if I'm braying the harmony as loud as a gall-sore mule, she said. It was the truth she had a voice you could hear a mountaintop away. She had that old-timey drone that would cut through the air like throwing an ax. It's the old Irish way of singing, somebody told me. We sounded silky together, though, and might have made something of our music. Because I was a better fiddler than her, and everybody knew. People told him, Ward Purgason, you ought to let that gal follow her music, but my daddy said no ever and ever. It would make me flighty, he said, and turn my head. It grieved me to put away my bow and hang my fiddle on the wall and it made Samantha sad, too, because she'd brooded fancy plans for us to be doing big in the music world. Years later when Cora heard about it, she got mad at her grandaddy, and him dead by then longer than I remember.

Die. I hate that word. I wish it had never come to my mind. But it is the truth. Mama is lying down to die. Right here is where she wants to die, and as soon as she can. So it must be mighty hard with her, because she wouldn't do a selfish thing like that unless she simply could not help herself.

Sam has done big things in the music. She is on that radio show—the "Grand Ole Opry," they call it—a lot of times. But I won't have it on in this house—it would make me too sad and dissatisfied to hear her. And I would still get mad at my daddy. After all these years. You'd think a body would get over it. I've got over harder things. Like losing Rowe and Frank, my husband, and our good house burning down and Johnson Gibbs getting killed in the war. Things lots harder and lots of them. But they were part of my life, the life that was to come to me. The music was my other life, the one I never had and never would have once my daddy said no. So I was always bitter about it and held it against him, and that's a sin against me, and I wish it was the worst one.

I reckon Mama has done selfish things in her life, I reckon everybody has, but I never found out one she'd done. I have always thought she was all the world, that the sun and moon and stars all turned about her. Now that she has decided to leave me, it will be an empty sky above my head. I know I can go on, Joe Robert will stand by me, and I've got Jess and Mitzi, but it won't be the same. I'll be a stranger inside my own life because Mama was a chief part of it. I'll be a little bit of a stranger to myself and there will be some things I will have to learn to do different, to think about in different fashion.

I guess that on this dark and perilous way I'm treading I will meet all my sins and have to face them one by one. It won't do any good to say I did the best I could, because there's nobody to listen and it might not be true. There were times I could have done better, I will admit. But mostly I tried my best, I do believe. And when I did wrong to others, it was mainly because I didn't know better.

She is no saint, I will acknowledge. When Mama makes up her mind about something, there she stays. Doesn't matter what you say or do, doesn't matter sometimes what the facts may be. She doesn't give. Got that from her daddy, I expect. I've always heard he was such a stern person. It was John Howard Early told me that the first time and he said it in such an odd way, it stuck in my mind. He didn't say stern; he said sternd, with a *d* on the end of it. Your grandaddy was a sternd old man, he told me. There's a dark vein of willfulness that runs in your family. But Grandaddy didn't seem that way to me. He died when I was five, so mostly I only imagined him. I pictured him as being sweet and kind and gentle and not smelling of snuff and cow shit and stale whiskey breath like Uncle Burleson that lived to be ninety-three. In my mind, my grandaddy was anything but sternd, yet they tell me when he was set upon a thing, he always got it to go his way.

The window has lit up again and I can see the outside plain. I can't hardly see the inside of the room at all, I can't see Cora good, but I can see the outside. It is full daylight now and the light is the light of a fine May morning you would never mistake. One morning one morning one morning in May. There again. That's another line from an old song and it goes perfectly with what is in the window, the blue sky with one fluffy cloud and rounded green hills with perfect trees stuck here and there about. Of course it is not the real outside. The window is showing me some country where I've never been, the kind of country you see in your mind when you're a child and read in a storybook or if someone tells you a happy tale about when they were children. It's not real to walk in, but it's a real place. I don't know if my soul will be traveling in a place like that or not. The only thing before me now is this scorching creek bed. But the window shows me this other place, so maybe there is a chance.

John Howard Early, he was a case. He would stand right in your face to talk to you and if you backed up a little, not being able to help yourself, he would just move in on you some more. And looked as hard and deep into your eyes as any creditor presenting a long-due bill. I don't know that he meant anything by it. That was just a way he had. Probably he couldn't see real well. But it made an impression on you and you'd remember something he'd say where you'd forget it if it was anybody else. Looked so grave and solemn, you wouldn't believe he'd think of mischief. That's why he got away with so much. Not like Joe Robert. He's such pure mischief, you can see it coming a mile.

One morning one morning one morning in May, I met a fair maiden a-walking my way.

That's why you don't mind; that's what makes him so irresistible to my heart. Because I know he's nothing but mischief and I see it coming and I know it's harmless because it's so open. It's an education to watch people meet Joe Robert for the first time. They become all attention. They know something is coming, but they don't know what.

Good morning good morning good morning my dear, Where are you going so sweet and so fair?

That man, I tell you I don't know. Twenty years married and I still don't know.

It wasn't only that Holme Barcroft took songs from us here in the mountains to put into books and share with the wide world. He taught us songs, too. He taught me a little song in the French language I can't remember now. Not a word. And it had the liltingest tune to it, as light as a sparrow's feather, but I don't remember. One I remember well, all too well, is Oh Shenandoah, I love your daughter. That was the one Frawley Harper brought back to our hills from his travels as a handsome sailor to bewitch all hearts, even mine a little bit, I will admit, though I was married to Frank by then, held with bonds of love as strong as iron.

It nigh wears you out, though. Every day with Joe Robert being so new and fresh, it's almost like you have to wake up with a new man each time and wonder what in the world is going to happen. I was crazy about him from the start, but Mama was afraid at first, thinking maybe he wasn't quite right in his mind. Then she decided he was only an overgrown boy of a special sort. I'll say it, though, we'd never have been married except for Mama. You have to be patient with men and wait for them to settle down, she told me more than once. That's the way she did with Joe Robert and the hired help and maybe even Daddy, too. With Luden, she waited and waited, but it never happened. It might yet, I keep telling her that, but she only smiles gray and sad.

O Shenandoah I love your daughter, All away, you rolling river, I have come this day to greet her, Away, I'm bound away, Across the wide Missouri.

But I don't know that she ever had a closer friend, man or woman, than her son-in-law. They will go on and on at each other, or pretend to. He's always trying to get her goat, but it usually works the other way. My husband is a strong, brave man, I expect, but this will break his heart, he admires my mother so much.

When I hear that song in my head, I hear the high silvery voice of Holme Barcroft. He had an accent that was simply winning. It sounded more English than Scotch to me, but how could I know? He teased me. Never never ever tell a Scotsman he sounds English, he said. Don't you know there's a history of blood between the nations? I could have told him all about Mary, Queen of Scots and the Battle of Culloden and the Bonny Prince. I told those stories many a time to the pupils I taught on Long Branch. But in the presence of Holme Barcroft I only smiled and shook my head. It was my wish that he would tell me the stories in his own tongue.

There have been some sharp times and some sharp talk, too. Some of Joe Robert's rusties could have got mean if he was a different sort. Mama has never forgotten how Joe Robert and Johnson Gibbs switched pullet eggs for her fancy chocolate candies and made her so embarrassed in front of her lady friends. She has never ceased to laugh about it, either. Sometimes a look will come on her face that shows she is trying to hold back a giggle and I'll know she has remembered those pullet eggs wrapped up in colorful foil and put back into the candy box where the boys had eaten the real chocolates. That goes to show how close they are, that she'll still laugh about that fifteen years later.

I had better not be thinking now about Frawley Harper and Holme Barcroft. I had better be getting ready to meet my Lord. And don't say Scotch, he told me. Say Scots. Say Holme Barcroft is a Scotsman, not Scotch. Scotch is something to drink.

No one could count the nights they've sat at the table after supper and argued religion. Not that Joe Robert is against it—I don't believe he is. Only that he can't resist teasing anybody who seems dead certain about anything. I believe he only takes personal things seriously. Big ideas like religion and politics and science he only likes to play with.

Oh Shenandoah. The path is steep and crooked and rocky and burning and it hurts my knees and the palms of my hands to be crawling along. In the burning silver rocks there is the sound of one kind of wind and in the blue rocks the sound of another and in the red another. In the silvery rocks the wind sound is the sound of women weeping. All the women who ever lost their men are crying inside that sound. In the blue rocks it is the sound of children who have lost their mothers.

In the red rocks the wind sound is hottest of all. The wind in the red rocks is flame and it is the sighs and moans of everybody who lost their way in life. It seems like the window is farther away than ever now.

But I don't know what we'll do with Mama gone. Can't bear to think. I will be distraught. Joe Robert will be heartsore for I can't guess how long. And Jess. And Mitzi. Jess, I think, will understand, but Mitzi . . . I don't know. She's ten. I can't remember what it means to you at ten. I know you never forget, but I can't remember how you feel.

Now the window is a mirror. Dark and peeling. It shows me this room with me lying in the bed and Cora sitting by, but that's all I can tell, because I don't look like a woman lying down and Cora looks like she's wearing a dark brown robe with a hood over her head. She looks like she is praying, but I am the one praying, yet I don't look like a person, but like something drifting on a river. I am being carried away from Cora praying by me.

Don't leave me yet, they thought or said together at the same time. There must be time left for us to say things we never got said and to make sure we know the lights and shadows in each other. It is cruel how the power of time is a power only to separate. We were mother and daughter before time came upon us. We only want to be together a little while longer. There are many things between us we still don't understand.

Mama, I can't go much farther. I have to stay here with Joe Robert and Mitzi and Jess. The way for me turns back to this world now.

O Cora, don't try to go this pathway of rock and ember. It is too soon for you. I would not be struggling away if I could help it. I would rest in the bosom of my family and spread on the table a fresh, clean tablecloth and lay out shining plates and in the morning sweep the dust off the steps and the cobwebs out of the ceiling corners of the porch. But I feel the darkness or the light, I don't know which, pulling at me with such an awful strength that I cannot go anywhere but toward the window with its light or darkness, whatever is there.

Mama, I'm afraid. My throat has closed up and my tongue feels thick and mushy. "Would you want some water? Could you take another sip or two?"

What is that sound?

"Mama?"

Somebody is calling my name, but I can't tell which shore they are calling from. Both shores are as dark as the night I laid down in to begin with. I don't know which shore to turn toward. Is it you here, Cora?

"Co."

"It's me, Mama. I'm still right here. The doctor hasn't come yet. Would you like to have another little drink of water?"

Reach out your hand and touch me so I'll know which shore you are calling from.

"Here. I'll just put the palm of my hand under and raise your head a little bit. Now. Try to drink some. Try just a sip."

Something is happening to me in darkness, but there is a light coming into my mouth that feels good.

"That's good. That's fine. Now I'll let your head down. That was real good."

O Cora, I'm bound away.

"Just you rest now."

I need to rest and breathe a little, they said or thought together. There is a mighty power of time in the room that is taking all my strength to fight. I need to think there is someone alongside me in the struggle.

THE SHOOTING WOMAN

"Your mother tells me," my grandmother said, "that you're sweet on that little Sarah Robinson."

"I wish she wouldn't say that," I objected. "I don't see how it is anybody's business but my own. What makes her think so, anyhow? I never said I was. I wish—"

"I can tell it's the truth," my grandmother said. "Your stuttering and muttering gives you clean away. You might as well wear a valentine heart pinned to your shirt that proclaims your sentiment to all the world. You don't think liking a girl is something to be ashamed of, do you?"

"Maybe not. But I don't want to be talking about it."

"Well, it's been going on for a mighty long time. It's nothing but natural for men and women to pair up together. You can understand that much, I reckon."

"Yessum." I remembered how my father had told me the story of Helen of Troy and how I'd later discovered that Helen still haunted the dreams of all men everywhere. I remembered all the women that streamed to Uncle Luden like black ants to a sorghum stir-off. I thought of Romeo and Juliet. But these skirmishes with history and legend little prepared me for the turmoil that rose smoky within me each time I saw Sarah or heard her name spoken or thought of her plump pink hands and neatly pointed chin. Those were her cardinal points, I judged, but I also devoted happy reverie to her billowy ash-blond hair and dark blue eyes that turned violet when she brooded over some injury or slight, fancied or real. I had to concede that her ankles were fat and didn't seem to belong to the rest of her body—what I'd seen of it, anyhow—but I figured I could accustom myself to them. Over a period of time, I'd get so I didn't notice how they bulged over her shoe straps and turned purplish in cold weather. Then when I realized that I was thinking about a "period of time"—which meant a *long* period—I became apprehensive and began to wonder why I was keeping secrets from myself and how dire those secrets were.

"Have you planned out what you're going to do about that pretty little miss?" my grandmother asked.

"No, ma'am. I didn't figure I needed to do anything."

"Well, maybe you don't. It's better to make your mind straight and clear in these matters before you act," she said. "You don't want to play the fool." She held a jar against the musty ivory glow of the twenty-five-watt bulb that hung above us, wiped it with the dirty old pink flannel rag, and peered into it again.

We were in the storeroom off the kitchen hallway. It was a windowless little space with big wooden bins for flour and cornmeal on the left-hand side; ranged above these around three walls stood tiers of shelves holding mason jars of edibles, the products of long, steamy canning sessions in summer and autumn. There were gallon jars of grainy-looking chopped cabbage and cob corn and whole tomatoes in brine. My favorites were the squat half-pint jars of relishes and preserves and the red-speckled gold chowchow and the dark ruby strawberry preserves and the tarry blackberry-jam jars with their silver helmets of hardened wax. Most of the jars were quarts of vegetables: whole okra and chopped, mustard greens and turnip greens, pudgy lima beans. There were meats, too: sausage balls in fat that looked and smelled like library paste, Brunswick stew as livid orange in color as fresh-cut pumpkin. Cherries gone gray-pink, vegetable soups, hot-pepper relish—shelf after shelf.

It was as if my grandmother was planning for our survival through a new Ice Age. But some of the jars had been there for maybe decades, and every year she and I or someone else in the family dusted and inspected them, discarding the ones that looked suspicious, pressure-creviced or spoiled by faulty seals. After a few years the jar rubbers could stiffen and crack and air would seep into the spicy applesauce and turn it to vinegar mush, a metamorphosis my grandmother greeted with bitter lamentation. She hated waste worse than a hard-shell deacon hates sin, but if our family had multiplied like barn rats and eaten for a generation, we would hardly have made a dimple in this store of provender.

She handed the jar to me. "What do you think it is? It's turned so dark, I can't tell."

I held it up. Lumps of vague shadow swam in a blue-pink murk. "I think it's beets," I said, and gave it back.

She smelled around the seal, turned it to the light once more, and gave it a vigorous shake. "We'll keep it through the winter," she said, "but if we don't eat it this year, we'll feed it to the hogs next spring."

The pigs were in for a treat. She didn't trust the jar enough to bring it to the table, but she couldn't yet bear to part with it. Whatever it was—beets or baby turnips or purple plums from the old tree by the stone bridge—it was going to enjoy one more anniversary at least.

I took another jar off the shelf and gave it to her. She wiped it absentmindedly and returned it. "These next six are all grape juice," she said. "They're sound. We don't need to look at them."

Oh Lord, her famous grape juice. She never checked the seals for leaks on these jars, even though they were often found to be loose or cracked. My father claimed she did it with cunning aforethought, that my teetotaling grandmother was making wine accidently on purpose by letting her grape juice ferment. At the end of a long day in the hayfield or tobacco patch she might send me to fetch a jar of her cooling grape juice. One jar out of two would be sour wine. "Oh my," she would say, "air must have got into this jug. Maybe I'd better pour it out." But she would be prevailed upon to forgo such shocking waste and we would pass the jar around, and the fuzzy glow we felt at sunset was not entirely that produced by a task well done. She never gave up the ritual, and over the summer weeks those of us laboring with her, or under her persnickety direction, would glance at one another during jar openings and silently mouth her unchanging benediction: Oh-my-air-must-have-got-into-this-jug.

When we moved on to a row of sweet pickles, she said, "But sooner or later you'll have to do something."

"About what?"

"About your sweetheart."

"She's not my sweetheart."

"Well, if you want her to be your sweetheart, you're going to have to plan what to do and then carry it through. If you keep on piddling around, some other young buck will come along and take her out to a barn dance and then begin sparking on her and she'll be his girl. Then you'll stand at the gate and moan."

She often confused me with her old-time thoughts and expressions. As soon as I'd felt a flash of vanity at hearing myself considered a young buck, I had to picture myself standing at a pasture gate mooing to be fed and milked, like a forlorn Guernsey at twilight. "Well, what do you think I should do?"

"You should declare your affections," my grandmother said, "and then take steps to impress them on her heart."

"But what if she turns me down?"

"Then you'll know where you stand, which is a lot more than you know now. Oncc you know whether or not she finds you likely, you can plan to spend time with her or with another girl. Somebody whispered in my ear that Sarah Robinson wasn't the only fetching young thing in Harwood County."

"She's the only one for me."

"If that's how you feel, then you'd better load up your shotgun and go kite hunting." She held another jar up to the light and inspected it as closely as Charles Darwin ever examined a trilobite.

"I don't know what that means—kite hunting," I complained. "I hear you and Mama say that, but I don't know what you're talking about."

"You don't know the story? You don't know how your daddy and mother courted each other? You never heard about Ben Franklin's kite?"

"Not exactly." I wasn't really fibbing. I'd heard the story several times from my fathcr, but never from my mother or grandmother. I'd understood from listening closely that the various stories I heard about specific events didn't always match; sometimes, in fact, they were totally contradictory. I never gave up on finding out the truth of any of them but considered that extraordinary measures would be required to discover it. The truth was like one of these mysterious jars we were flanneling. My grandmother would hold it to the unrevealing light and declare the contents to be peaches; my mother would surmise that they were beets; to me they looked like green tomatoes. Then when the jar was opened, with red-faced exertion and partially suppressed profanity, by my father we would be assailed by the smells of sugared vinegar, allspice, mustard, dill weed, and strong pepper. Pickled crab apples awaited our pleasure; grayish in color—like most of the foods my grandmother canned—they were welcome sour-sweet company for sausage biscuits or scrambled eggs or pork chops fried, according to custom, terra-cotta-hard. I generally found these surprises of truth agreeable, even when I'd had my mouth set for green tomatoes.

For thirty years I've carried conflicting versions of many stories in my mind and have come no closer to discerning the truth than when I was fifteen.

It was no use asking my father about the truth. He'd gaze at one of these jars long and hard, as if it was full of silver dollars and he was counting each and every. Then, in a voice grave with deliberation, he would aver that the vessel contained thousand-year-old eggs from the Kiangsu province of China, brought to America at great financial expense and at the further cost of the lives of two sailors who had sacrificed themselves to save these eggs when their junk was swamped by the great feckless pleasure yacht of the Rockefellers during a drunken bribery orgy for twelve U.S. senators, including especially North Carolina's own Jack G. Horsebun. That was my father's variation on the senator's real name, and it was so apt that it long ago supplanted his official cognomen in my mind.

So I'd heard the story about the courtship of my parents and the wonderful kite of Benjamin Franklin, but I'd never heard my grandmother's particular account and expected it to differ, in some of the details at least, from the one I'd garnered from my father. But having broached the subject, she didn't seem eager to pursue it. She kept peering into the mystery she held against the puny wattage, as if some secret figuration there would help her decide whether to tell the story or not. Then she smiled one of her private smiles and wiped it away with her characteristic gesture and said, "Well, you know that your daddy and mama started out as schoolteachers up the river at the Bigelow community. Joe Robert always claims he didn't like schoolteaching and never had any knack for it and thought it then and now a profession fit only for the female gender, as he calls us women. But he was a pretty fair schoolmaster, after all, from what I hear tell, and if he'd stuck with that, he might have been county superintendent by now. Of course, he'd have to settle down from his flibberty ways and not back-sass one and all in every rank above him, and I expect he was never going to do that. It's not in your daddy's nature to travel in any fashion except against the current, and the stronger it tries to push him back, the better he likes it."

She sighed a small gray wisp of a sigh and paused a moment before going on.

"But of course that was the main quality that drew Cora to him. Just as soon as he arrived for his first year of teaching, he showed himself no great respecter of the rules, sneaking down to the boiler room for a cigarette and maybe a nip of whiskey with the old colored janitor that was always there. And not fibbing about it, either, but admitting it straight off when Jake Silverside brought him to task. I reckon he felt he knew all about Jake, the way all the young bucks thought they had his number. Jake was going on sixty years then and had just married Agnes Rorty from somewhere down around Spruce Pine. She couldn't have been more than twenty, if that. So there was a lot of sniggering about Jake behind his back. But that all stopped when Agnes gave birth to a strapping eight-pound man-child, some say nine months exactly to the day of the wedding and some say not quite.

"Jake learned from asking him that your daddy wasn't the kind to weasel but would look him right in the eye and tell the truth whether it might harm his own interest or not.

About something like that, your daddy is as straight as Honest Abe, though not otherwise, I am ashamed to admit. And your daddy learned he wouldn't be able to hoo-raw Jake; the principal wouldn't be persnickety about every little regulation, but he expected all the teachers, including Joe Robert, to abide by the reasonable ones.

"You know, I never thought before, but they were right much alike, Jake and Joe Robert. They both felt they were only filling in time at the schoolhouse, waiting for Hoover's Depression to pass away so they could get on with their real business. Jake was going to start up a construction company that would take on the upkeep of a lot of private roads and driveways way back in the hills where the big outfits didn't care to go, the money too scant for their notice. And your daddy was waiting, too; he wanted to be . . . well, I don't know what Joe Robert wanted to be. I'm still hoping to find out. Maybe he is hoping, too, since he's trying so many different things.

"Anyhow, he told the truth and took his reprimand in front of the other teachers and didn't bad-mouth Jake Silverside afterward. His manliness in the matter impressed your mother. From that day forward she kept her eye on Joe Robert, and it wasn't long before she conceived a warm affection for him that soon ripened into a passion.

" 'Oh Mama, Mama,' she said to me one Saturday morning, 'what am I going to do?' She was as mournful in the face as any grave-digging sexton.

" 'Now, daughter,' I told her, 'you must listen to the dictates of your heart and do what your better nature allows.'

" 'But I don't know what to do,' she said, 'for I want Joe Robert to love me as deep as I love him.'

"I thought she might burst out wailing then and was glad she didn't. I brought her up to be an independent woman, as independent as any man. Our family has never harbored crybabies, male or female. I expect you to remember that, Jess. I said to her, 'You must do something so he'll take notice. We could invite him here to supper, but then he'd figure you've got your cap set for him. If you're too forward, you'll scare him off like a buck deer in hunting season. Why don't you find out what he's interested in most of all and strike up conversing with him on that special subject? That's how he will center you in his sights.'

"She heaved a sigh so deep it might have turned a weather vane. 'He's not interested in anything at all except his dreary old science,' she said. 'I don't know the least thing about chemistry and atoms and all that.'

" 'You're a shining scholar,' I said. 'You took high honors at Carson-Newman College and the University of Tennessee. If you think science will help you to attract his gaze, you must learn all about science.'

" 'I've got no head for it,' she told me. 'As soon as I look at them, the numbers and facts run together in a soup. And besides—'

" 'What, then?'

" 'Well, I'm just not pretty enough,' she said. 'Every other teacher there is prettier than me. I believe Joe Robert has already got his eye on that new Frobisher girl that teaches home ec. I don't stand a hoot owl's chance against her.'

"Then I gave her the facts in no uncertain terms. 'Just hush,' I said, 'hush up that kind of talk right now. Men don't know what pretty is; they don't have the least faint glimmer of a notion. All you have to do is keep yourself clean and fresh and groom your hair and walk with your shoulders straight. Good character is what makes a woman handsome,' I said, 'and your character will show in your face like lamplight behind a window shade.'

" 'But Mama,' she started, and I wouldn't hear any more.

" 'No,' I said. 'You round us up some books of science to commence with and I'll help you. I'll quiz you every night on what you've read.'

"I could tell she wasn't satisfied, but that was the plan we followed, reading in the evening after all our chores were done and she'd graded the papers she always brought home from school. I washed the dishes in order to help her out a little. Then we'd slap open a book and stare at it together. We couldn't have been more mystified if we'd been looking at the ancient Hebrew language. But we didn't give up.

"Whether that was the key to Joe Robert's attention or not, I don't know. But something was, for he began to take note of Cora. His notice wasn't strong enough to suit her, but it was something to work on, she told me. She had a clue to his interests and thought it a telling one. That's what she said, and I was relieved to hear the happy sound in her voice that so long had been downcast.

"At that time, she was teaching English and history and Spanish to the ninth and tenth grades. So she had quite a store of work ahead of her every morning from the hour she arose from bed, what with her chores here at home added to the tasks of teaching. I knew what she faced because I'd done the very same thing myself at her age, rising early to do the farm and household tasks, then riding my bay mare Sookie up the mountain to the Long Branch school. Of course, that was just a little one-room schoolhouse, but my twelve or fifteen pupils were a rare handful for me to manage, I can tell you that. And I never had the advantage of learning a foreign tongue, as Cora has done. She knows Spanish and French to read and speak, but all I ever gathered was a scrap or two of Latin, and that mostly by accident. I hear tell, Jess, that you take a keen interest in the ancient tongues, and that's something to admire, because it's so close to how Moses and Jesus and Paul spoke in the Bible. I always wanted to learn the language they spoke but had no opportunity. . . . I do recall some Latin words, though. *Agricola,* that means 'farmer.'

"Anyhow, her Spanish class was on the second floor of the proud new building out at Bigelow and it so happened that Joe Robert's class in general science was located on the third floor, right above the room where Cora taught. Many's the time she'd come home shaking her head. 'I wonder what scientific facts that wild man claims to be teaching his students today,' she'd say. 'There was the awfulest commotion up there. I thought the ceiling was going to come down on our heads.'

"But that was her cue to get him started talking, I'd say. She asked him what he'd been teaching and he explained to her all about his 'demonstrations,' as he called them. He told her how he liked to get the students involved in his demonstrations so they could see and do for themselves what the great men of science had done over the ages to bring the marvels of the twentieth century into being. One of the things he wanted to do was fly them Benjamin Franklin's famous kite, the one that proved how lightning rods work. But, he told Cora, he hadn't been able to find the right material. He needed silk, he said, and he, being a bachelor, had no old silk clothing and did not wish to spend money at the store on such cloth. When she told me this, I struck upon a notion. 'When does he want to fly this kite?' I asked Cora.

" 'He'd hoped to do it next week,' she told me.

" 'Well, then,' I said, 'today is Thursday and you'll be seeing him tomorrow, so inform him then that you think we might be able to supply him with what he needs. On the way home, stop off at Virgil Campbell's store and get some red dye to dye cloth with. Say to Virgil that we need the reddest dye he's got. I'll tell you next what to do after that.'

"So she did, and while she was at school that day, I went through the back bedroom closet upstairs and found an old-fashioned silk petticoat that used to belong to my aunt Emmaline Trowbridge. It was all yellowed and musty and spotted with mildew, but I didn't mind. I took my shears and cut it down to Cora's size, more or less; didn't need to be exact. And snipped off some of the old-timey furbelows but left on all the lace I could.

"Saturday morning we got out the big washtub and set it in the front yard. I fetched Aunt Emmaline's old petticoat that I'd cut down and the packet of dye and handed them to Cora. 'This is to be your slip next week,' I told her. 'You'll want to dye it as bright as the dye will color. We want to see it the brightest scarlet since the days of Babylon.'

" 'Why Mama,' she said, 'I can't wear any such slip as that. You know it wouldn't be becoming for me to wear a red slip. I would feel silly all over.'

" 'Never you mind about that,' I said. 'You just dye this silk as scarlet as the sins of Salome.'

" 'But it won't even fit me. No matter how red it gets, it's not going to fit.'

" 'Never you mind,' I said.

"So she poured in the water and dye and vinegar and let that old rag soak. Every time she'd dip it out with the wash paddle and hold it up to look, I'd say, 'Not yet. Let it take some more color.' Finally along about milking time, I judged it to be satisfactory. Red enough to suit me at last, it would put a raging fire to shame. If there was e'er a man with blood as red as that silk, he would be acclaimed a stalwart hero far and wide. It kind of hurt my eyes to look at it. 'All right,' I told Cora, 'now lay it out to dry and set and don't mind if it streaks a little. That won't much matter.'

" 'Mama,' she said, 'I will state plainly that I'll never wear this scarlet scandal. Why, I'm ashamed to be in the same county with it.'

" 'Never you mind,' I said. 'Let's get the milking done and the other chores and sit us down to a bite of supper.'

"So we did, and at the supper table I unfolded my mind to her. She was to tell Joe Robert, come Monday, that the only silk she had been able to lay hands on was the very slip she was wearing. 'You tell him it's seen its best days,' I said, 'and that you are willing to contribute it to a worthy cause like science, only you don't know how to give it to him without occasioning gossip. Then he'll figure out some way to get hold of it and you tell him you're going into the teachers' cloakroom or somewhere and take it off right there and deliver it. If you do that, I believe it will start up a chain of events leading to a fortunate conclusion.'

" 'Mama,' she said, 'I will tell you once again that I shall not wear that scarlet slip to school or anywhere else.'

" 'I'd be ascared if you did,' I said. 'All you have to do is tote it to school in a paper poke. He won't know you didn't wear it.'

" 'You want me to lie to Joe Robert?'

" 'Well, I'll admit that it's a fib, and a pretty good-sized one,' I said. 'So you must promise me that when you two are married and living content together for a while, you'll open up to Joe Robert and tell him the whole truth.'

" 'Even about my mother putting me up to it?' she asked.

" 'If need be,' I said, though I'll admit to you, Jess, I hoped it wouldn't come to that.

" 'And you think this will do the trick?'

" 'Daughter, I believe that it must.'

"And so it did, for she recounted to me how Joe Robert took an interest in her silk and how his eyes lit up when she told him she would secretly disrobe and deliver the slip to him and how round as saucers his eyes got when he peeped into the paper poke and saw that silk as scarlet as the flames of Sodom and Gomorrah. He peeped down in that paper bag she sneaked to him under the table in the lunchroom and when he raised his head, he looked at her with an expression she had not seen on his face before, nor on the face of any other man besides.

"Don't ever imagine, grandson, that an old woman like me doesn't know what's on the minds of hotblood lads like your daddy was and you pretty near are. If women couldn't figure out things as simple as that, where do you think the human race would be? Perished off the face of the earth, is where. And science would have to wait a mighty long time for another set of monkeys to turn into human people again. Not that that's the way it happened we got here. It's only one of your daddy's bright ideas that will cause more trouble yet, if he's not careful.

"Anyhow, it turned out like I thought it would. Your daddy opened up that brown paper poke and I expect he closed it again quick as a flash. But even before he got it closed he was thinking thoughts about that Cora Sorrells wearing a slip of such color. Red flag to a bull, that was, though of course it didn't make him mad. Only wondering and curious and eager as a shirttail youngun to see Christmas come.

"I had a strong notion that scarlet slip would catch his interest, but Cora said, 'And what will he be thinking of me now, do you suppose? I'd give a pretty to know. He will consider me to be one of the easiest sort.'

" 'It'll all turn out well,' I told her. 'There's a lot of stop and go in a courtship. With Joe Robert, we've had to get him going strong before we'll ever need to stop him.'

" 'But what will he do? What's going to happen now?'

" 'He'll have to teach his demonstration about Benjamin Franklin's kite. Tonight he'll be up late putting it together and tomorrow you'll see it flying through the sky.'

" 'Then what?'

" 'On your way home from school tomorrow afternoon,' I told Cora, 'I want you to stop by Virgil Campbell's store again and get three boxes of twelve-gauge shotgun shells.'

" 'What in the world for?'

" 'Never you mind,' I said. 'Everything's going the way we planned. You just bring home those twelve-gauge shells.'

"She looked at me like I was a woman insane, but I knew she'd do as I asked. As soon as she went off to school and I got most of my Tuesday-morning chores out of the way, I went up to the attic and moved some old tobacco canvas and other truck out of the way till I uncovered your grandaddy's shotgun. It had been up there since the week after he died, but I knew it would be in good shape. Uncle Uless had cleaned it and oiled it and wrapped it tight in oilcloth and put it away for me. I took it out in the yard and unwrapped it in the sunlight so I could see it clear. I didn't spot a speck of rust, only a little grime and attic dust, and of course the oil had leaked away from some parts. I cleaned it the best I knew how with some rags and a curtain rod and thought it would shoot well enough. It is a striking-looking shotgun with a curly-maple stock and some gold engraving along the barrels. . . . Well, you know what it looks like; your daddy has let you hold it once or twice, I reckon.

"When Cora came home after school, she told me how Joe Robert had wasted no time before flying his kite. He took his science class out into the schoolyard and told them to run it aloft. 'Be sure and feel that red silk, boys,' he said. 'It came from Miz Silverside's silk panties that I believe to be left over from her years as a cancan dancer in the wicked haunts of Paris, France.'

"So they flew it in the air and he made sure to pass it by Cora's windows, where she was teaching her Spanish class. Back and forth, back and forth—like a redbird building a nest, she said, and she told me it made her feel peculiar. 'What if it really had been my slip that I took off for that man?' she asked me. 'How would I feel then? And what if somebody else thought it was my slip? What if he told one of the other teachers it was?'

" 'Never you mind about that,' I said. 'Did you bring home those shotgun shells like I asked you to?'

" 'They're in the back of my car,' she said.

" 'Well, let's get them,' I told her, 'because you're going to need to practice up.'

" 'Practice what?'

" 'Your marksmanship,' I said. 'I'm going to teach you how to be a shooting woman.'

" 'I don't want to be a shooting woman,' she complained.

" 'Yes you do, Cora. Tell me the truth—hasn't everything happened just the way I told you it would? Have I misled you so far?'

" 'No,' she admitted to me.

" 'Then let's just keep on with my plan,' I said.

"And so we did, and you know the rest of the story. Joe

Robert wouldn't give up on Dr. Franklin. He ran that kite past Cora's classroom windows every day for a solid week. Meanwhile, she was out in the pasture every afternoon shooting away at tree limbs, thistle heads, daisies, squirrels—anything that would serve as a target, sitting or moving.

"I have to say, though, Jess, that she wasn't born with a natural talent for firearms. I'm a pretty steady marksman myself, but your mother was always a little ascared of the shotgun and couldn't stop from flinching and jerking the trigger. But practice makes perfect, you know, and if Cora never actually got to be perfect with her twelve-gauge, she finally didn't need to. That red kite flying so close, just about anybody could bring that contraption down, and that's what Cora did.

"She let go both barrels, she told me, and there wasn't anything left of that silk kite but a red snow flurry. Then she leaned out and looked down at your father, and his mouth was open so wide, it looked like somebody had dug a hole in his face. That's what she told me, anyhow, and I can well believe it. He wasn't expecting any such force of arms. Then she hollered at him to stop distracting her Spanish class and slid the window down and left him standing foolish in the middle of the schoolyard, looking like he had been lightning-struck."

"So that's how she won his heart," I said. I had heard about shooting the kite down. My father liked to tell the story and now and again my mother would allude to it. I'd heard other accounts, too, some confused and partial, some elaborate and fantastic, from the loafers down at Virgil Campbell's Bound for Hell Gro. and Dry Goods. But I had never heard how my grandmother had planned out the whole drama from day one and how her strategy had worked every step of the way as perfect as a waterwheel turning.

"No. That's how Cora got Joe Robert interested enough to start up a fiery courtship and lead her on to marry him. That's not the same as winning his heart."

"But I thought—"

"No," she said. "The mind is swift to passion, but the heart is not an easy learner. She won his heart on their wedding night."

"Oh," I said, swallowing. I was pretty sure I didn't want to hear anything about that part.

"That's when he saw her left shoulder undraped," my grandmother continued, "the way I'd been looking at it for four days. It was blue and purple and downright black in places, the way any girl's soft-skinned shoulder would be who had fired off fifteen boxes of shotgun shells in less than a week. Looked like she'd suffered more than one stout kick from Johnson's old gray mule."

"Fifteen!" I said. "I thought she only bought three."

"I kept sending her back for more."

"Why? She didn't need that much practice. You told me that almost anybody could have shot down that red kite."

"Yes, but only three boxes wouldn't have left much of a bruise."

"Why would she want a bruise?"

"She didn't. She complained about it hourly. But I wanted her to have it."

"Why?"

"To win your father's heart for good and all. When he saw how bad her shoulder was bruised, he'd understand how much she loved him and was willing to endure to get him. That would make him feel proud of her and would be the beginning of a love as deep as she desired."

"So it was your plan that brought them together. Did you ever tell my daddy how you worked it so he'd marry my mother?"

"Do you think that would be a wise thing to do, Jess?"

I thought for a full minute of time. "I guess not."

"Well," she said, "while you're guessing, why don't you tell me what you think this jar contains?"

I took the quart of thick muddy brown liquid and held it against the lightbulb, but no rays could pierce that murk. "I think this one is thousand-year-old eggs from the Kiangsu province of China, brought to this country at great financial expense."

She took the jar from my hands and looked it over again. "I believe you must be right," she told me. "Your daddy said the very same thing about it last year. I'd plumb forgot where I'd placed these Chinese eggs."

She slid the jar back into its niche and turned to pull the chain to cut the light. "I'm getting old and forgetful. Pretty soon I won't have the least spark of memory left."

"No, ma'am," I said. "You're wrong about that. What you forget ain't worth remembering."

THE FIGURING WOMAN

"Aunt Sherlie Howes was known in our western North Carolina hills," my grandmother told me, "as hands down the smartest woman there was. Only she wasn't—she was the smartest *person,* man, woman, or child. Of course, the menfolk would never say so; they say women rush at a problem with their feelings and don't think. But Aunt Sherlie was not only keen-witted; she was orderly in her thoughts. Folks called her 'the Figuring Woman' because nobody could beat her at figuring things out.

"You, being of the masculine gender, wouldn't think so, but it is true. Many a woman you'll meet as you go along in life that has orderly thoughts and many a man disorderly, and yet you'll come out at the end like your daddy and grandaddy, believing that it's men alone can think a puzzle through.

"Yet Aunt Sherlie sat out there in her little house on Devlin Road, stitching and stitching in light good or bad, having taken up as a seamstress after her husband, Ben, died of a flock of heart problems. And people would bring their conundrums to her and she would listen and then lay aside her sewing for a little and, might be, would take a pipe of tobacco in Ben's old black briar and wait in her chair a spell and then deliver her mind. She spoke softly, so softly you'd sometimes have to hold your breath to hear her, but whatever she said was gold or, at the least, silver. She couldn't solve every problem, but her near misses were valuable, too.

"She had a gift for listening and the patience to draw out facts that looked as little as liver pills until she put them in a proper light. Then they rose as big as boulders. Some feller might desire to know if it was worth breaking up his farthest-off patch of ground for a cornfield or was the soil too grudging. How many bushels would that rooty hillside yield? The questions she asked didn't seem much to the point. Wasn't there a thorny hedge that ran all down the east side? Didn't that gateway down by Miller's pond marsh up with September rains? Hadn't Dummy Pendleton busted the axle on that three-quarter-size wagon he had? Never a query about the kind of seed or the slope of the hill or anything that would make sense. Until she said at last, 'Well, Harley, if you plant where you're thinking about, you'll feed the crows and the jaybirds, but not one grain of meal will come to your table.' Because she'd understood, you see, that Harley Stansberry could get into that piece of ground with his team and his plow, but there was no way he could drive in with a full-size wagon to pull his corn and haul it out, being as how the one other way in would be hip-deep in rain-season mud and being as how the one small wagon in the settlement was incapacitated and so was

Dummy Pendleton, in a manner of speaking, that man never having mended a broken thing in his life.

"That's just an example of the way Aunt Sherlie thought, and I could give you many another.

"But it wasn't only practical problems, farming and carpentering and money matters and so forth, that she was asked about. The young women—and some of the young men, too, though they were a little shamefaced—would come to her about affairs of the heart. It is the affection of love that causes most perplexities in the world, and you will come to understand that in about five years. Because I don't see you as a natural-born bachelor," she said, and gave me a smile.

My grandmother always smiled slyly, furtively, almost secretly. Then she would wipe the smile off her mouth with the back of her hand, as if she were erasing some naughty word from a schoolroom slate.

"The one I best remember," she said, "was the problem of Daniel Rathbone's daughter, Vonda, who had two beaux to her string, as we used to say, two boys as different as night and day and no love lost between them. Now that's a situation not wayward at all with a fresh-looking young thing like Vonda Rathbone, her hair shining like oat straw and bound up with a ribbon red or pink, and her gray eyes as clear as raindrops, and her way of walking that made her modesty flirtatious without her seeming to know. She was the prettiest girl in the county.

"But she wouldn't give her say, not to Jimmy Keiller so big and strong and willing, nor to Paul O'Dell, who was as wiry and clever and sharp-eyed as a terrier. The reason she would neither yea nor nay was because of her daddy. Daniel was not a cross-grained man except with his daughter. She was his honey darling, the apple of his eye, the one earthly treasure he cared about except for his wife, Martha, and, I suppose, his two ungainly lunkhead sons, Perce and Harry. But Vonda was his favorite. Whenever she came into the room, his face lit up like a jack-o'-lantern and looked mighty nigh as silly as one, to hear Martha tell it. But she was only funning—or, she was mostly funning, being fond of Daniel's fondness. She did foresee trouble coming with Vonda's courting days and had advised her daughter to stay quiet and keep her own counsel. 'Because, daughter,' she told Vonda, 'you know your daddy don't want you to wed, not now nor in time to come. He will have to bow to it someday but will be long a-bending. So if your heart is set on one of these boys, whether it's Paul O'Dell or Jimmy Keiller, your daddy will be dead against him and will play up the virtues of the other. You had better let him make a choice, and once you've seen how the wind blows, you can begin to plan how to do for yourself. And if you do favor one of them, don't tell me, or your daddy'll be worming at me night and day to find out.'

"So that's what she did, Vonda knowing how canny and experienced her mother was in the ways of her daddy. She smiled at one suitor and she smiled at the other and elsewise kept her mouth still. Her mother might've guessed which way her affections tended stronger, but she never said a word, either, and they both waited for Daniel to make some little signal. The boys, Jimmy Keiller and Paul O'Dell, waited, too, but of course didn't know what they were waiting for and after a while grew impatient, and the warm rivalry began to change into black looks and ugly feelings.

"Which was a shame because they were both of them worthy young gallants and not the least bit alike. Jimmy was a big strapping lad, dark-haired and pale-complected except when his feelings ran high and his face turned as scarlet as beet juice on a white dinner plate. He was renowned as a fighter in the hamlets and hollers and would go a bout with any boy that looked at him sideways. There was plenty that did; the boys of that generation loved ginger soup and would scrap with one another just to see the stars at noontime. He was well-off, too. His daddy owned the gristmill in the big crook of Buckhorn

Creek and had amassed a fortune, according to the rumor. I have doubted about that fortune myself, but the mill brought in a brisk business, and Jimmy was there every day to help his daddy, shouldering the sacks of cornmeal and growing stouter and stouter.

"His rival for the hand of Vonda was of a different breed. The O'Dells were a silent tribe that mostly kept away from other folks. Not dark and mean and suspicious like the Buggses that lived up by Beaverdam—I'll tell you about them sometime. But only just quiet and watchful and as poor, as the saying goes, as Job's turkey. They got to be so silent, I expect, from living on the edge of the forest, where it pays to walk soft and be observant. But you never heard a word against them, not one. People wondered about them but didn't gossip much. They made their living off the woods, hunting and trapping and collecting herbs and, like as not, learning to go hungry when they had to. Paul was the youngest of four children and didn't show any sign of breaking with the O'Dell ways. He had spent most of his days and many of his nights deep in the mountains, under the trees. But once he'd glimpsed Vonda Rathbone, he came out into the open like a groundhog to a kitchen garden.

"So you can see how the choice was not between a Ben Davis apple and a Stayman apple but between two creatures altogether opposite to each other. Between, you might say, a sturdy workhorse and a swift-coursing hound. And you might take for granted that Vonda's daddy would light on the Keiller boy as his favorite, him blessed with a family business and being a big stout feller like Daniel himself and right well-spoken, too, though maybe a little too loud inside an ordinary dwelling house.

"But when Daniel made his first little remark, it seemed he was more interested in Paul O'Dell. Of course, the truth was he'd rather have the both of them in the bottom of a well deep in the land of Jericho than mooning around his daughter, but they'd been coming to the house for so long that finally he must've reckoned he had to take some notice, so he said, 'I wouldn't've thought it right off, but that O'Dell boy has some sense in his head.'

"That was the clue that Vonda and her mother had been waiting for, and they began to examine it as anxiously as a fice dog at a rat hole. What did he mean, saying such a thing? What was Daniel's plan? Was he trying to smoke Vonda out, or was it just a remark he happened to make between a bite of corn bread and a swaller of coffee? The two women would wait until all the menfolk were out of the house and then they'd debate that one sentence like it was some new verse of Holy Writ. Of course, Martha didn't tell everything she knew about Vonda's daddy and his plans, and Vonda was careful to argue both sides of every point equally because she wasn't going to let her mother know which way she was leaning, not yet. The discussions were fascinating but fruitless, the impasse not breaking until Vonda said, with as careless an air as she could muster, 'Well, Mama, it seems to me that Jimmy Keiller has advantages as plain to see as the nose on your face.'

"Martha nodded, just like she had expected all her life to hear this sentence spoken, and then said, 'I believe the best thing would be to drop a hint to your daddy that you share his interest in Paul O'Dell and then watch him swing over to Jimmy. Then if we can keep him straight in that furrow for a while, we may make some headway.'

"So that's what they did, Martha and Vonda both. They began to play up the O'Dell boy, praising his quiet manner and evident thoughtfulness and his clever ways in the woods. Vonda said it was sweet the way he cast his eyes down to the floor when he talked; she didn't care much for these big old boys with their bold stares. Martha claimed she'd heard he was the best rifle marksman in the region; it was a talent she had never praised before in anyone.

"When they began to talk in this vein, Daniel turned his mind around, just as his wife had said he would do. He began to speak, though grudgingly, of the favorable qualities of Jimmy Keiller, that boy who was as stout almost as a horse, and showed the spirit he had by speaking out like an honest man, and who possessed no fear to fight any man or boy in Harwood County. Besides all which, there was Jimmy's daddy and his gristmill and those sacks of money you heard whispers about. But he sang these lauds with such a melancholy air, they sounded like a funeral dirge. He had seen the inevitable coming but hadn't adjusted his mind to it yet.

"So, things were going about like Martha expected, pretty much the way she hoped they would. Trouble was, they had not and could not tell the boys what progress was being made, and the situation between those young bucks was not cordial. In fact, it was so stormy, it had to come to blows, and on Tuesday, March eleventh, 1911, it did.

"Jimmy and Paul betook themselves to Jason Crouch's old falling-down barn up in Ivy Cove—that was a favorite battling place for youngbloods in those days—and had it out with each other. If money had been bet, it must undoubtedly have been placed on the head of Jimmy Keiller, but the boys told no one about the fight until afterward, and then we learned that it was a battle royal and went on from two o'clock in the afternoon till sundown. That little Paul O'Dell had more grit in him than the bravest fighting cock and managed to score a split lip on his opponent, but the struggle ended the way everybody thought it would.

"Jimmy was not a brutal boy, but when Paul showed up at Plemmons's little grocery store in the settlement next day, it was obvious he had got the worst of it in a most unmerciful way. His head was swollen up like a candy roaster and lumpy as your aunt Ticia's mashed potatoes and was a rainbow of suffering: red, blue, purple, yellow, and even a little green about the cheekbones. It was startling to think a young man could take such punishment and still stand, and you could see, of course, only the outside of him. No telling what ruination he had experienced on the inside. But he hobbled around the store, smiling the best he could with his puffed-up mouth and broken teeth, trying to put a cheerful face on his dreadful defeat. The look of him might have turned some folks against Jimmy, but they knew he was the stouter and it was a fair fight with feet and fists and maybe a handy stick or two, but no weapons made of iron. All that being so made it Paul's personal business and he had invited nobody to poke into it.

"Anyhow, Jimmy sent word to Daniel Rathbone—along with a sealed private note to Vonda—that he was coming over Sunday to begin his courting of the girl in the formal manner, sitting with the family in the parlor till it was time to go home and then bidding good-bye to Vonda out on the porch. In summer or winter she would have walked with him down to the cow-lot gate by the barn, but now in March the ground in front of the house was awful muddy. Daniel had been proud to build this fine two-story house with a southern exposure, it being so cold in winter back there where they dwelt in the holler. And he never could get a stand of grass in the front yard, and in the thawing spring and the rainy fall it was pure mud. But they had a big deep front porch that ran the length of the house and in mud season everybody left their boots out on the porch and went inside in their stocking feet. Might be, when they had visitors, you'd count a dozen pairs of muddy boots out on the porch amidst the other truck: plow points and washtubs and dinner pails and a broken-down little coal stove and even an old corn sheller Martha had told her boys a score of times to lug down to the barn. But they were lunkhead boys and couldn't remember.

"Jimmy had won his fight with Paul and he seemed to believe that made him the one eligible suitor, and when he sent word to Daniel he was coming courting, he knew Daniel wouldn't like it but would have to bear it. What nobody expected was the effect this news would have on Vonda herself. She swooned dead away when she heard it was Jimmy ready to come to her parlor. Turned as white as buttermilk and sank to the floor as graceful as the virgin maid of a melodrama and had to be put to bed. There she turned her face to the wall and went as dumb as any stone.

" 'What is it?' Daniel asked his wife. 'Was she favoring that little Paul feller all along?'

" 'I'm not real sure,' Martha said. 'Maybe she's overcome with joy.'

"That was clearly not a correct diagnosis, because Vonda was not to be moved from that bed on Thursday or Friday or Saturday. She had read Jimmy's note and wadded it up and flung it away. Quiet and pale she lay, her eyes beseeching God or the plaster ceiling to deliver her from her hideous fate. But her daddy was not pleased. No daughter of his was going to be afflicted with sinking spells and convulsions of the spirit. If he could get used to the notion of Vonda marrying, then she could, too. It might be harder for him than for her, he told Martha, and so he wanted Vonda out of that bed by Sunday evening; he wanted to see her sitting modest and proper in the parlor upon the hour that Jimmy Keiller came to call.

"When Martha delivered this command, Vonda at first made no response but to leak silent tears like an icicle melting. Then, with what seemed the mightiest of efforts, she told her mother she would acquiesce, as an obedient daughter, to her father's will. It would cause her pain and sap her vital strength, but she would do it. Only she begged to be let off from going to church Sunday morning. 'Don't make me go, Mama, where people can stare at me like a marvel. I couldn't bear it.'

"She gained that one little point, at least, and when Martha and Daniel and Perce and Harry started for church on Sunday morning, they left Vonda supine in her bed of sorrow, her eyes still searching the ceiling for aid and comfort. They boarded the wagon that Perce drew up to the porch steps so they could avoid the mud and, with heavy hearts and maybe a little resentment toward Vonda, they rode away. They hoped the preaching and the hymns would lighten their souls.

"But when they arrived back home as hungry as grub worms, Vonda was absent. Her bed was carefully made up, the room was clean and neat, but her new button-up shoes and three prettiest dresses were gone off with her.

"Her daddy thundered and her mother rained. 'She has run off with that little O'Dell weasel and it's your fault for spoiling her,' he said, and she said, 'You was always too hard on her and now we've paid the price.'

"They searched without success for a letter or a note. She had only just put a few things in a paper poke—not having any valise of her own—and departed, leaving no more trace than smoke going up the chimney.

"But then when Perce drove the wagon to the barn and unhitched the horses and stalled them and was slopping back to the house, he noticed something and called them all out to have a look-see. In the yard mud and leading up to the porch steps were two sets of tracks, one set going and one returning.

" 'That's it!' cried Daniel. 'That just proves it. It is the sneaky little O'Dell boy that has abducted her away.' Then he named Paul some bad names and expounded upon the damage he would wreak upon the lad and upon all his kin.

" 'But looky here, Daddy,' Perce said. 'This wouldn't be Paul's track.'

"His observation was just. The boot track was a large one, clearly outlined in the red mud, and with a row of double *x*'s cut into the heels for traction.

" 'Too big for little Paul,' Perce said.

"Then Harry remembered he had seen that same exact track before but disremembered where. They pondered on the fact for a while, until it came to the three men at once that they noticed it every time they carted corn to the mill for grinding. There in the dust of those meal-slick floors the double *x* heel marks followed Jimmy Keiller every step he took.

" 'And looky here again,' Perce said. 'You see his tracks going to the house and you see them coming out, headed the other way. Look how much deeper the second set is than the first. He was toting a right fair weight when he left.'

"They looked at one another and knew it was Vonda. Jimmy had kidnapped her without getting a speck of sticky red mud on her.

"Perce follered the tracks as far as he could, but they ended up in the grassy patch below the barn by the rocky road that led out of the holler. He thought he spotted some scrapes on the road stones but couldn't be sure because they'd just brought their own team and wagon up this way.

"Well, to tell the truth, Perce wasn't what you call an eagle-eye tracker.

"So it was evident what had happened. What they couldn't figure out was why. Jimmy had established himself as the one and only suitor and that meant—barring divine intervention—that he and Vonda would declare before the preacher in a month or two. Daniel had got mollified to the situation, Martha favored whatever her daughter desired, and Perce and Harry didn't count.

" 'If we was willin' to the marriage, I don't see why he had to abduct her. I could've got used to Jimmy. We ain't got nothing against the Keillers,' Daniel said.

"Martha said, 'Well—'

"Daniel began storming afresh. 'You mean you think the Keillers might have something against *us*. Like we ain't good enough for them. Like Vonda ain't. By God,' he said, 'we'll be seeing about *this.*' It was his thought to go on the instant to the Keiller house and call out whoever was in it and face them down. Nor was he going without Perce and Harry and two pistols apiece and a shotgun.

"Martha held him back from his bloodthirsty urge and talked quick but soft, trying to gentle him down. She kept saying they couldn't do nothing till they had found out what had truly happened. 'You wouldn't want to start bad blood over just a set of boot tracks,' she said.

"He vowed he wasn't going to set around driveling when his only baby girl, his honey dumpling Vonda, had been kidnapped and no telling what would be happening to her right this instant. What did Martha expect them to do? What was her idea?

" 'We'll go see Aunt Sherlie Howes and ask her advice,' Martha said. 'You must promise not to do nothing till we've heard her out.'

"He grudged and grumbled but finally agreed, saying he would do it if it was done within the hour. He was a patient and forgiving man, he told his wife, but he wasn't going to be looked down on by the Keillers nor nobody else. Then he told Perce to rehitch the team and bring the wagon back around to the porch. And to be quick in the doing."

"Aunt Sherlie Howes received the four of them with quiet courtesy into her trim little cottage. She offered herb tea and cider and other such comforts, but the Rathbones were not taking, Daniel being so all-fired headstrong. Martha spied the piece that Aunt Sherlie was working on, a christening dress of delicate linen laid out on the sewing table by the window. She admired it for a while and the women conversed about the Bartons, whose infant the dress was going to grace in church two Sundays hence. The men stood glowering and looking foolish till Aunt Sherlie seated them in the straight chairs that ringed the wine-colored armchair where she sat sewing and offering advice. The right arm of the chair was like a big pincushion, stuck full of gimlets and needles dangling threads of different colors.

"When she asked about their business with her, Daniel and Martha told the tale by turns, the boys looking on with expressions that did not suggest total comprehension of the narrative.

"In truth, the story did get rather confused with husband and wife telling it at the same time, backing up and shooting forward and contradicting each other as often as not. But Aunt Sherlie listened patiently and you could see she was used to sorting out such tangled skeins. When Daniel and Martha reached the stopping point—or maybe just gave up talking—she said nothing for a long time and only sat meditating. She took a silver thimble from the arm of her chair and began turning it in her fingers while she thought. If you could look into her mind, it would be like watching her at her needlework, patient and careful to make her stitches neat and straight, piecing swatches together almost seamless.

"Finally she said, 'And was it only just this morning that Vonda disappeared? How much time has passed since you-all went off to church?'

"Daniel tugged his pocket watch out and flipped it open. 'It's one-thirty now and I'd say we left home about nine-thirty. So that's four hours.'

"She nodded and turned her attention to Perce. He squirmed and reddened under her gaze when she said, 'You was the one to see the tracks. Is that right, Perce?' When he admitted to it, she asked, 'Were all the tracks sharp-edged or were some of them streaky—like whoever made them was sliding about in the slick mud?'

" 'Sharp-edged,' he said.

" 'Sharp-edged. Both coming to the porch and going away?'

" 'Yessum.'

" 'Is the mud soft all the way down or is the ground froze underneath?'

" 'We've had some frosty nights,' Daniel said. 'It's a covering of mud over frozen ground in most places.'

"Aunt Sherlie didn't even glance at him, but kept looking steady at Perce. 'How about the back of the house?' she asked. 'Did you think to look around back?'

"He colored up again and said, 'Yes, ma'am. I did look. But there weren't no sign. Hadn't been nobody back there.'

"She smiled at him in friendly fashion and spoke softly. '*No sign* and *nobody* ain't the same thing.' Then she inquired of the four of them if any had seen Paul O'Dell after his fight with Jimmy, and Harry said he had seen him the day after the fight down at Plemmons's store.

" 'How did he look?'

" 'Poorly.'

" 'Took a sound beating, you'd say?'

" 'Worst I ever seen,' Harry said, adding proudly, 'and I've seen many a one.'

" 'What kind of fighter would you take Paul O'Dell to be?'

" 'He's quiet,' Harry said. 'He don't much scrap.'

" 'Never?'

" 'Well, sometimes. Sure.'

" 'How does he make out?'

" 'He don't like to fight and he don't never win, but . . .' Harry paused, waiting for words to come to roost.

" 'But he don't never say Calf Rope?' Aunt Sherlie suggested.

"He nodded, relieved. 'Yessum. Once his mind is set, he don't never say Calf Rope.'

" 'How about Jimmy Keiller? If he was to fight a feller and whup him, would he just keep on thrashing him?'

" 'Not if the other'n would give up,' Harry said.

" 'If the other boy said Calf Rope, Jimmy wouldn't keep on a-pummeling?'

"Harry shook his head. 'I don't believe he would.' He grinned, clearly pleased with himself for being able to talk sense to Aunt Sherlie.

"She then began to question Martha, asking her if she was satisfied that Jimmy was the one Vonda was sweet on. Martha said that all the signs pointed to Jimmy, though Vonda had never declared outright.

" 'Would she have reason to deceive you? I know, Martha, that Vonda would never lie to her mother, but mightn't she mislead you without saying anything?'

" 'The only reason she would deceive me would be to deceive Daniel through me. Because I don't mind which one she wants, but we knew that whichever she favored, Daniel would be against that one. So we tried to throw him off the track.'

" 'So if Daniel seemed to cotton to Paul O'Dell, she'd let on she liked Jimmy Keiller,' Aunt Sherlie said. 'And that would throw Daniel off the track. But if she wanted to throw *you* off, she must've been favoring Paul. Do you think she could like Paul better than Jimmy?'

" 'I don't know,' Martha admitted. 'You never can tell what's in a young girl's heart. But she did say to me one time that Jimmy had advantages as plain as the nose on your face.'

" 'That's not the same as saying she liked him better.'

" 'No,' Martha said, 'it ain't.'

" 'I'll ask you this,' Aunt Sherlie said, 'because you're around the house all the time and would know. Has anything been taken? Is there anything missing out of the house?'

" 'No.'

" 'Nothing at all? I don't mean a teacup or a ball of twine. I mean something heavylike and maybe pretty big.'

" 'No. . . . Well, I finally got that old busted corn sheller off of the front porch. Harry or Perce must have carried it down to the barn like I've been asking them to do day after day for months on end.'

" 'Is that right, Perce?' Aunt Sherlie said. 'You moved the corn sheller?'

" 'No,' he said, 'but I saw it in the barn when I went for the team. Harry moved it, I reckon.'

" 'Harry?'

"He shook his head.

" 'Daniel?'

" 'Me neither,' said Daniel.

" 'Well now,' said Aunt Sherlie, 'I believe we know all we need to know, don't we?'

"Then the four Rathbones looked at one another and the puzzlement was mighty thick amongst them. Finally Martha spoke. 'Well, I don't know nothing more than I did already. What are you talking about?'

"Aunt Sherlie turned to Daniel and looked him straight in the face with those sharp blue eyes that would see to thread the eye of the littlest fine needle. 'I want to get a promise from you, Daniel, if I can,' she said.

" 'What kind of promise?'

" 'If I tell you how to get Vonda back all safe and sound, I want you to promise me that you'll be satisfied with her choice of man and be reconciled to her and treat all concerned with generous kindliness.'

" 'Do you know who the man is? Who is he?'

" 'That don't matter just now.' Aunt Sherlie spoke soft and patient. 'You'd have to settle to her choice sooner or later, anyhow. If you do what I tell you to do, everything will work out for the best. For that reason, I want your promise. What do you say to me?'

" 'He'll promise,' Martha said. 'He'll promise and he'll stick by his word.'

" 'I don't know what I'm promising,' Daniel said. 'It's a pig in a poke.'

" 'I'm going to tell you exactly what will happen,' Aunt Sherlie declared. 'And then I want your promise to do what I say. In about a week or ten days, Vonda and her new husband will come riding on their horses up the settlement road and probably from the south. There will be a third person with them, mounted on a big roan horse. Without a doubt, somebody will come running to tell you about it because people around here will be expecting you to start up some mischief. But you and Martha and Perce and Harry are going to meet this party of three and invite them in to dinner and feed them good and a few days after that you will have a social in your house and your kinfolks and friends and neighbors will come and greet them and make them feel settled and at home in the region here. And there won't be no bad blood on any side. And everything will just hum along like a top.'

" 'Daniel,' Martha said, 'listen what a pretty picture Aunt Sherlie has painted for us. If you don't give your promise right now, I don't know what I'll do. But I do know you won't like it and won't be liking it for a long time to come.'

"'Well, then,' Daniel said, and squeezed out a tight little smile, 'I guess I'll give my promise. I want to see my Vonda again. I will do what you say to do.'

"And that's what he did, and he was not a man to go back on his word, and, as the old story says, they all lived happily ever after."

My grandmother smiled her sly smile and then rubbed it away with the back of her hand.

"But what happened?" I asked. "I don't understand. Which one did she marry?"

"You're the male person in this room. You can figure it out with the orderly thoughts a man has in his head. Which one do you think she married?"

"Jimmy Keiller."

"Why do you say so?"

"Because he was big and stout and won the fight."

"No. She married little Paul O'Dell. Because he loved her the most."

"How did she know he loved her the most?"

"He took the bloodiest drubbing he could stand, that just about anybody could stand, and it didn't daunt him. Nothing would stop him but killing. Not the marriage vows, not threat nor refusal. And maybe even after his life was over he might come back for her. A lot of hants are dissatisfied lovers, you know."

"Who was the third person that came back with them?"

"That was Jimmy Keiller on his fine roan horse sixteen hands tall that everybody admired. That Sunday morning after he got his little ruses completed at the Rathbone place, he rode like lightning six miles down to Bitter Springs Baptist Church, where he stood best man, muddy boots and all, for his friend Paul O'Dell. He had pummeled the little feller till he thought one more blow would end his earthly existence and he saw there in that falling-down barn up in Ivy Cove that no matter if he won the fight, he was never going to win the girl.

So the boys rested and blubbered together a while and then made the best of it they could. They planned for Paul to carry off pretty Vonda and for Jimmy to lay a false track."

"How did he do that?"

"Now I know a smart boy like you figured that part out the very first thing. Jimmy just walked up to the porch, lifted up the corn sheller, and toted it to the barn so that his tracks going back would be deeper than coming. The footing was slick as grease, what with the mud on top of frozen ground, so he had to step mighty careful for people to read his tracks with no mistake. The other tracks around were smeared and messy as folks slid and slipped and nearly fell. His were the only tracks sharp and clear."

"What about Paul O'Dell? How did he get Vonda out?"

"They just went out the back door and up the hill a ways, then down through the woods to the road, where he had two horses tied."

"I thought Perce looked behind and didn't find any tracks."

"Back in that icy holler, Daniel Rathbone had built his house to catch the southern sun. On the front side it did, but the ground back of the house was froze solid. Wouldn't take a track till almost May. That was where his warm southern exposure tripped up Daniel Rathbone. But it all ended well and it wasn't long before a grandbaby made him happy as a king. . . . Now don't you think Aunt Sherlie Howes was a smart person, woman or not?"

"I reckon so. Did she tell you how she figured it all out?"

"As far as I know, she never told a soul. She wasn't the bragging sort."

"Then how do you know what she thought?"

"I figured it out for myself, following in her tracks, so to speak. Trying to think in an orderly fashion, the way she did."

"Then you are as smart," I told my grandmother, "as Aunt Sherlie Howes was."

"Not quite," she said. "Aunt Sherlie unpuzzled it all while

the Rathbones were telling the tale. I pondered on it off and on for four years. Not every hour of every day, mind you."

"Still, you got to be smart to figure it out at all."

"Well, I guess maybe I've learned a thing or two in my time," she said, and smiled once more and wiped it away again.

THE SILENT WOMAN

My grandmother and I sat at the table in the cozy alcove off the kitchen, peeling and coring and slicing Romes into quarters. These moon shapes we dropped into a big kettle of water she had brightened with a few drops of vinegar—"to keep the fruit from browning up," she told me. She was making what she called a "run" of applesauce, enough to last a week or longer.

We looked out the windows upon a cold February day with clouds dark and low and voluminous. The grove below the road had unleaved and we could look into the bottom fields with their patches of sheet ice and the tall, shriveled goldenrod where sparrows found uncertain perches. What we had been talking about I don't recall, but we fell silent for a long space and there was only the sweetly teasing sound of blade and fruit flesh. The smell of the apples rose about us like a strain of ancient music.

It was the silence that caused my grandmother to fall to reminiscence and the story she told took silence as its theme. It has remained in my memory for some thirty-odd years now, but the nature of it sometimes makes me think she never told it at all, that she communicated the whole of it without speaking a word. Such detailed recounting is not possible without vocalization, I'm sure, and yet so many messages passed silently among the members of our family that I can almost believe I learned this story without hearing it.

It concerned a woman named Selena Mellon, whom my grandmother had known when she was twelve-going-on-thirteen. Some of her elders dismayed her with their incomprehensible ways, but she stood in perfect awe of those she admired.

"I had not come to the age of good judgment," she said, "but I had no trouble making up my mind what I thought about Selena Mellon. She was wonderful. She was like a personage you might hear of in a fairy tale and I never met anyone else like her the least little bit.

"Women have got a blame name for talking, but I don't know that it's a right and just one. If we're bad to gossip and tattle and trot our tongues unendingly, why, I can say the same about plenty of menfolks and I can number some that have embraced the vice more warmly than any female of my acquaintance.

"The worst I know of was Cam McInery. That man was so bad to tell tales that he even spread rumors about himself. Some people said he even started a few of them, as black as he'd put off on another. He must have known his wife would get wind of these whisperings. . . .

"When I hear menfolk accuse women of loose tongues, Cam McInery comes to mind as a worse example than any woman. Selena Mellon comes to mind, too—but for a reason exactly opposite."

"In a gathering of people, you might not notice her at first. She was not tall or bold or striking . . . Well, yes, I suppose she was striking, but not *loud* striking. If you didn't see her immediately, after a while she'd be the one person you did see. She'd just naturally draw your gaze the way that candlelight does or a cat dozing in an empty room. But when she looked at you, you wouldn't meet her eyes and would turn your face away.

"That's the way it was with me, anyhow, and not only because I was young and shy and skittish. I saw the same thing happen with gray-headed, sharp-tongued women and big, red-faced, loud-talking men. Even a horse dealer one time. What you saw in her face and eyes was so different from what you saw in anybody else that it overcame you. Took a while to adjust your mind and ready yourself. Then it was all right to trade glances, because there was no harm in her, no ill will; she could never harbor malice. Only the kind of person she was made her so unexpectable that you had to prepare.

"Maybe I'm not being clear.

"She was middling tall, with coffee black hair that came down in a widow's peak over her left eyebrow. She was pale-complected, but it was a warm paleness; some said like ivory, but I always thought of scrubbed pinewood. She would wear pale gray dresses or light blue and there was always a touch of snowy white about them, embroidered collars or broad cuffs or sometimes just piping. Her hands were smallish and white and soft as a cotton handkerchief.

"Her eyes I was going to say were gray, but that's not right. They were actually silvery; there was a cool light in them as calm as a saucer of water and you could feel it when her gaze came to rest on you. She took you all in, not in a warm fashion but not unfriendly, either. I don't know how to express what I want to say, Jess. . . . When she took notice of you, you felt that you had changed and were not the same person as you were before. Not worse, not better; not more comfortable or uncomfortable. You just felt *known*—and by someone who had no way to know you and no particular reason to do so.

"Her face was roundlike, but not a moon face, and her lips, too, were pale. Her expression was never lively; her mouth would only hint at a smile or her forehead suggest a frown and that would be enough. Just those little traces of expression spoke volumes. An orator shouting and waving his arms on a flag-bedecked platform would appear as lacking in expression beside Selena.

"But those traces were necessary because she never spoke. . . .

"No, I'm serious. No one had ever heard her utter so much as a lonesome syllable. You hear it as an expression—'That Miller Simms never says a mumbling word'—but it's not true. The most closemouthed people turn out to be mile-a-minute talkers if you bother to keep accurate count of each sentence. We're so used to chatter that we don't notice. But Selena never spoke. No one could recall that she had ever spoken. Sometimes it was thought she might be crippled of speech, like Dummy Pendleton. But somehow you knew she wasn't. She could hear very well indeed; you caught her listening to sounds most of us would never pay any mind to. She wasn't deaf and dumb. And besides, there was something about her demeanor, about the way she held herself in company, that let you know she could speak if she so desired, that she was aware of the conversations in all their twists and meanderings.

"The reason she was silent was a topic of grave and complicated speculation. Some conjectured that she had a deep dread secret like the one that caused Aunt Chancy Gudger to lose her mind—whatever that secret was. They thought that it was a secret so full of itself that if Selena ever spoke one word, all the rest would come tumbling out in a terrible confession that would shame her forever. Others fancied that she had taken a vow of silence, maybe for Bible reasons. I've heard of a hermit who vowed never to speak until Jesus returned; he didn't want to take any part in this sinful world. Or maybe she'd devoted to a vow of silence for reasons of the heart; maybe it was a deep-sworn lovers' vow. You hear of lovers taking vows of silence sometimes, but it usually doesn't take long for those to wear off. That's because they begin to imagine slights and then these turn into hurts, and when people hurt enough, they must talk.

"For you should understand, Jess, that it takes forethought and practice and strength of character to make silence mean something. All these Selena possessed and no one ever felt mocked or put-upon or injured or ill-used because she wouldn't speak to them. It was a way she had of making folks accept her the way she was. And more than that, too: She got them to respect her silence without knowing the cause of it, and it's the rarest man or woman who could do that.

"She was alone in the world but pretty well set up. Her mother had died of consumption not long after Selena was born and the grief of loss bowed her father plumb into the earth. He pined and dwindled and finally died of something they couldn't name. Her grandfolks on her daddy's side took care of her till she turned eighteen, and she couldn't have learned much habit of speech from them. In Grammer Mellon's gloomy stone two-story house I expect you wouldn't hear six words spoken from Sunday to Sunday. And the Lord's day they would keep in complete silence.

"Try to picture her in that dark old house. Grammer and his wife, Tennie, had lived so long together, they looked alike. He had a greenish face; she had a greenish face—like they had mildewed from being long out of the light of the sun. They both had balded in the back, showing splotchy heads. And they both had the same tight little crack of a mouth. There was something wrong in the head with both of them and they looked at Selena like spies peeping from shadows. Nobody ever much cared for either of them. . . . Well, you can see how Selena came by her strength to be alone.

"I mean, to be herself all the time, to be Selena when she was alone and to be Selena still when others were nigh. That's another uncommon thing. You'd be surprised how much we change in the company of others, how we stand different and talk different and think of ourself in a different way. She didn't.

"A woman like that is bound to have a marked effect. Selena impressed every person variously. One feller would be struck lovesick after a bare minute of her acquaintance, while another man—just as readily disposed toward the tender passions as the first one—would begin to ponder upon the notion of celibacy. A swarthy outdoorsman might suddenly think of the peaceful advantages of the studious life, while the bookish scholar might dream of dwelling in some lonely fastness with only the tall pines and the stately moon and his rifle for companionship. The straitlaced preacher would remember the pleasures of youth and the red-eyed reprobate would recall the empty broken promises he had made to his departed mother. It wasn't that she searched your soul with those silver-glancing eyes; you did that yourself—only her gaze had prompted you to it.

"Upon the passing of her grandparents, all the Mellon property came to her. That was four hundred fat acres down by Buie's Bend with that big stone house and three spacious barns and I don't know what-all livestock and equipment. She lived in the house and managed to lease out the farming, and her income from that was more than sufficient to tide her into her gray years. She kept the house herself—spotless, too, according to those few who saw it. That would be Lawyer Jenkins, who handled the bulk of her affairs, and Bob Brendan, the Republican banker that she trusted when nobody else would, and Hiram Belcher, who leased the land from her and made the both of them a pretty penny on the arrangement. She went out to parties and socials and weddings and funerals and church dos when invited and seemed to have a pleasant time.

People had got used to her and they thought they could read her moods pretty well—though they have been dead wrong sometimes about that.

"Not that people wouldn't try to fuss her now and again, try to tease her into breaking her silence by saying something cheeky to her. Not straight to her face, of course, because when she turned her eyes on them, they couldn't do it. But sigogglin, looking away toward the window or toward some other person to say something smart-mouthed or even a little rude sometimes. One time when your uncle Harold Roark was stationed at Alexandria, Virginia, he told how people were always making faces at him when he guarded the tomb of the Unknown Soldier. They'd say impertinent remarks, trying to cause him to forget his discipline.

"That was the way people tried to get at Selena, hoping to crack her rule of silence. But they only did it once, because when they gained her attention and she looked their way, they changed their mind about many things and especially about deviling her again ever."

"But there was one exception—seems like there's always one person who won't fit the pattern. This time, it was Lexie Courland. She was a handful, Lexie was, a double handful, with a lot of spillover. She was a tall, loud woman in her flaming forties, with wild red hair and as full of mischief as schoolchildren on Halloween. No respect for beast or human, man, woman, or child. Raucous and free-talking.

"Now your aunt Samantha is a free-talking woman and picked up the habit on purpose to kind of protect herself in the business she's in. Yet anybody can tell just by listening that Aunt Sam is harmless with her words, thoughtless, in fact. But the coarse words that Lexie Courland uttered were meant to be coarse and not matter-of-fact. She wanted you to hear coarseness."

"Why?" I asked my grandmother.

"Well, she'd been widowed twice and separated and I guess finally divorced at least once. Those circumstances are bound to work damage on a woman's spirit. But probably it was just her character to be the way she was, from the beginning and always. She liked fuss and trouble; she liked to rake up the coals just to see the sparks fly.

"One thing I must say in her favor—she was no hypocrite. She let you know she supped her whiskey straight, would paint the town from dark till sunrise, and was ready for any man. Straight-out about it. 'I don't mind who the menfolk are or who they're hitched to,' she said. 'It's the wife's duty to hold on to her man. Happens he comes my way and I like the looks of him and the jingle of his purse, I'm after him like a chicken hawk on a hatchling. The women that don't want their men stuck in my flypaper had better warn 'em stern and treat 'em sweet. For I'll snatch at any old corn pone that crosses my path.'

"She didn't say *corn pone* and I won't say what she did say.

"You can't speak plainer than that, seems to me. Of course, it was a conflagration scandal all over the township. One after another, no less than five preachers came to call on her, carrying their Bibles in their strong right hands. They knocked and she opened to them and shut the door behind. When it opened again, out came the preachers white-faced and trembling and clutching onto the Good Book like it was a failing handhold on the side of a high and rocky cliff. They shook their heads and sucked for breath. Two or three delegations of women made visits, too, but the result was different. When the women came away, they had switched to Lexie's side. . . .

"Well, they weren't exactly on her side. They were not conferring upon her any man-hunting license. But they were satisfied that she was just what she said she was: a scandal to behold and not the least concerned who did the beholding. They figured they could live with the danger of Lexie Courland. Any man with plain good sense ought to see that she had detour signs written all over her: Warning—Rough Road Ahead.

"Men being what they are, a few of them fell into her clutches anyhow. She kept her promise of being a good-time girl, but her kind of time was too good. They couldn't keep up. Soon enough they were panting in her dust, like a dog chasing a car on an August afternoon. She'd run them ragged, then send them home, where their wives would snatch them bald-headed.

"Wouldn't you hate to be some old buzzard that had to drag home shamefaced to his wife after a rowdy time with Lexie Courland? You'd feel as low and gloomy as a red worm. I hope you'll remember that, Jess, in your days to come.

"So when Lexie met Selena Mellon the first time at a social that was given for Morissa Cannon when she was a bride-to-be, she behaved just like those irreverent creatures at the tomb of the Unknown Soldier. She tried with all her might to discompose Selena because she'd heard all about her and was overcome with raging jealousy.

"Or maybe it wasn't jealousy. Now that I've said that, I wonder if really it might have been nothing more than an irresistible impulse to upset everybody's settled notions about Selena. That's more in line with her true character—just to be raking up the coals.

"So at the party, she arranged to stand well within Selena's earshot and said, 'I hear there's somebody at this party who thinks she's too good to talk to the rest of us. Who could that stuck-up person be, I wonder?' She didn't look at Selena; she was standing sideways to her and gazing off at the far corner of the room.

"When she said that, the other women there drew away from Selena and Lexie, leaving them a space all by themselves in front of the hearth. They understood that Lexie had chosen to confront Selena and they wanted no part of it. They truly didn't want it to happen, but they knew better than to cross Lexie. She was not above hair pulling, that one.

"For, you see, Selena's strange silence and her modest reserve and her calming influence had come to be important. Though Selena was not a part of the tight circle of these women, still she *was* one of them, only with a soul more pure and noble than any of them possessed, her spirit large and her mind clear of every least fear or shadow.

"That's the way they thought about her, right or wrong, and Lexie knew what they thought and that was why she was causing such a spectacle.

"Selena, of course, did not reply to Lexie's rude remark. She did turn to look at her, but Lexie wouldn't respond to her gaze, only staring off at the far wall. Then she struck again: 'Or maybe this certain someone don't say anything because there's nothing in her head except empty air.' She let little time pass before she made another trial: 'Or maybe it's pure laziness. I've heard of lazy, but somebody being too lazy to talk—that's a new one on me.'

"Well, she could hurl these taunts into the distant corners all she wanted to. Everybody knew that Selena wouldn't respond and that the true test of strength would come when Lexie turned about to face her and they locked eye beams. Lexie knew it, too, and so put off the moment as long as she could, standing there with her hands on her hips and saying vain, ugly things in the direction of the ceiling. Finally, though, the time had come to look her destiny in the face. Still with her fists dug into her hips, she wheeled slowly on her heels and looked at Selena square.

"Concerning this awful moment, everybody gave a different account. Some say that for once Selena's expression did change, and with surprising quickness; she looked upon Lexie with such a melting compassion it would stop the heart of a slow-thoughted ox. Others say no such thing, that Selena gave her a glance of such cold contempt that it would freeze the water in a steaming teakettle. And there were those who read anger in her face and others who read curious friendliness. And there were some who said her expression never changed at all, that it was as calm and placid as the moon, just like always.

"Lexie's face was easier to read, all her feelings being outsized anyway. First a sudden fury overcame her; her face went red and her eyes got wild and she dropped her fists to her sides and began clenching and unclenching them. It was like a campfire that has burnt down to embers and then somebody throws on them a dollop of kerosene and they flame up head-high but then die down again as quick because there's no fuel to feed on. So it was with Lexie; her red rage drained out of her almost as fast as it had flared and left her feeling I couldn't say how. Shaken, I'd think, all-over trembled, down to her foot soles. Like everybody else that Selena took notice of, Lexie understood that she was *known,* her body and spirit understood for the first time in her life, seen through as simply as you and I see through this window we're looking out of now at the storm building up.

"Then as soon as the anger passed out of her, Lexie filled up with sorrow. She dropped to her knees in front of Selena and bowed her wild red head. She started sobbing, too, quietly at first and then in that full-throated way you see sometimes at funerals or maybe when a child has lost her favorite dolly. The weeping went on quite a while.

"Nobody knew how to act. At first the women pretended not to notice and tried to converse among themselves like this strange occurrence was not taking place in front of them. But that was a pretense impossible to keep up and they soon fell silent and gathered in a circle around that pair of women to see what would happen next.

"Selena looked down at the weeping Lexie and made no motion for what seemed the longest space. Then she bent down and grasped her upper arms and pulled her to her feet. She hugged Lexie and patted her on the back, the way you've seen comforters do a thousand times. After Lexie quietened, Selena stepped by Lexie's side and took her right arm in her left and they went out of the room together. In the foyer they paused to gather their light wraps, then joined arms again and left the house and went down the walk to where Selena's rig was tethered to the picket fence. She helped Lexie up into that trim little buggy and climbed in herself and took the reins and off they drove.

"The others watched from window and doorway and they all declared that the hooves of Selena's bay mare made no sound on the dusty gravel road, that they struck the hardpan as light as thistledown and the two women drifted out of sight as noiseless as a dream overtaking a parson's sleep.

"They drove straight to Selena's big stone house and nothing was seen of either of them for at least a good five weeks.

"What they did, Jess, was set up a life together. In that one glance of Selena's, Lexie Courland found what she had been looking for with all her unbridled behavior. She had discovered her true friend, her soul mate, and it flooded her mind with strong amazement to understand that she had a chance to be happy and leave off toying with those puny-spirited men that were but as chaff in the wind."

"And this pair of women lived together in peace and contentment till the end of their lives. To the end of Selena's, I mean. She died first. There was never any anger or bitterness between them and, as far as anybody was able to tell, not even passing irritation. It was an arrangement that must have been made in heaven—that's what I say. We all know for a fact that not one hard word ever passed between them.

"Because Selena did not break her silence. After the pair was joined, people all said, 'Well, now Selena will begin to talk and she's going to be the noisiest chatterbox that ever donned a petticoat.' But they were wrong on that score, just as they had been wrong about so many things.

"When they went out in society together, Selena never spoke and Lexie only rarely. She had absorbed a lot of Selena's character. She quietened considerable and stopped her ugly, rude comments about people to their face and behind their back. She dressed different, more ladylike and becoming, and of course showed no sign of interest in any menfolk. She washed the henna out of her hair. I won't say she sweetened; there was too much gall in her nature for that. But she kept her sword in the sheath, so to speak.

"She did take it upon herself to became a kind of interpreter, telling folks a little of what was in Selena's mind. When a foodstuff of one sort or another was offered at table, she might overpass her friend, saying, 'Selena doesn't care for creecy greens.' Or when some social gathering was proposed for a future date, she might declare, 'Selena believes that we'll be busy with housework in the afternoon but would be glad to show up along about sundown.' Things like that, but nothing about her friend's deep feelings or broader opinions. In fact, she was much less free with her own notions now, not having to let everybody know at the top of her voice what she felt and thought about every little thing that took place.

"Yet she was frank and open when questioned—up to a certain point. I don't expect she would've answered questions too warmly personal, but she was willing to satisfy a reasonably polite curiosity.

"What was it like living in a house with someone who never spoke? She vowed it was the most graceful existence a person could envision.

"How did she know when Selena needed assistance or had some minor want? She said that it didn't take long to pick up slight signals and that if anybody else would observe her friend attentively, they, too, would decipher them.

"Did she and Selena perfectly agree in every point about religion and politics and such topics? She replied that they did not agree on every detail but that these matters rarely came up. When you lived in silence for a good while, you learned not to bother much with trivial matters.

"But surely the Lord and His works were not trivial? No, but talking about the topic was pointless unless you had something better to add than what the Bible said or Preacher Hardy could explain.

"Well then, what was there that had importance? What matters loomed large enough to occupy their communion with each other? Quietness, she explained. Silence. Silence itself had a deep mystery in it. Many mysteries, in fact. And these she and Selena explored together, sitting side by side in their chairs, never exchanging a word.

"Nobody understood what Lexie was talking about. But they were mightily impressed with her saying the things she said, uttering such solemn words on such grave matters. Your father likes to talk about the ancient teachers and philosophers; Joe Robert will go on about Socrates more than a smidgin. Yet I have thought, Jess, that Lexie Courland turned into a deep-thinking woman just by being near Selena Mellon all the time. I don't expect your daddy would agree with me. He would ask where her learned tomes were to be found and her big ideas. She changed into a different person, is all I know. One day she was a heedless, rip-raring thing as impulsive as a young bull and then in a short time with Selena she became longheaded and seriously inclined. Living with Selena was a course of training for her, and I've met more than a few others I would desire to be educated by the same method.

"They lived together for many a year, more than thirty all told, I believe. Then, like I said, Selena died first, and it was no easy going. She got the cancer and it began to eat up her insides, and the torture of it is something I can't imagine or bear to try. It didn't break her spirit until the very end, and I'm not sure about then. She still never spoke except that one first and last time, but she moaned a moan that would climb into a keening wail and then trail off into sobbing. Lexie sat by her every minute, her heart wringing inside her like a rope twisting around a well crank. She reported that Selena did speak—once only, as I said before. The pain had let up a little in the last day and a half, but when Dr. Anderson looked at her, he shook his head and foretold she only had hours. Lexie said—and I've always believed it the truth, Jess—that in the last peaceful time before the end Selena murmured to her. 'Goodbye, my dove,' she said.

"The wonder was that Lexie could tell about it cool and dry-eyed. But can you think how she must have been feeling?

"She went into mourning then for a long period, wearing black and sometimes veiling her face. She and Preacher Hardy had made all the necessary final arrangements and he performed the funeral rites. Lexie saw to the stone. Maybe you'd like to visit it sometime with me over in Pleasant Hill Cemetery. It is unusual because it only has that one single word on it—no dates and no inscription and not even a last name. 'Selena.' That's all it says, but Lexie was right. It is one word that speaks libraries."

"After a decent time had passed, Lexie did a most surprising thing. She asked a few people in for a ladies social at her house. She called us long distance and I went over to the settlement with Aunt Ona Caslin and a few others and we were all burning with curiosity.

"Lexie met the five of us at the front door and brought us into the foyer. 'Before we have our tea and sweetmeats,' she said, 'I thought you might like to see the house, the rooms where we lived together, me and Selena.'

"We followed her up the stairs and inspected their bedrooms. I won't describe all she showed us, except to say that everything was scrubbed clean and as neat as a pin and without the least touch of luxury. It surprised us to see how sparely they lived. We expected a more showy style from Lexie.

"She took particular care to point out a little sewing room that must have been a favorite place with its two comfortable stuffed chairs facing close together under a lamp. On one of the footstools lay an embroidery hoop with a pattern half-finished. Lexie explained that Selena had been stitching a flower piece for Granny Martin's birthday. 'But of course that occasion passed by many months ago,' she said, and dabbed at her eyes.

"Then she led us downstairs through the shining kitchen and the big guest bedroom they had dutifully kept up, though it had never been occupied. There was a cozy reading room off of one of the smaller hallways. Then we went into the front parlor and sat to sip our tea and nibble the cinnamon cake Lexie had baked.

"As we were eating, Lexie sat down and gathered herself, straightening the bodice of her black wool dress and crossing her ankles. 'So you see how we lived,' she told us. 'As quiet as mice. I can't think that any Quaker ever lived more quietly than Selena and me.' She looked at each of us for a long moment, then said, 'Now I know you've all been curious about us and I'm here this afternoon to answer any question you might care to ask.'

"Well, naturally, nobody would own up to being curious, but after an embarrassing minute Aunt Ona spoke up with the question that had been on our minds since always. 'Is it really true that Selena never talked? That she never spoke a word, even when you-all were alone in the house?'

"Answered Lexie: 'She never did.'

" 'Why was it that she never spoke? Was she afraid of somebody, or did she bear a deep-seated grudge?'

" 'No,' said Lexie, 'she never held a grudge against a living soul. And I'm not real sure why she didn't talk. A guess is the best I've got and I don't have any idea whether it's close.'

" 'What, then?'

" 'I believe there was something she wanted to say but didn't trust any words she knew to say it for her.'

" 'What was it she wanted to say?'

" 'It wasn't a thing for words. It was more like a picture. One time we were sewing together in the room upstairs. I was mending a tear in an old work dress and Selena was knitting I don't remember what, something dark blue. Anyhow, I noticed that she laid her work aside and closed her eyes for a spell. That was something she used to do pretty regular and I always took notice because she wasn't just resting her eyes. There was a matter came to her mind at these times and I could feel the silence deepen all around. When she closed her eyes like that, everything went dead quiet. There was no sound to be heard in the sewing room or anywhere else in the house or coming from outside. When she closed her eyes, all the sound everywhere stopped.'

"She unfolded the bitsy linen handkerchief from her palm and dried her eyes again. 'So this one time I thought to myself, If I close my eyes, too, and think real hard, maybe I can see in my mind what Selena is seeing in hers. So I tried it out. I shut my eyes and concentrated with all I had in me.'

"Aunt Ona asked if the trial succeeded. We all five leaned forward, holding our breath.

" 'I don't know,' Lexie said. 'There's no way to tell for sure. But a picture did enter my mind as powerful as the electric coming on. Nothing I'd ever thought or remembered in my head, so I thought it was Selena's picture. Anyhow, when I opened my eyes and heard the sounds of the house again, I saw that she was looking me full in the face with the sorrowfulest expression you'd ever see on anybody.'

" 'What was the picture?'

" 'All right, I am going to tell you,' she said, 'but I won't be able to make much sense out of it. It was the picture that came in my mind, but whether it was the same one in Selena's, I can't know.

" 'What I saw is this little girl. She is about five years old, maybe six. She is naked and her lips are purple with cold and she is sick with I don't know what illness. She is lying on a heap of smelly old rags in a dark place. She has been lying there a long time and she will go on lying there. She cries sometimes, but if she makes any noise, some green-faced creatures come out of the shadows and put their claw hands on her and in her. So she weeps and tries not to make a sound. She does not move her arms or legs. She will go on lying in this foul place forever and her suffering will never come to an end.'

"We couldn't figure what to make of it all. 'Who is she?'

" 'I don't know,' Lexie replied. 'I don't know anything but that picture in my mind. It was there clear as a bell till I opened my eyes. Now it never goes out of my head. I wish it would, but it won't.'

" 'Is that little girl anybody we know, somebody in our settlement?'

"She shook her head. 'No. Wherever she is, it is far away in a strange land that is cold and dark.'

" 'But—'

" 'And now,' she said, getting up and going to the teapot, 'you've heard my last word on the subject. I'll never mention it again and I'll thank you not to ask me. But I want you to have some more tea and to try one of these sugar cookies I made yesterday with some vanilla drops I put in them.'

" 'But we wanted to hear more about the little girl. Where—'

" 'No,' she told us. 'You've heard my last. No use in asking.' "

The ruby curls of Rome apple peel lay heaped on the table and the quarter-moon slices floated in the pan of water. My grandmother and I looked not at each other but into the snow that was funneling down in tiny bitter flakes, twisting around the tree trunks in the grove and whispering against the windowpanes. Looking through the grove, we could see the snow wild above the fields, flaring in thin curtains like cheesecloth tattered and torn. The ground was beginning to whiten, the sheet-ice patches furring over. The fields were otherwise empty, no animals, no birds, only the snow tingling the wind with noiseless tumult.

I started to say something but she forestalled me. "No, I don't understand it, either, Jess, not anything about it. Lexie Courland said it all that one time and never said again. Lexie is gone now and Selena before her and Aunt Ona has passed on, too. Most of the women of that generation are gone and their loss is a destruction to us all, for they were a good and faithful company and the generations that have come after don't seem to me to have their hardiness or savor." She began brushing the peels off the table into her aproned lap. "Maybe I'm wrong about that. I'd like to think I am."

I felt like I ought to say something, so I said, "No, I don't think you're wrong." But even that was too much and I hushed and looked out again into the snow that was coming down harder, the wind raw behind it now.

THE FISHERWOMAN

My grandmother was not partial to the story of Earlene Lewis because it was speckled with profanity. It was only a mild spring-scallion type of profanity, nothing like the raw, hot Spanish-onion oaths that have lately become so common a part of discourse. But cusswords irritated my grandmother; she called them "bywords" and avoided the tales in which they were necessary. My mother, too, kept her modest distance from warmly seasoned diction, but she admired Cousin Earlene so much and was so pleased with her story that she could not resist telling it to me one long November afternoon while we waited for my father to come home for supper. He was engaged with his friend Virgil Campbell in a project that was either serious business or sheer deviltry; we wouldn't know which for weeks, and maybe not ever.

"Earlene Lewis was different from all the other girls," my mother told me, "because she was a trout fisherman. That was what she was born to be. Mighty few women at that time took an interest in fly-fishing, and most of them were so clumsy at it that all nature shuddered to glimpse them on the stream, fat in their hot waders and with their hair all in fancy dos. They took few fish and didn't much care, since they were only trying to impress boyfriends.

"But Earlene owned to a genuine interest from the start. In fact, she met old man Worley because he had spotted her in the back of Ronnie Dacy's Western Auto store one Saturday morning in early March while she was looking at fishing rods. She admired the colors—the dark green and the malt brown and the splotched gold-and-black—and she was tapping a red one lightly with her fingernail to feel it throb along its length.

"The old man stood behind her and, just as she was turning away, spoke abruptly. 'What's your name, girl?'

"Mr. Worley was a picturesque old fellow. His face was weathered to the color of a cured burley leaf and so wrinkled it appeared to be caving in, but his blue eyes were alert and as bright as the shine on a table knife. He wore faded brown coveralls and a beat-up black felt hat pulled low on his brow. The colorful patch of his costume was the clean red bandanna knotted around his neck.

" 'Earlene Lewis,' she said.

" 'Who's your folks?'

" 'My mother is Maidy Lewis. She works at the Challenger factory.'

"He nodded. 'So your daddy would be Jimmy Devoe Lewis. I know Jimmy Devoe. Know your mama, too. Know all your folks for a long time back. You never saw your grandaddy, did you?'

"She shook her head, staring at the knot of his red bandanna. When he talked, it bobbled up and down like an apple on an October limb. The way it moved seemed part of his voice.

" 'Where is your daddy now?'

"She answered this question straightforwardly, though it required a kind of courage that Earlene was learning young. She looked old man Worley right in the eye and said, 'He had to go away for a while. He was drinking too much and it made him sick.'

"Mr. Worley nodded again. 'That's what I heard,' he said. 'But I'll tell you, around these goddamn parts I never expect to hear anything that's half the truth. How are you and your mother getting along? What shift have they got her working?'

" 'Three to eleven,' Earlene said. 'We're doing okay. She says if I'll keep the house, she'll bring in the money and we might do better than before.'

" 'Maybe so,' he said dryly. 'But here you are, looking at these fishing rods. Have you ever been fishing?'

" 'Yes, sir. My daddy took me.'

" 'Where?'

" 'We went to the lake one time. And we went to Brumley's Trout Pond.'

" 'That ain't fishing. That ain't even a proper way to drown worms. Did you catch you a fish?'

" 'Yes, sir.'

" 'What was the biggest you ever caught?'

"She held her hands out.

" 'That ain't very big.'

"She looked away from him, out the window of the store, at the sleepy railroad depot across the street, dingy in the morning sun. 'I guess not,' she admitted.

" 'If you don't learn to tell a lie, ain't no way can you be a fisherman. Here—' he said, pulling her hands a yard apart. 'Every fish you ever caught is this big.' He spread them a yard and a half. 'And every one that got away is this big.' He let her hands go and leaned down to peer at her solemnly. 'That's the first thing you have to learn.'

"Then she smiled at last. 'Yes, sir.'

" 'About how old would you be?'

" 'Twelve.'

" 'Going on thirteen?'

" 'Yes, sir.'

" 'Do you like to climb trees? Do you like to get up in a big old cherry tree and climb all the way to the very tip-top?'

"She nodded, not admitting to anything, and was relieved to find he liked her answer.

" 'Thought so,' he said. 'I thought I might be looking at a tomboy when I spotted you with these rods. How would you like to go fishing? I might take a notion to bring you along sometime.'

" 'I don't know.'

" 'Tell you what, I'll talk to your mama. If she says it's okay, we'll go one of these days, you and me. But I don't go to no little pissant pond. I go in the mountains where it's rough, up to the real fish. You reckon you could scramble over them big old rocks?'

" 'I guess so.'

"Suddenly he bent down and held his face close to hers. 'Take a real good look,' he said. 'How old would you say I am?'

"She shook her head. 'I don't know.'

" 'Take a guess. How old?'

"She imagined an astronomical figure. 'Fifty-three years old.'

"He cackled like a treaded hen and straightened up and announced with grand pride, 'I'm seventy-five. Three-quarters of a century. You think about that. Seventy-five years old.'

"She thought, but seventy-five didn't mean anything. He might as well have claimed a thousand. She looked glumly at the dull toes of his boots.

" 'I'll talk to your mother when I get a chance. We'll see if she won't say you can go. You're a peart-looking youngun; we might could make you a fisherman. I'll have a little talk with Maidy.' He turned and walked away. Halfway down the aisle, he spun about and called to her. 'What was the biggest fish you ever caught?'

Without hesitation she showed him her whole wingspan.

" 'All right,' he said. 'It's a keeper.' "

"In this way, Earlene met the old man she never afterward called anything but Mr. Worley, and she had remembered for three years every detail of that encounter and she expected she would remember all her life. She had become his fishing partner, just as he'd proposed. He was not some filthy old man thinking to do shame on a young girl. He was Mr. Worley, whom everybody knew, cranky and good-hearted and famous for his devotion to the art of trout fishing.

"After Mr. Worley had spoken to Maidy, she came to ask her daughter if she actually did want to go off every Saturday morning before daylight. 'He's a dear old soul,' she said. 'He'll treat you good. But he goes into some tight and rugged spots and he's getting on in years. It could be dangerous. You'd have to use your good sense not to get hurt.'

"She looked into her mother's face, searching for a hint. She wanted to ask if it would be any fun but was not certain the question was polite. Maidy seemed distracted, as if she was thinking hard, but not about the subject at hand.

" 'That's if you want to go, I mean. Do you want to?'

"They were sitting cross-legged on Maidy's bed and Earlene began to pluck at the blobs of pink chenille. 'I don't know,' she said. 'I guess so.'

" 'Well, don't tear up the bedspread just because you can't make up your mind.'

" 'I don't have any fishing stuff,' Earlene said. 'I don't have any . . . tackle.' She mumbled the word shyly and for the first time. She had gleaned it—along with words like *trolling, walleye,* and *duck blind*—from the pages of *Field & Stream,* the magazine she used to read in the barbershop while her daddy got his hair cut. She liked the bright covers with flushed birds in flight or big fish breaking water in the foreground and the handsome, capable men in the background taking the excitement in stride. She studied the advertisements for telescopic sights, oilskin kayaks, snowshoes, and Johnson motors. She memorized the photos of hunters and fishermen with their trophies, because they looked like people she might know; the rich people pictured in *Look* and *June Bride* appeared unreal.

" 'Mr. Worley says he'll loan you something to fish with while you learn,' her mother said. 'All you'll need is some old blue jeans and tennis shoes. Your feet would be wet all day long, and no telling how much else of you.'

" 'I don't have any tennis shoes.'

" 'Well, I reckon we can manage a pair of those, honey. But first you'll have to make up your mind. I'm not certain why he's asking you along. Over the years he's taught a lot of boys all about the streams, but you're the first girl he's took an interest in.'

" 'I am?'

" 'That's what I hear.'

"So she decided yes. She wanted to be the first girl to do anything. She'd always hoped to strike upon adventures, and now she was twelve and had her chance. No other girl she knew of went trout fishing. Of course, she didn't know them very well. She had no close friends at school, probably because of her daddy's reputation. But she didn't care about that, either. She liked Jimmy Devoe. When he was drunk, he wasn't cruel or ugly, only sad and helpless and lonesome. A long time ago something dreadful had happened to her father, something that caused him to drink like he did. Earlene knew she was too young to understand what that might be. She'd have to grow older to find out, and she wasn't looking forward to that. There was a time when people said, 'You'll understand when you get a little older,' and she had taken it as a promise. Now she heard that sentence as a threat. 'I want to go fishing,' she said.

"Her mother warned her. 'It won't be easy.'

"But she was steady in her mind. She wanted to learn how to fish for trout. Maybe she would be the only girl who ever did, the first in world history."

"And three years later, now when she was fifteen, she was still the only girl she knew about who fished. She hardly knew her schoolmates; her situation at home prevented an active social life and, anyway, she preferred to go fishing. Her mother pretended despair, saying that she was bringing up a daughter whose only ambition was to be like old man Worley, a crazy old coot nobody could get along with. 'You used to be a nice young lady, but you've gone sadly downhill.'

"There was a melancholy tone in her mother's teasing, though. Jimmy Devoe had disappeared; he had run away from Pleasant Acres and the police could not locate him. Nobody could. To Earlene, it was as if her father had fulfilled his strongest ambition: He had always been lost in almost every way and now his body had wandered off like the rest of him. She knew better than to hope he would return, but sometimes she imagined that he did—that he came in late at night and sat silent, full of whiskey and sorrow, on the foot of her bed while she kept her eyes shut, pretending to sleep. Just the way it used to be.

"Yet she was not deceived. She was a sensible girl and thrashing the creeks and rivers every Saturday in fishing season had toughened her. That's what her mother said, but Earlene thought it wasn't the waterfalls and thickets, the rocks and brambles that had made her wiry in spirit and body. It was keeping company with Mr. Worley, whose temperament was as barbed as blackberry vines and gnarly as willow roots. If she could take what he dished out, the trout streams would be the easy part. In fact, the man himself was a headlong stream and everybody who knew him had to toil against his current.

"He was impatient of everything but Earlene and fishing. These days in midsummer the mountain streams were overloaded with tourist anglers, plump, red-faced Floridians who smoked cigars and carried expensive rods and Swedish lures. Mr. Worley detested their fancy equipment, their big new cars, their blowhard talk, their tastes in fashion, and, above all, their manners on the streams. When he drove his clatterbang old Ford pickup over the gravel roads to his favorite spots, he and Earlene would pass troops of outlanders casting in the easy lower stretches. He noted one of them wearing a soft tweed hat decorated with dry flies. 'That feller had better hope he don't fall in,' Mr. Worley said. 'The fish will gnaw his head off.'

"Earlene had learned to get along with him. He went easy on her for the most part, though he never tired of calling her 'a child of her time.' He had an unbounded contempt for the present time. According to Mr. Worley, all the strong men and beautiful, brave women had died out, all the tall, sound trees had been cut down, and all the champion fish had been taken by scoundrels or smothered by pollution.

" 'Just look at this guy,' he said, indicating the oversized camper lumbering slowly in front of them on the tortuous mountain road. 'If this son of a bitch went any slower, he'd roll backwards on top of us. Couldn't decide what he ought to bring along with him, so he brought his whole goddamn house.' He stepped on the accelerator and swung around the obstacle, taking the outside of a blind curve. 'Goddamn things are a menace to life and limb,' he said.

"Earlene let out her breath. She had tried to resign herself to the notion she was going to meet her doom in this clankety pickup when Mr. Worley plowed it head-on into a church bus or spun it over a cliff edge. But her stoicism faltered as the wobbling side of the camper came within inches of her window. 'You're right,' she conceded. 'They're dangerous.'

"He gave her a quick foxy glance. 'I don't let 'em buffalo me. A man would die of old age before he got to the fishing place.' He pushed his crooked wire-rimmed glasses up the bridge of his nose. A month ago he had decided his eyesight was weakening, so he'd rummaged in the tool chest behind the truck seat until he found a pair of spectacles in an old steel case. He had no idea how they'd got there but claimed they improved his vision one hundred percent. 'Better than a hundred percent. I can see a mite on a flea on a tick on a hilltop three miles off. I'd be ashamed to tell you what they're doing to one another.'

"His sentences were well seasoned with words like *hell* and *goddamn* and *son of a bitch,* but those were generally his strongest oaths and he wouldn't tolerate even these in Earlene. 'If you took to cussing while we was out here, we'd just have to turn around and head back. Fish can't stand to hear a woman cuss. They hide under the goddamn rocks.'

" 'Well, *you* cuss.'

" 'They're used to my ways. When they hear me coming, they say, Damn if it ain't that old low-life Worley again, and when is he ever going to get tired of whipping this water to death? That's what they say.'

" 'Maybe they could get used to me cussing.'

" 'No. Don't nobody get used to a woman cussing or mining coal. But I reckon they've done just about everything else.'

" 'What about trout fishing?' she asked. 'You don't see women trout fishing.'

" 'That's so.' He appeared to study the problem. 'I knew maybe five or six I'd call real fishermen. One of them I was married to.'

" 'What happened?'

" 'Well, we found out we liked each other right well, so we went to a preacher and he said, "Do you?" And we said, "We sure do." And that was that.'

" 'I mean, what happened to Mrs. Worley?'

" 'She give up on me,' he said. His face went solemn and the wrinkles around his eyes smoothed out, but this only made him look older. 'All three of them did.'

" 'Did what?'

" 'Give up,' he said, and she knew that was all he was going to say and that whatever other information she found out would have to come from someone else.

"They pulled around a curve and Mr. Worley pointed to another gaudy angler standing hip-deep in a pool. 'Look at that one,' he said. 'He don't want no fish. He only come so they could admire his shirt.'

"She smiled, having got used to his humor, cornball and waspish. She understood now how he used it to deflect irritation and tedium. She discovered, too, that she was picking up the habit, along with others of his, making little jokes to ease tensions with her mother.

"They were headed up the river to a spot so troublesome to reach that it was almost never fished. To get to this three-mile stretch of water, they had to go straight down the mountainside through shale and blackberry vines. The stream was choked with boulders and flood-piled timber, but there they could take the long, lean, pink-fleshed rainbows the old man described as having gone native, and not the pasty, fat Park Service stock. It was thrilling to tumble down through the riprap and copperheads but not thrilling to climb back up after a day on the water.

"But this was where they came now that he'd taught her how to fish, because it was the best place. The rocks and low bushes were obstacles she overcame now, placing her fly almost anywhere she desired, settling it on the surface as gently as a blown thistle seed. It had taken a while, but she had learned.

"Mr. Worley used to counsel patience. 'That's what you need and you ought to learn some. I'm the one that ought to lose patience, what with one foot in the grave up to the knee joint. Slow down. You can't have a good time if you go too fast.'

"He spoke of death so often and so cheerfully that she became assured he could never die. Maybe men didn't die, but only disappeared—like her father. He and Mr. Worley were the only two she had ever known; she had no uncles and no boyfriend and at that time her mother had no boyfriend, either. Even last year Maidy was still in love with Jimmy Devoe, wherever he was, alive or dead. So Mr. Worley was Earlene's one man and he talked as if he might expire at any moment.

" 'I don't see how you're in any great danger,' she said.

" 'At my age, every breath is a mortal danger.'

" 'But I hear you're only as old as you feel.'

" 'Don't believe it,' he said. 'If I was as old as I feel, I'd've done outrun Methuselah by a generation.'

"Yet his strength and endurance were extraordinary. He suffered a shortness of breath and a slight palsy, though this latter affliction did not hinder his tying a Royal Coachman to a nearly invisible nylon leader with a deft twiddle. He traveled the streams with enviable alacrity, careful not to outdistance Earlene, who was surely no weakling.

"And no tenderfoot. He had taught her patiently and thoroughly how to read the streams, how to approach the fish, how to use her rod and line. These nights she dreamed of taking a huge brown trout on a leader as slender as a horsehair. He had told her about horsehair.

" 'That's what we used to use,' he said. 'They're stronger than you'd think, but hard to handle. But I found me a method. They're brittle, you know, so I soaked them in Johnson's baby oil. You might want to remember that.'

" 'This is the modern age,' Earlene said. 'We've got nylon leaders nowadays.'

" 'But what are you going to do when the nylon factories break down? This modern age of yours is just a passing fancy.'

" 'When do you think the factories will break down, Mr. Worley?'

" 'Be a while, I reckon,' he said glumly. 'There's still a few streams they ain't poisoned yet.' He pulled the truck into a wide-out under a tall walnut and cut the ignition and gave Earlene a sly wink. 'Let's you and me go down,' he said, 'and engage in the hopeless cause.'

" 'You say that every time.'

" 'Bad luck not to. Ain't nobody but a goddamn tourist will think he can actually catch trout.'

" 'Well, you catch them. A lot of them.'

" 'They feel sorry for me,' he declared. 'So will you when the time comes.'

"They got down from the truck, both a little stiff from the early ride, and paced about to loosen up. Then they stood silent, side by side, looking into the gorge through the treetops below and listening to the river.

"They made a pair. Mr. Worley was age-bent now to the same height as Earlene, but she still felt that she looked up into his face. She was a pretty girl with freckles and green eyes and dark red hair she had learned to pile on top of her head and tuck under her hat brim. She had a deep contralto voice, startling in its masculine timbre, and she wore jeans and an old corduroy jacket and she imitated the old man with a beat-up felt hat jammed down. She envied his bandanna but hadn't the nerve to wear one.

"Their friendship was in the nature of a religious confraternity, bound not by the fish but by fishing, by the stony peaks, the shadowy hollers, the deep pools and the shallow white water, and the urge of the discipline. Never just the fish—they could have gathered those with live bait or even, as Mr. Worley said, 'with a big goddamn truckload of dynamite.' Tourists might do something like that; they were missing the point. 'Because they don't understand how God did not put us on His green earth to blow up trout or bash them with baseball bats. He put us here to test us against a smart creature that lives in the water and He wanted us to use a lure that looks like a piece of lint you found under the bed.'

" 'Why does He want us to do that?'

" 'For the same reason He give Job boils and Adam a wife. To learn us some patience. Just like I've been trying to learn you some patience.'

" 'I have learned patience,' Earlene said. 'You just don't know.'

" 'I know better'n you do. One of these first days some big old no-good trifling boy will come along and look at you sideways and off you'll go. You won't half think. You won't remember patience or nothing else. Off you'll trot like a bird dog that's been whistled for.'

"She sighed. 'I don't know. No boys have been looking at me sideways or frontways or behindways. No telling what I might do.'

" 'You'll go running after him like a bloodhound.'

" 'Well,' she said, 'if he's good-looking. Real, real good-looking.'

"Because she wasn't going to say, I'll never do that, like the silly girls in my high school. Like my mama these days. At first her mother had been guarded and secret after Jimmy Devoe was lost and gone, but that had lasted only two years. Now she was all moony-goony about a man who might as well have had LIAR spelled on his forehead in green paint. He called himself Kyle Kelvin, and Earlene kept all the distance from him she could. If she'd been a praying girl, she would have entreated the Lord for her mother's sanity to be restored.

" 'Are you about ready?' Mr. Worley asked.

" 'I reckon,' she said, thinking that boyfriends could come later, after she had caught the big fish she dreamed about. And then Earlene and the old man stepped off the level gravel road into the steep mountainside and went down as awkward as new-foaled colts."

"They fussed about together at the river edge, getting their feet wet and their tackle ready, and in a few minutes Earlene struck off upstream, leaving Mr. Worley to follow after her in a while. She found a dim trail above and followed it to a picturesque waterfall about twenty feet high. The fall had a spindly stream on either side of its one powerful pour-off into the deep onyx pool below. She decided to try her luck here; she could tell no one had fished it that day.

"It looked good. The boil of the waterfall spread into a calm water fanning outward, black in the middle but with sunken logs and rocks beneath, all furred with cocoa-colored tannin.

"There would be a trout in there. She smiled, thinking how Mr. Worley would sniff the air, saying he smelt a good un. She debated about a choice of flies and decided to stay with the female Adams she had already tied on.

"She knew where she wanted to place it, at the point where the pour-off smoothed out into ripples that would bob the fly up and down. She took her time stripping line off and cast easily, almost casually, and put it where she aimed. The fly rode silkily down the current, gathering speed as it neared the outlet of the pool.

"She had decided to take it up for another cast when she felt the strike—a hard one. For a moment she felt nothing, and then a powerful steady pull as the fish made a run for the rocks at the pool head. She groped with her feet for balance and made sure the hook was set. Then she took four breaths to the bottom of her lungs and began to think with the fish, just the way the old man had taught her to do. She could tell it wasn't the fish of her dreams, but it was big enough, the biggest either of them had caught in three years.

"It must have been an epic battle with that fish," my mother said, and she told me, too, how sometimes she liked to think of her cousin as a young girl, there among the boulders of the Upper North Mills, struggling to land the trout that would earn old man Worley's admiration and maybe his envy. "It took her a good half-hour, but land it she did, fighting for every inch of line, then scooping it up at last with the net that was looped around her belt with elastic cord.

"The part Earlene always hated was knocking the head of a fish against a rock to give it a quick death, but she did this, too, and sat down on a mossy boulder to gut her catch with her little Boker pocketknife. She was wet and chilled to the waist, but all above she was hot and sweaty. It had been a little like a wrestling match; at the end she'd felt her forearms tiring, but she'd outlasted the trout and made it her trophy.

"She rinsed her knife and closed it and slipped it into her pocket. She washed her hands. Thirsty, she removed her hat and got down on all fours and sucked from the river. It tasted of rocks and leaves and moss and she imagined it flavored with fish guts, too, fresh and raw. She put her hat on and stood and held her trout up. Pretending she was another person, a stranger to the fish, she whistled in amazement. It was too big to go into her little homemade creel, so she dropped it into the net and slung it over her shoulder and started back downstream.

"She hadn't realized she'd come so far; it was a good twenty minutes before she spotted Mr. Worley. He was sitting in the sand with his back against a rock. When he saw her, he waved his hat and she knew something was wrong. She hurried the best she could, the big fish flopping against her spine.

" 'What's the matter?' she said. His strained face frightened her, pale and tight. 'What happened?'

" 'Turned my goddamn ankle,' he said. 'I took me a little tumble over there while my foot was wedged in between them rocks.' His voice was stretched thin.

" 'Does it hurt bad?'

" 'It's broke,' he said, and tried to make a joke. 'So it don't feel as good as it looks.'

" 'Let me see.'

" 'No,' he said. 'Don't waste your time. You're going to have to go for help because we won't be able to get out of here, just you and me.'

" 'Where do I go?'

" 'Head out toward the ranger station. You're bound to run into somebody before too long. Tell them to come and get me. You know where we are, don't you?'

" 'I think so.'

" 'You'll have to hurry along. If it was to rain up a flash flood, I'd be a goner down in here.'

"She glanced at the sky. 'I don't think it'll rain for a while yet.'

" 'That's a pleasure to hear,' he said, 'because it's a right far piece to get there and you'll be going slow. Leastways I hope you will.'

"It took her a moment to catch on. 'But I never drove,' she said. 'I don't know how to drive.'

" 'I'm going to tell you how.'

" 'I don't think I can.'

" 'Sure you can. Anybody that can catch them a big old fish like that one can drive. Let me see that thing.'

"She held it up and he wagged his head in wonderment, just the way she'd hoped he would.

" 'I'd call it a keeper,' he said, but then he grimaced. He opened his left hand to show his key ring ready for her. 'This here's the ignition key,' he said, and went on to explain, patient and salty, just as if he was in no pain or danger, how to drive. He answered all the questions she could think to ask. 'There's easier trucks to learn on,' he said, 'but if you can drive my old Ford, you can drive anything. I was planning on learning you anyway.'

" 'I don't know about this,' she said.

" 'Yes you do,' he said. 'Because you've got to. You'll be all right. Just keep your head like you had a big old fish on your line. You understand me now?'

" 'Yes, sir.'

" 'Hurry along, then. Leave your stuff here with me. Try to make some speed, but be mighty careful. Stop the first people you see and tell them what the trouble is.'

" 'All right,' she said. 'I'll be back as soon as I can.'

" 'You better be quick,' the old man said. 'Because if I get hungry, I'm going to eat your fish.' "

"She struggled on the mountainside, pulling herself up with any handhold she could find, but slipping backward on the shale. Once she went down on a patch of sharp gravel and tore her jeans and when she saw her knees bleeding, she tried not to think about it. Already her mouth was dry and she wasn't halfway up to the road.

"When she got there, she had to pause and think which way to turn and she began to talk to herself aloud, being her own old man Worley. 'Slow down,' she said. 'Think it out. We started up on top of a ridge where that walnut tree was and the road goes uphill here to the right, so it must be in that direction.'

"Her reasoning was sound. After the second curve she spotted the truck under the towering walnut and let out a noisy sob of relief.

"She climbed in on the driver's side and for a brief moment crossed her arms on the steering wheel and laid her head there and wept a little. Her legs ached and burned, her throat was sandpaper, and she was frightened.

"Then she collected herself and tried to get her thoughts in order, though the strange sensation of sitting on the wrong side of the truck cab distracted her. On the passenger side the seat was firm, but on this side it was butt-sprung. And the litter underfoot—the broken tools and paper cups and soft-drink cans—confused her feet as she tried the pedals.

"She dug the key ring out of her shirt pocket but couldn't fit the right key into the ignition until she thought to turn it upside down. 'If I can't even get the key in, how will I ever drive this thing?' she asked. And answered: 'By learning me some patience, the way God gave Job boils.'

"When she twisted the key, the starter whined and the truck lurched forward against the walnut tree. 'Wait,' she said. 'Remember you've got to push the clutch in.'

"She had to balance forward on the edge of the seat with the steering wheel brushing her chest in order to reach the clutch. When the motor caught at last, she concentrated on finding reverse. Not an easy task. She kept putting it into second, rocking against the tree, and killing the motor, but finally she backed it out into the road, wrestled it into low gear, and rolled away.

" 'Somebody could have come around the curve right then,' she said. 'They would've hit me smack dead-on. There wouldn't be nothing left of us but license tags.'

"It was dreadful to push in the clutch and feel the truck speed downhill. This time she couldn't find second and skidded around a gravely curve, holding her breath when the rear end fishtailed. The gears scraped mercilessly.

" 'Slow down.'

"She hit the brakes and slid toward the ditch and almost killed the motor again. 'I'll keep it in second,' she announced. 'If I keep trying to change gears, I'm going to roll off the mountain.'

"A drop of sweat made her nose itch and she tried to wipe it off on her shoulder but was afraid to take her eyes off the road. She knew she was swinging too wide on the curves, but when she tightened down, she was always late. The washboard stretches of road bounced her so high off the seat, her foot would slip from the accelerator and the truck would lurch almost to a standstill. It's not many times a girl will wish for more lard in her bucket, but this one time Earlene knew she was too light where she needed heft.

"She risked a glance at the speedometer. Thirty miles an hour. She would have sworn she was going sixty, the gravel spraying up behind her and the truck leaping up and down like a jackrabbit and the flowery roadsides whizzing by. Thirty was still too fast, but when she braked on the curves, she slid the wrong way. And when the road climbed again, she had to floor the accelerator to keep going at all. She would rather chance a wreck than have the motor die on a steep upgrade. 'I don't know what I would do. Roll backward all the way home, I guess.'

"But then on the next curve there was a car headed toward her, a rusty red station wagon bearing down fast. She swerved to the right-hand side, rubbing against the clay bank with big tree roots protruding. There was a tearing noise and the truck rocked fearfully, but when she tried to pull back onto the road, the ditch kept crumbling away so that the truck was leaning against the bank and digging in. Then she saw it coming, the big rock sticking out of the bank, big as a corncrib, but there was nothing she could do. It took out the window on the passenger side and crumpled the door and skewed the truck halfway around, setting it crosswise in the road.

" 'If a car comes through here now, we're all doomed,' she said. 'Just a red spot in the road.'

"She twisted the steering wheel to the left as hard as she could and gentled the acceleration and the truck straightened out. It was hard to turn and she was sure there was something wrong with the steering. The right fender would be rubbing against the tire, but there was something else wrong, too. 'He is going to have an A-one conniption fit when he sees his truck,' she said, and began to wonder if she could impute the damage to the crazy driving of some splatter-shirted tourist.

"The safety glass of the broken window flapped like a pillowcase in the wind and gritty dust stung her face and made her thirst more acute. She thought she heard the engine making strange noises, sounds no truck on earth had ever made before, and she could only hope the motor would hold out until she reached wherever she was going. The downhill grade had become pretty steep, so she knew she was nearing the western valley. There was a bridge there at the bottom and from the bridge straight up the river it was only about a mile and a half to where Mr. Worley lay in pain. 'They'll probably go up from the bridge to rescue him,' she said, but the optimism of this sentence sounded hollow and she shook her head. 'I'd just better mind keeping this old busted truck in the road.'

"She had come to the last and steepest slope of the mountain and she knew it to be full of hairpin turns, so she stopped and put on the emergency brake and wiggled, sweating and muttering, into low gear. Steam was billowing from the radiator and it blew back in her face when she let the brake off and went slowly down, the engine roaring like a thresher in an oat field. 'I hope this thing won't blow up like a big firecracker,' she said.

"But she was getting close to the bottom. She could hear, or imagined she could hear, the river dashing against its boulders down there beneath the treetops. She hated crawling along like this with Mr. Worley hurting and maybe in danger of drowning. 'But what good would it do him if I drove off into the river?' Still, she was glad he couldn't see her inching along.

"The road leveled out now that she had reached the bottom, so she stopped again and got it into second gear and went bumping along. Her jaw muscles ached from clenching her mouth shut; every time she talked to herself, her teeth clicked together and she bit her tongue. The crippled truck was shaking violently. Like a cat trying to pass a peach pit—that was what Mr. Worley would say, and Earlene nodded at the thought.

"Because she felt a sweet relief. She could hardly believe she'd got down off the mountain alive in this busted-up old truck, but here she was on level ground. All she needed to do now was find somebody to send after Mr. Worley and save his life.

"She spotted the bridge ahead and two vehicles pulled off beside it. One of them was a ranger. He was questioning a tourist in a red-and-yellow Hawaiian shirt and they both turned around to see her coming. They heard this engine about to blow up, she thought to herself. Just look at their faces. I'll bet they never saw such an old wreck of a truck still traveling on the road. They look like they're seeing Frankenstein's monster.

"When she got to where they were standing, she stopped the truck dead center in the road and cut the motor and climbed down. Me, too, she thought. I'll bet I look like something they never saw before, either. Worse'n the truck. I'll bet they think I'm a certified crazy person.

"The ranger was coming toward her, with the tourist following tentatively, and she stood her ground, though she dreaded trying to answer any questions about her driving. But her legs kept trembling and finally buckled and she plopped down on the running board and gazed up in mute appeal into the ranger's face. He was a middle-aged man with a bright complexion and his eyes were full of concern.

" 'What's wrong, young fellow?' he asked. 'Have you hit another vehicle back there on the road?'

"When she tried to answer, she couldn't. Her mouth and throat were parched and she couldn't seem to get her breath. She looked down at the gravel and her damp tennis shoes, thinking, All I did all the way down the mountain was chatter to myself like a monkey and now I can't speak a word.

" 'Take it easy, son,' the ranger said. 'Take your time. Is there anybody hurt back there where you came from?'

"She looked up now at the ranger, intent on his question, and at the plump tourist gawking at her with his mouth open, and stood up so quickly and with such an intense expression on her face that both men, with a concerted startled movement, stepped back from her. Wildly she looked from one to another. Then she ripped off the old felt hat all stuck to her head with sweat and flung it down in the dust and banged her fists against her hips. Her pretty red hair tumbled down on her neck as she cried out, 'I ain't no goddamn boy!' "

"Now I don't think that was what she meant to say first thing off the bat," my mother explained. "But it must have been foremost in her mind at that moment, because the sentence shot out of her mouth like a rock from a slingshot."

"What did those men say to her?" I asked.

"Nothing. She told me they just stared at her like a person that had escaped from Bakersville Hall still dressed in a straitjacket. Of course, she went on to tell them about old man Worley and the peril he was in and where he was located. She even had the presence to mention her fish and ask them to bring it out, too."

"Did they bring it?"

"They sure did."

"How big was it?"

"Just a little over ten pounds."

"I'd call it a keeper."

"Wasn't she a brave young thing?" my mother said. "She's my age now and still a spirited woman. Everybody knows what Cousin Earlene is like."

"How come you know so much about it? The things she was thinking and talking to herself?"

"She told me a lot and then I put myself in her place so I could tell the story to you. That's what storytellers do. Maybe you'll remember that if you ever take a notion to tell stories. Do you think you'd like to be a storyteller?"

"Maybe. But I don't hardly know any stories."

"Don't worry," my mother said. "You'll learn some. All you have to do is listen."

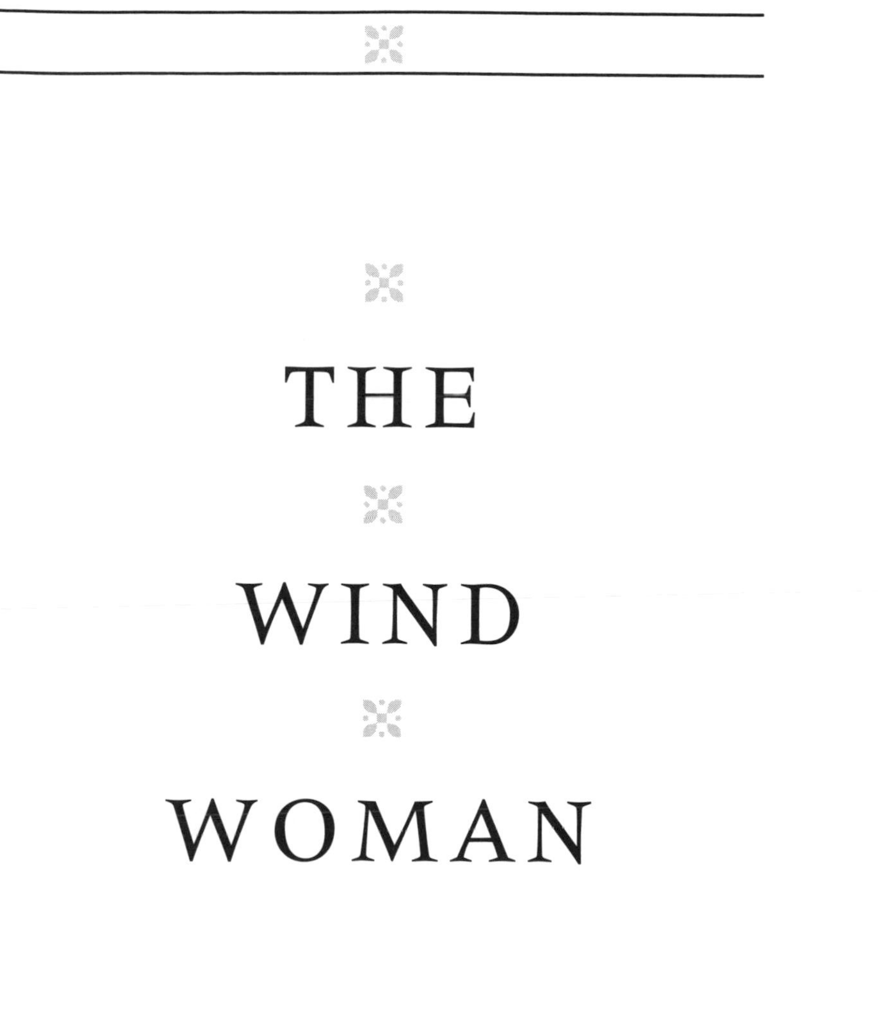

THE WIND WOMAN

It seemed that my mother told me she had a number of duty calls to pay and asked if I would like to accompany her. And it seemed that I was younger than I actually was and said yes and we set out westward toward Hardison County in the old wooden station wagon we used to own and not in the new green Chevrolet sedan. It seemed that we were soon off the main highway, following rattling gravel roads squirming between mountains taller and bluer than any I remembered. My mother was wearing a smart linen dress and white gloves and white shoes and kept her gaze on the road, which went continually bright and dark with tree shadow. It was like she was not looking out a windshield but peering into something, a dim corner or a deep well.

"We must pay our respects," she told me. "First to the River Woman, who lives in the grassy bottom acres by the Little Tennessee. Then we must visit the Cloud Woman and the Fire Woman. The Moon Woman lives in a cave on the far side of Ember Mountain; I hear she has been ailing and has had doctors in, so we mustn't stay long, but we have to make our call. If Aunt Priddy is home, we will stop by for tea but then must travel on to see the Deer Woman and the Happiest Woman. But I am most particularly anxious for you to meet the Wind Woman. Do you know why?"

"No, ma'am."

"Well, I saw the other day that you were writing poetry in one of your notebooks. I don't know what you were writing about, but if you ever take a notion to write about our part of the earth, about the trees and hills and streams, about the animals and our friends and neighbors who live in the mountains, then you must meet the Wind Woman, for you'll never write a purposeful word till you do."

"Who is she?" I asked. "I never heard of her."

"That makes it all the more important."

"Where does she live?"

My mother turned then to give me the pitying stare she reserved for those whose ignorance locked them in a darkness as extensive as the nightside of Mercury. "I thought you knew that. She lives on Wind Mountain, right there on the knob beside the sawtooth gap. I thought everybody knew at least that much."

"Not me."

She looked away. "I used to write poems. They were about the affections of my heart. My heart was always selfish, but my head has been clear. I have a good head for business, better than anybody knows. That comes later. When my heart was foolish and untamed, I wrote many poems."

"I'd like to read them."

"Oh, you can't read them, Jess. No one can. I set them down in pokeberry juice and oak-gall ink. I wrote out the words with many a flourish on the petals of mallow and dogwood petals and morning glory. Then I gathered them all up in a great bedsheet and walked down to the iron bridge over the Pigeon River with them slung on my

back. I emptied them out onto the waters. I can still see them floating away in the air like butterflies and then settling on the river in a sunny glistening and floating away down to the boiling rapids. It was a pretty sight, believe me."

"So nobody'll ever know what you wrote."

"No."

"I'll bet they were real good poems."

This time when she looked at me, shadows from inside her mind rippled over her face like furls in a breeze-raked silk banner. "Excuse me," she said, and pulled over to the side of the road and got out of the station wagon and wept.

She stood weeping in the road for a long time.

When she got back in and started driving again, I could tell she felt better. She said to me, "There is a difference between a young woman writing lines of affection and a poet writing true things to be known and seen in the world. That's why we must call on the Wind Woman and you must open your heart to her."

"No," I said. "No, ma'am. Please."

"Oh but Jess," she said, "there is no choice. I never did it, you see. I never spoke my mind to her. I never opened my mind to the Wind Woman and listened afterward to what she had to say. So when my passion for love was calmed in marriage and when my own family was ringed cozily about me, I laid my pen aside, feeling I had little more to tell. It is passionate affection or sorrow that makes most of us poets, and when those feelings are smoothed down by the hand of time, we all become like one another again and only see and know the same things. But when our passions are high, we are different from one another and see all things more furiously."

"Why couldn't we be passionate all the time?"

She sighed a withering long sigh. "Some can. A few poets can. The rest of us can't. I don't know why."

"Maybe I can," I said.

"Maybe so," she said. "But that would be all the more reason you must talk to the Wind Woman. Passion must feed on something, Jess,

and a poet's passion must feed upon truth. And that is what she can supply."

"Well then, I'll talk to her. But I have to tell you, I'm pretty scared of the idea."

"As well you should be," she said. "But that's the way it was with me, and so I never did. And for that very reason, you have to. . . . Oh, here we are at Aunt Priddy McCamus's house. We really must stop in to call on her."

Aunt Priddy was more like a hummingbird than a woman, and she ushered us into her shiny-floored front room and perched us on the hard edge of a yellow settee and made us drink sassafras tea and eat honey cake off little plates no bigger than thumbnails. The cake was sweet and flavorsome but had no more substance than the perfume of the tea.

Then we went into her garden in back, where roses yellow and white caused it to seem this plot of ground contained a sunshine all its own, not borrowed from the sun in the sky. A tall whitewashed plank fence surrounded it and great sunflowers with mustard-colored faces and saffron collars looked blankly down upon us. They were ranged along the fence in straight lines and my mother took pains to admire them. "They are so all-out gorgeous," she cried. "Aunt Priddy, you are a wonder, you are."

"Why, thank you, Cora," said Aunt Priddy, and turned her blushing countenance aside.

"Have they begun to sing yet?" my mother asked.

"These? Oh, no," Aunt Priddy explained. "These are those Dying Swan sunflowers that sing only once, late in the season, when they begin to wilt and shrivel."

"I'd like to be here then to hear them," my mother said.

"Well then, you must come, Cora," Aunt Priddy replied. "You have a standing invitation. But I should tell you that it is a sad occasion. Their final, only song attracts the crows to come and they tear them all apart. I have been frightened at times."

"Oh my."

* * *

I don't remember how we made our departure manners and got back to the station wagon, but there we were, rattling along the foot of Forgetful Mountain, with Worrisome Creek following us on the right-hand side. The water was clear and in most places the sand at the bottom shone red, but the pools below rock ledges looked deep and black and I thought of the lean brown-mottled brook trout lurking there and imagined I could smell the fishy clean smell of them. Then the road climbed one way and the creek another and soon the water was screened from sight by the tops of oaks and hickories.

"Where are we headed now?" I asked.

"Why, to see the Wind Woman, just as I promised."

I swallowed some of my dread and tried not to think of what might be coming, but when we rounded a deep curve that brought us below a neat red cabin cocked up like a rooster comb on the smooth hummock of a hillside, she could not resist.

"Oh, let's stop in for just a minute," she said. "We won't stay long, I promise. But the Happiest Woman would never forgive us if she knew we'd passed her by."

She pulled the station wagon into the wide sandy shoulder and we began the climb toward the cabin. The steps were quartz rocks lumped into the grassy hillside and some of them were uneven, so that we had to support each other as we went up. There looked to be many many steps to climb, but I was surprised to find us soon at the top, standing on the clean porch boards.

The door opened before we could knock and the Happiest Woman came out. From the name of her, I'd expected to see a tall, blond, smiling woman, but she was short and dimly complected. Her black hair was threaded with silver and she was so tiny that I looked down upon the neat part that ended in the homely bun done up in back. She was round and buttery and wore a long gray dress with a plain white apron.

Nor did she smile. Her face was as solemn as a pulpit and, though lined with humor crinkles about the eyes, seemed expressionless at first. Her brown eyes were lively and it was in reading them that I un-

derstood why she was known as the Happiest Woman. They were warm with a melting light as calm as a starry June sky. The smell of her reminded me of oatmeal muffins fresh from the oven and it seemed that this smell grew stronger when she rubbed her hands on her apron.

She buried her head in my mother's bosom and they hugged for a long time. My mother looked over her head, down into the holler with its dark oak grove, and her eyes misted again. "It's been such a long time," she said. "It's been too long."

"Yes it has," said the Happiest Woman. "And it needn't have been—because you are welcome here at any time, Cora. You know that."

"Yes, but so many things seem to get in the way. It doesn't make sense, does it?"

"No."

"And sometimes . . ." she hesitated, as if making an unwilling confession. "Sometimes I simply forget. That doesn't make sense, either, does it?"

"No, but you're not the only one to forget." She turned to look at me. "Now who is this fine-looking young man?"

"This is Jess. You know about him, of course, but you've never met him."

"Now is the first time," she said, and searched my face with her brown gaze and then looked at the rest of me as if I were the most serious object in the world. After a while she spoke, her voice firm and quiet. "I hope that you will have a serene and happy life, Jess."

She must have discovered everything she wanted to know, for after this examination she took little notice of me. I remained silent during the visit; I could feel that words were not expected of me, that this was a time for women to be together in some strong way I would never fathom.

She ushered us inside. This front room was dim but looked comfortable; in fact, it looked comforting—and that is the impression I gained from the whole house. There was a cushiony wine-colored sofa with frilly doilies on the arms and across the back. There were footstools aplenty and wooden chairs worn smooth and two hooked rugs with flower patterns. On one of the rugs a gray tabby opened one eye and then the other to take us well in; finding us harmless, it rose and stretched and poured itself into a different shape and settled to sleep again. There were few knickknacks on the shelves, but there were dull pictures of ancestors all about and against the far wall stood a stately harmonium with two rows of keys and wide pedals with frayed baize treads.

I went to inspect it and found that the ivory of the keys had discolored and that the music book in its place in the holder was titled in a language I could not recognize. I stood looking at the harmonium while the women talked, now and again hugging each other warmly. When they wandered into the kitchen, I didn't follow. I didn't feel unwelcome, only unnecessary, and so I decided to go back outside and sit in the green rocking chair on the porch and watch the goldfinches that glittered in the poplars off to the right.

Perhaps I fell asleep in the rocking chair. At any rate, my mind was brought back to itself by strains of music. It must have been the Happiest Woman playing the harmonium, because I think my mother did not know how. The sound of the instrument was like nothing I could have expected—not groaning and wheezy and turgid, as I'd heard so many parlor organs sound, but fleet and light and inspiriting. She played beautifully, keeping the melody line firm and clear while embellishing it with intriguing figures and odd flourishes.

Then they both began to sing, and again the sound was surprising. I couldn't tell who sang lead and who harmony; in fact, the parts must have been interchangeable almost from one measure to the next. And I was uncertain which voice was my mother's. Finally I decided she was the one who sounded so much like Aunt Samantha Barefoot. The Happiest Woman possessed the lighter voice and would range it silvery in the high registers to take the melody or plunge it below the lead to sing supporting tones.

Maybe they sang quite a long time, yet it seemed but a minute or two. I sat unrocking and watched two monarchs at play on a shaggy abelia and a nuthatch upside down on the trunk of a white oak, busily gleaning the scabby bark of its morsels. I could have listened a long time and I did not rise from my seat when the music stopped. I imagined the women inside, hugging and murmuring their good-byes, and knew that my mother would come out alone.

In a little while she did and down those awkward steps we stumbled and found ourselves back in the station wagon. We didn't speak. The music was still vivid in my head, cool as springwater and bright as an October beech leaf, and I did not want to disturb it. I desired to hear it in my mind for a long time—for always, if I could. But little by little it left me as we followed the road down into the valley. At last I could hear it only very small, as if I were watching it through a reversed telescope.

When my mother spoke again, she opened with a compliment, and this was so rare an occurrence, I knew to be on my guard. "Your manners seem to be improving, Jess, and that's something to be proud of."

I made no reply.

"Now if you would only do something to improve your appearance, you'd be a more-than-presentable young man. But your shoes are often a disgrace and your hair . . . well, I don't see why you can't learn to train it the way your father has trained his."

I maintained my prudent silence, figuring to let the familiar harangue run its course.

But she veered off. "Still," she said, "manners are the more important thing, and I'm glad to see you seem to understand that. But we need to brush up on them a bit before you meet the Wind Woman. She is a special person and special manners are required to get on her good side."

"What kind of special?"

"Well, you mustn't ask her any questions. She has many valuable secrets and if she wishes to unfold them to you, she'll do it in her own good time. But you mustn't pry."

"Yes, ma'am," I said, thinking that here was something I needn't be told. I had not been brought up to quiz my elders.

"But you must answer her questions fully and truthfully. Some of them may be embarrassing. It is her habit to cause you to think of things you don't care to think about and don't want to admit to out loud. But if you are not open with her, the visit is of no use."

"Will you be there when she asks me these questions?"

"Now why do you ask? You're not keeping secrets from your mother, I hope."

"Not exactly."

"Then why shouldn't I stay through your visit?"

"No reason, I guess," I said, vowing that if my mother sat in on this interview, I wouldn't say a mumbling word.

"Well, maybe I won't," she said. "I'd have to be invited to stay, and she may not invite me."

I felt a gushet of relief.

"There's another thing you shouldn't do. Don't eat anything. No matter how often or how sweetly she offers, don't take a drink of milk or eat a biscuit or anything else. Do you understand what I'm saying?"

"Yessum."

"And don't stare. Some people find her appearance unusual—especially young people. But she's likely to take offense if you gawk. That's not nice to do under any circumstances."

"Yessum." By now my curiosity was mounting to a towering pitch and I began to look forward to this visit I'd dreaded so earnestly. What would she be like, the Wind Woman? Scary, I thought. Like nothing I'd ever seen before.

We had reached the foot of Wind Mountain, though I was unsure how I knew this fact. The ascent seemed gentle at first, the road well graded, and the bordering woods pleasant with light and shade. But the mountain hung above us like a great purplish cloud and I knew there would be steep climbing ahead.

I was right. Sooner than I'd expected, the road narrowed and there were breath-shaking washboard stretches and in some places deep, hardened clay ruts. My mother drove with stern purpose, not glancing at me anymore. I'd thought she'd made this visit many times, but now it was apparent the road was mostly unfamiliar to her and she had to concentrate on every curve and bankside. The road had narrowed so straitly that I prayed we wouldn't meet a car coming down. Such an encounter could only be head-on.

Up and up we went and climbed above the tall trees into hillsides of scrub brush and knolls so closely grassed over, they seemed to be painted green. Among the groves below, breezes had made the treetops waltz, but up here the wind was stronger and we could feel it push against the station wagon.

"What kind of things will she ask me?" I said.

"I don't know." Her voice was uneasy and caused me to misdoubt all her explanations.

"You say you never opened your heart to her. Did you ever talk to her at all?"

"Not precisely."

"What do you mean?"

"I visited her just once, a long time ago. But I was too shy to begin, and when she pressed me, I went away. So I'm a little anxious she'll remember me and think of me as that rude girl who came once to visit."

"Oh," I said, as if I understood.

"Well, this is as close as the road brings us," my mother said. "We'll have to walk on to the top."

I looked up and saw a weathered old cabin right on the grassy tiptop of the mountain. It looked so ramshackle and makeshift, I found it hard to believe it could withstand the winds that swept this abandoned knob. Yet it had obviously been here for many years. I knew already there was no one who could say when it was built.

We got out and started up the slope at an easy pace. Then we had to work harder at it because the wind that poured down upon us was powerful and steady and we could make but a slow thrust uphill against it. We bent into the wind as if we were leaning over the edge of a pool to see our reflections in the water.

I found it difficult going; my legs were tiring and it was hard to get a good breath in the face of that wind. It was like the breath was sucked out of my mouth before I could get it into my lungs.

Suddenly my mother sank to her knees. She shook her head. Her short, fine, dry hair flapped ugly in the wind.

"Are you all right?" I asked. "Come on."

"This is as far as I go," she said. It was hard to hear her in the wind moil.

"Come on," I said. "It's not far."

"You'll have to go on by yourself."

"I'm not going alone."

"You have to. I can't make another step."

"I can't leave you here by yourself."

"Yes you can. You must. It's better for you to go alone. Go ahead. I'll be all right." She stretched her legs out before her and pulled her hem down and began a deep study of the landscape below, with its fields and groves and rivers, its houses and barns and haystacks. She must have needed to stop or she wouldn't have sat white linen down on that green grass.

"Are you sure about this?"

"Go on, Jess," she said.

I went on, but the hike became no easier. The wind had got stronger and now was full of mutterings, not animal, but not quite human, either. I closed my mind against them and staggered on.

The cabin, when I reached it, was just as unsteady-looking as it had appeared from below. The shingles were warped and split, the rock chimney leaned three ways at once, the steps were chewed and sagging. There were six lard-can flowerpots lined up on the porch edges; gaily painted red and blue and green, they held no impatiens or geraniums and their soil was dry and shrunken.

I knocked on the door but could tell from the hollow sound that the house was empty. That wind that had been against my face now forced at me from behind, streaming up out of the valleys and hollers of Hardison County. It was fresher now with green smells, not raw as it had been out upon the mountain bald, and the mutterings in it had turned to human language, though I could not make out the words.

I knocked again and was about to turn away to go back and join my mother. I could see her heading down the mountainside to the station wagon; this old windy hill had been too much for her. I was thinking how glad I'd be of the shelter of the station wagon myself when the door of the cabin swung easily open.

I debated only a moment before entering. I'd come this far and I knew my mother would be dissatisfied if I made no effort at all to meet the Wind Woman, so I stepped inside and waited for my sight to adjust to the dimness.

The place was as empty as I had expected, but it was not deserted. I could tell that someone lived here—sparely and cleanly and intensely. There was no sofa and no cushions, only four sturdy oaken straight chairs and a rocker. A mandolin lay in one of the chairs, gleaming black and golden; I could tell it was often played. Since the cabin offered little relief from the wind, the rocking chair tipped eerily back and forth. There was a narrow shelf by the window, in which sat maybe two dozen renowned volumes, Homer and Milton and Shakespeare and the others. And Virgil, of course.

I visited the Spartan bedroom and then went into the kitchen. Washed dishes were piled on a drain board by the basin—there would be no electricity here and no running water. In some nearby cranny of the mountain the Wind Woman would have a wonderfully cold spring. The ashes in the firebox felt faintly warm, but there was nothing in the oven or in the bread warmer above. Stove wood was stacked neatly in a wooden box beside the range. The gray tin pot was coffeeless.

I went back into the front room and tried to decide what to do. Finally I thought I would wait a bit. I could tell that the Wind Woman wouldn't be coming, but if I tarried, I might mollify my mother. I stopped the rocker's motion with an index finger and seated myself.

When I closed my eyes for a moment, the wind swelled up all around the cabin and inside it, making a great music of speaking voices and voices singing and instruments playing and the sounds that the horses and cows and dogs in the fields make and the trees and birds and stones in the woods. The commotion in my head was frightening and intoxicating. I was lost in bewilderment.

In a while—short or long, I don't know—the different sounds gradually sorted themselves out and I could understand what some of the voices were saying but knew nothing of what they meant. It seemed there was the wild, desolate, heartbroken voice of a woman crying away away away, so that the hair rose prickly along my nape. There was square-dance music joyous and copper-bright and music of bagpipes and drums and harps from over all the seas. A man's voice sang a river song slow and deep while another was singing a high-tenor mocking song:

I see blackbird fighting the crow
But I know something he don't know.

I heard in the wind in that room houses and barns, ropes and straps, gunshot and sword slash, iron and calico, jubilation and lamentation, country and city, old age and childhood, birth and death, the whole of the world below the mountain, and in the midst of it all, like a pallid queen in a silver throne raised above a clamoring multitude, the great round silence of the moon that looked down pitiless on Hardison County and all the surrounding counties out to the horizon.

My head swarmed with the hurt of it and I clapped my hands over my ears. It had come in a torrent too sudden and overwhelmed me so that my heart leapt and struggled. My breath wouldn't come.

Then it all went silent except for that single round, silent tone of the moon that I could hear as clearly as if it were a distant bell upon a deserted planet. That sound was a mercy and a marvel.

Now I understand, I thought. This journey was for me to come here to this cabin and let these sounds come upon me. I can't figure them out by myself. The Wind Woman will teach me how to lay out these sounds in proper fashion. I will wait here for her to come and beg the favor of her aid. I will wait here as long as it takes.

And that is the last sight I have of myself at that time—sitting alone in the cabin up on Wind Mountain with my eyes closed and patient to consort the sounds of the hollers and slopes and valleys below into music.

THE

MADWOMAN

When my mother remarked how I must have noticed that our aunt Samantha was a free-talking woman, I said yessum and no more than that. Aunt Sam's colorful speech was one of my keenest youthful delights and I didn't wish to say anything that might hint disapproval—or approval, for that matter. If my mother realized how sweet it deep down tickled me to hear Aunt Sam declare that Preacher Andy Garvin had less true religion than a rooster fart or describe Lem Turley as being so short that his face cheeks were not well divided from his ass cheeks, she might find some way to shut off that source of pleasure. But probably not. We all stood in awe of Aunt Sam and would as soon tell the rising sun its proper business as advise her on the social graces.

She was a famous mountain musician. She played a fiddle that could tear your heart out and then with another tune give you a brand-new and more joyous one. She could play other instruments, too, guitar and piano and maybe a little banjo, and she could sing lead or harmony in her burgundy contralto voice in such a way, you felt she was stroking your cheek with a velvet glove. She was to be heard fairly regular on the "Grand Ole Opry"—though my grandmother never allowed us to listen to that program—and she traveled all around the South with her band, the Briar Rose Ramblers, playing high schools and armories and in between baseball doubleheaders and county fairs, you name it. Anywhere she went, she was as welcome as August rain.

"That's how she got into the habit of strong language," my mother explained. "She was traveling with a bunch of male musicians before she was married and while she was married and after she was widowed. That is a situation uneasy for a woman and Aunt Sam decided she might protect herself by being one of the boys. If they thought of her as one of themselves, they wouldn't be trying to take advantage of her as a female. So she spoke as they did."

"How did it work out?" I asked.

We were climbing the steep grade of the mountain just this side of Betsey's Gap and my mother took her eye off the road for a brief moment to glance at me. "I think it worked splendidly," she replied. "She has as upstanding a name as any church organist or sewing circle leader. Nobody holds her lightly and nobody talks trash about her."

"Then it's a smart thing to do," I said.

"Well, yes. But it gets to be a habit and sometimes she forgets who she's talking to, and that can be awkward. Or sometimes she'll say something just for devilment. Like when she told her bass player's wife how she felt right sorry for her."

"Why did she say that?" I asked, and watched my mother's face turn a dark mottled red.

"Because—" She was trying so hard not to laugh that she choked on her sentence and tears streaked her cheek.

"Watch out," I said as she veered toward the ditch. Luckily, we were at the top now and there was a wide-out, and she pulled into it and tried to regain control.

But the story was too powerful in her and she had to finish. "She said she was sorry for Marilou. Her husband's pecker had to be *awful* scrawny, she said, because that's where he kept his brains." She reached a Kleenex out of the pocket of her gray cotton sweater and blotted her face and breathed deep and we started off again.

Going down the mountain, she told me about when Aunt Sam was young. "It is a sad story," my mother said, "and you will remember that Aunt Sam never needed more sadness in her life. If there is an ordeal she has not endured, I would flinch to know its name. But it is a sweet story, too, because Aunt Sam is a sweet woman and found herself doing what not another person could do. It was too much for her, if the truth be known, because at that time she was just about the age you are right now.

"It was Aunt Chancy Gudger who needed her. Aunt Chancy had lost her mind and there was not much way to help her. Her brother Willie lived across the county in a little house on Chambers Mountain and he made sure to look in on her when he could and tried to get her to move in with his family, but she was not to be budged. She was a part of her cabin like its roof, she said. Her sister Amy had got married by then and lived down on Sawney Creek but wouldn't have anything to do with Chancy. She had abandoned her; everybody figured there must have been terrible bad blood between them, but Amy laid the blame on her husband. Benjamin just wouldn't put up with Aunt Chancy, she said—though nobody had ever heard him say a word against his sister-in-law. Of course, he was as closemouthed as a miser's purse snap and never would have spoken his mind except in his own backyard in the dark of night.

"Aunt Chancy wasn't dangerous to herself or anyone else. That's what everybody thought at least. And she could still look after herself pretty well, cook and sweep and keep her body halfway clean—except for her hair, which was a mess. You, being of the he-male gender, wouldn't know how that's a sign you look for in a woman. If she doesn't keep her hair shining and brushed and combed and put up, then she is suffering in her mind. Aunt Chancy could boast a full glory of honey red hair when she was a young woman and then long after that when she was married, but when her husband was gone, her hair turned a streaky white-and-gray color and she clapped her husband's ugly black shapeless felt hat on her head and that was that. She was never to be seen without that big black hat on her head. It became the living signal of what she was, the way a coon's mask tells what it is and a possum's pouch does.

"She talked, though, without ever stopping. Most of it was only nonsense, unconnected sentences or sometimes strings of words that didn't hook up or sounds only a little bit like words. She would howl, too. When the moon came sailing up behind Twichell and flooded down on her cabin there by Herndon Creek, she would howl like a soul lost to man and God. You could hear it on the mountain and in the hollers and some claimed they could hear it yonder in the valley. *Away away . . . away . . . away . . .* Well, I can't make the kind of sound she made and I expect nobody else can unless they're undergoing the secret burning sorrow Aunt Chancy endured. It was a howl that made you hold your breath as long as you could and your skin would go hard and cold on your forearms.

"I've said she was possessed of a secret sorrow, because that is what we all supposed about her. She was always a strong-minded woman before she lost her reason, as strong-willed as her husband. Uncle Dave was a willful man and a mean one, according to some report, but he wasn't cruel to Aunt Chancy, because she wouldn't put up with it. She said to your grandmother once that as long as Colt made pistols, there wouldn't be a man to beat on her, and it surprised your grandmother to hear a woman talk in such a violent manner and she never forgot Aunt Chancy's saying it.

"So she had a forceful steady mind and then she lost her steadiness. Or rather, her mind divided up into different parts. When you were little, you used to play at damming the small creek beside the house at the foot of the hill, the one your daddy built his famous bridge over. The water will flow right along in its channel, but when you choke it up with rocks and mud and sticks the way you used to do, it spills over the banks and takes a lot of different little courses, running every which way. That was what it was like with Aunt Chancy. Something had blocked the natural channel of her mind and now it wandered in runlets to no purpose.

"But her willpower was still strong. It was strong to begin with and it got stronger during all those years with Uncle Dave. It must have been a struggle every hour of every day between those two and it toughened her spirit the way grubbing stumps and breaking new ground make the menfolk tougher. And meaner, too, sometimes, you might notice, and that might be the case also with Aunt Chancy. When her mind was ill and they wanted her to move, she wouldn't. She told her son she wouldn't and her daughter and her friends and neighbors and even the preacher from Herndon Forks Baptist. . . . Well, to tell the truth, she'd never put much stock in preachers; she was kind of like your daddy in that respect.

"It was a rough situation. She kept house the best she could, I expect, but it surely was not spotless. And she would have all sorts of queer things about, dead mice and possum skulls she would find in the woods. Snakeskins and so forth. The kind of things you might think witches used in the olden times, and of course there were some folks who said she was a witch. That talk made your daddy spittin' mad. 'Witches!' he would say.

'This is the twentieth century. You have to work at it twenty-four hours a day to be so ignorant.'

"Anyway, Aunt Chancy was no witch. She was just a poor old woman whose wits had strayed and she was trying to find her way in the darkness of her mind and keep her independence. But it was a sore trial to hear her talk and howl. One time your grandmother went to visit her and came back so troubled and unhappy, she had to lie down. That set us to worrying about *her,* it was so unlike. For days afterward, Aunt Chancy stayed on her mind and she tried to think and pray a way to help. She spent long hours with her Bible and in the Book of Samuel she found her plan.

"You know the story of King Saul and David, how the king was troubled by an evil spirit and was advised to seek out a man who was a cunning player on the harp. So he searched and heard about a shepherd whose name was David, the son of Jesse, and he sent for him to come. Then always afterward when the evil spirit was upon Saul, David took up his harp and played it with his hand so that Saul's spirit was refreshed and the evil spirit departed from him. You know this story; I'm sure your grandmother has told it to you, and maybe when you were little she paid you a nickle to read it yourself and tell it back to her.

"Anyway, that was the notion that came to her—for Sam to go to Aunt Chancy and play the prettiest music she knew and see if her bad thoughts would go away. It took a while to arrange, but Samantha had no fear of Aunt Chancy and was as willing to go as if she was going to eat supper with one of her many beaux in that cabin on Twichell. She took her second-best fiddle with her and her guitar, too, and planned on staying as many days as Aunt Chancy would allow.

"And so she did. But I have to tell you, Jess, it must have been a harsh and discouraging ordeal, for there were bleak hours when Aunt Chancy's mind would run to filth, the kind of words and thoughts it would make a grown man heartsick to hear, much less a ladylike young girl like our aunt Sam.

And then there was the moonlight howling that made your blood run ice. But Samantha would take up her fiddle and her bow and play a sweet slow waltz or an old-time ballad like 'The Salley Garden.'

"Down in the salley garden
My love and I did meet—

"Well, I'm no singer; you know that. But Samantha could sing. Her voice was pitched higher than it is now, and she could make it clear and light when she wanted to or give it that lonesome drone that carries so strong. Sometimes she would have to sing for a pretty long time, all through two or three songs, before Aunt Chancy could seem to hear her. But when she did listen at last, she would grow quiet and her face would gentle and her hands would stop their sawing motions and she would look at Sam with a smile of pleasure.

"One thing Samantha learned was that she couldn't rely on her music too often. The distress that was in Aunt Chancy had to find an outlet and run some of its course. It was like steam building up in a pressure cooker; if some of it didn't leak out, there would be worse trouble. So Sam had to let her go on for a while in that terrible way, and when Aunt Chancy slacked off a bit, why, then she could take up her guitar and begin singing softly, as if she was trying not to attract any notice at all, and then gradually sing a little louder and pick out, and after a while Aunt Chancy would loosen and close her eyes and hum along. She wasn't able to carry a tune, but she could hum along, and Aunt Sam described the sound they made together as a strange wild harmony that only the moon could understand.

"She only made one mistake, Samantha told me, and it was almost a fatal one. She had heard a song she liked that was new to her and she was teaching herself how to play it. Of course, it wasn't really new; it was an old song that came from out west somewhere, but it was new to Sam. I'm sure you've heard it many times. They call it 'Oh Shenandoah.'

"Oh Shenandoah, I love your daughter
All away, you rolling river—

"See. I told you I'm no singer, and I don't need to embarrass myself by constantly proving the fact.

"Anyway, Aunt Sam started playing that song, faltering a little with the chords. When she sang the words, she didn't start at the beginning, but picked up at the last verse.

"And so farewell, I'm bound to leave you,
All away, you rolling river,
I'll be gone when dawn is breaking,
Away away,
I'm bound away
All across the wide Missouri.

"And when she sang those words—not really singing, but sort of half-singing—Aunt Chancy gave a howl such as had never been heard upon this earth before and she came at Samantha with black murder in her face. If she'd had a weapon handy, it might have been the last hour Sam had seen. She cried out against her to stop. 'It's me, it's Samantha,' she said—because she could tell by Aunt Chancy's eyes that she wasn't seeing her, no more than a blind beggar could see her. She was only seeing into her own mind and nothing outside. And for a miracle, Aunt Chancy heard her and did stop, not more than a yard away and with her right hand quit from its strange sawing motion that always occupied it and raised to strike. Then her mouth worked and spit dribbled out and she said in a voice that frightened Sam down to the soles of her feet, a voice that was piteous and hurt and broken, but mean and vicious, too, and full of bloodlust, 'Where's my Frawley, what have you done with my Frawley, where's my Frawley at, what you have done, what have you ever done?'

"They stood like that a long time, Jess. Samantha was so full of terror, she couldn't move, and Aunt Chancy was seeing a devil from hell before her and was willing to kill. Then the spell broke and they both stepped back. Samantha could feel the hot sweat on her brow and Aunt Chancy reached down and brought up her dirty old blue apron and covered her face with it, she was so brimful of shame. She turned away and ran into the bedroom, with her face still covered, and shut the door. But Sam could hear her weeping, weeping and weeping, and she stood there in the front room, she said, and looked at that door like it was trying to tell her something, she was that dumbfounded."

"She knew who Frawley was, you see. All the women did. He was Uncle Burton Harper's third son, who left our part of the world when he was a lad of sixteen or so and went to follow a romantic life all around the globe. He had been to far countries and strange climates and, to hear him tell it, had pursued many a thrilling adventure. He was a man of about twenty-five now, turned dark by tropical suns and seas, and with thick curly black hair. He sported a handsome black mustache, too, and an easy teasing manner that set the girls aflutter.

"Maybe I shouldn't tell you this, but it's the truth, Jess, that he caught the fancy of your grandmother."

"Grandmother Sorrells?" I asked.

My mother nodded slowly, careful to keep her eyes on the gravel road that was winding us down into the valley.

"I don't understand," I said.

"Well, I don't know how to make it plainer."

"But wasn't she married to Grandaddy already? She must've been."

"Indeed she was. In fact, I was fourteen years old then and had girlish thoughts of Frawley Harper myself."

"But if Grandmother was married—"

"Jess, they don't poke your eyes out when you recite the wedding vows. And there was nothing to it. She was just sweet on a young man fifteen years her junior. Your grandaddy had to be gone away on his building jobs so much of the time, she was bound to get a little lonesome for romantic company. But there was never a word or a glance that passed between them, I can assure you of that. Frawley wouldn't ever have had the least inkling of her sentiments. Which she recognized as foolishness anyway. She only had a sweet thought now and again and that was all it amounted to."

"I don't understand—" I began.

She gave me a sharp look. "Well, it's about time you started to understand. You're old enough. People have hidden desires, most of them passing desires that don't come to anything because they don't want them to. You have them yourself and I know what they are. If I wanted to make you squirm, all I'd have to do is mention them out loud."

"I don't know what you're talking about."

She smiled her sly and knowing smile, the one I dreaded most. "Sarah Robinson is what I'm talking about," she said.

My hands clenched and I felt my face go hot and I looked out the car window into the red clay road bank, where some hopeful sassafras bushes had got a toehold. It was one of those passionate instants when I wanted to kill all grown-ups, starting with my mother. I could see them in my mind, an endless plain of grotesquely twitching adult corpses, their headless necks gushing blood in torrents. "What do you mean?" I asked, my voice taut.

"You're crazy about that cute little Sarah Robinson and it just burns you up to hear me say so out loud."

"And I suppose you're going to go on and on about it."

"I was only trying to explain," she said. "My mother was just a tiny bit sweet on Frawley Harper and I was moony about him, and all the other girls and women looked at that fellow like he was a stick of peppermint candy with a magnificent black mustache."

The picture she conjured made me giggle.

"There, you see. You're laughing at me now and laughing at yourself, too. It's just natural for males and females to be attracted to one another. Now and then there's a man whose attractions are nigh onto supernatural. But any girl with an ounce of modesty will keep her feelings to herself and would rather die than let her thoughts be known. Of course, some girls don't have an ounce of modesty. I won't mention any names. I certainly won't mention Rhonda Hollings; that name will never pass my lips."

"Who?"

"Never mind. She's long gone from our mountains now and I've heard some people say good riddance. I wouldn't say so myself. I don't believe in judging people. We're all of us sinners in the eyes of the Lord."

I couldn't help giggling again. My mother and grandmother spent fascinating hours together, gossiping about neighbors near and far, of this generation and the others, weighing their nice qualities and totting up with special precision their foibles and shortcomings. My father once told me of a dream he'd suffered. "The last trump had sounded, Jess, and it was Judgment Day and I was about to shuffle into that great courtroom in the sky and I stood there before the tall doors, thinking, Well, if it's Saint Peter and the Archangel Michael and God Himself and Judge Lynch thrown in, I've got a slim chance, but if it is your mother and grandmother sitting on the bench, my ass is hickory-smoked Carolina barbecue."

"What are you laughing about?" my mother asked.

"Nothing."

My answer didn't content her, but she was anxious to pull ahead with her story. She told me that the woman who seemed to fall most deeply under Frawley Harper's spell was Aunt Chancy. "I don't know what exactly went on between them," she said, "but there were communications and there were secret meetings. . . . Well, as secret as ever meetings between lovers can be in small settlements where everybody knows all there is about everybody else. To tell the truth, I think that Chancy was willing to give herself to Frawley. I'm not saying she did, mind you; I don't know that anything so dire ever took place. What I do know is that she and Uncle Dave had not been getting along comfortable together since the first week they were married. In those very first days, Aunt Chancy must have found out things about her husband that sickened her to the core. And don't ask me what kind of things, because I don't know and will not repeat the horrible rumors that were going around.

"They'd been wearing on each other from the beginning. Lots of women would have worn down after six long years and given in and let the man have his stinking brutal ways with them, but Chancy wouldn't, and her refusal was the point of conflict, and it was a conflict ready to spill into outright feud. Then Frawley Harper showed up like a dashing movie star from a world we girls could only dream about, and his appearance might have saved Uncle Dave's life.

"For the moment, anyhow.

"Because, you see, it's like that pressure cooker I mentioned before. Aunt Chancy had built up so much red fury that something scary was bound to happen, but then when Frawley dropped down out of the sky, it let some of the steam out of the situation. Aunt Chancy's attention was diverted from her anger as soon as her eye lit upon the handsome young man when she saw him in Plemmons's grocery store and post office, sipping Co-Colas and singing pretty songs from faraway places. Songs in French and other strange tongues. His particular favorite was that western song 'Oh Shenandoah,' which he said he'd learned on a Mississippi flatboat. It was there in Plemmons's your grandmother first heard that song, and afterward she undertook to teach it to Aunt Samantha, but it's not an easy one to learn; they both said they had trouble getting it right.

"Anyhow, he'd sip his cold drink and tell tales of wild exploits, not only to Plemmons's usual crowd of tobacco-spitting loafers who infested that place like corn worms but also to others, who only wanted a breath from the outside world. We were short on novelty in those days, Jess. No radio or television, just talking and singing and preaching and playing instruments and practical jokes that folks used to call 'rusties.' We had to entertain ourselves. . . . Well, we had to do everything for ourselves, just about.

"So Frawley Harper fired the imaginations of men and women alike, but Aunt Chancy was the woman who gave him the straightforward inviting look. Which he answered with one as bold or bolder, like any careless sailor strutting a fiddler's green. Because she was a handsome thing in those days, Jess. She had those bright green eyes and that honey red hair and the confident carriage of a woman who knows her worth and will possess her desires. She had a fine laugh, too, frank and easy and unashamed. When people heard that laugh, they turned around to see.

"And that was all that was needed, really, just that one exchange of glances in Plemmons's store. They understood each other in a single moment. But everybody else who was there understood, too, and they could barely wait to get home to set their tattle tongues a-wagging. In fact, I suppose a lot of them didn't get home, but stopped off at a neighbor's house on the way so they could be the first.

"It won't sound like much to you, just a man and a woman and one look between them. But those were different times and old-fashioned ways and the grown-ups were serious in their passions once they gave them rein. Aunt Chancy was past flirting age and was a married woman. But that look she gave Frawley—well, she might as well have lit a signal brand and waved it over her head. Everybody knew, or thought they knew, what was going to pass between them, and those idlers were already looking forward to the next chapter.

"Because it was as good as a settled fact that Uncle Dave would hear of the episode and would slay one or both of the amorous couple if anything happened between them, and maybe whether anything happened or not."

"But the thing was, he could have stopped the course of events. All he had to do was tell Aunt Chancy about the tales he heard from every side and say that she had better not find herself in the same house or holler with Frawley Harper again or he would take bloody measures. Yet he kept silent. He didn't say a mumbling word to her, but only let her think, as blind lovers will do, that she was getting away with something. He wore a white straw hat, did Uncle Dave, wore it winter and summer, indoors and out, and when he wanted to sign that you were talking about a matter of no interest to him or showing him a thing he didn't care to see, he would pull that white hat down over his eyes—to let you know he had shut you out and was paying you no mind. It was the rudest thing to do, but we were resigned to the fact that Uncle Dave presented no study in edifying manners.

"They hadn't been married all that long. Six years, because they both married late. But Jess, he must have hated Aunt Chancy with a brimstone hate, because he planned to let the foolish lovers have one sugar taste of each other, just enough to make their appetites restless, and then he would slaughter Frawley Harper and Aunt Chancy would live the rest of her days with that single precious hour of passion haunting her. Or maybe after the memory had tortured her a while, he would murder her, too."

"Why didn't Aunt Chancy just divorce him?" I asked.

My mother eyed me in startled disbelief. "Divorce? Jess, folks in that time and place had never heard the word *divorce*. When you got married, you made a vow to God and you kept your vow whatever the cost."

"Sounds like the cost could get to be awful high."

She shrugged. "You took the vow and you kept it."

"Anyhow," my mother continued, "the illicit loving pair had

kept their secret appointment and planned to meet again in the shining Maytime, with all the dogwoods abloom. It must have been the happiest day of Aunt Chancy's grown-up life, the happiest she had been since she was a pigtail girl playing in the creek or dressing up a baby doll. I don't know what went on during their hour together on a fine Saturday morning, but for Aunt Chancy all the world was wrapped up in that hour.

"Then her heart nearly failed her when she came down the trail through the pine grove and saw her husband sitting on the little porch of their cabin with his thirty-thirty rifle laid across his knees. That must have been the evilest sight she'd ever seen, even after six years with Uncle Dave Gudger. But she would never show that man any fear, you will count on that. She stopped for a moment at the edge of the woods and breathed a deep breath and walked out into the yard as easy as she could, knowing that of course he knew about her and Frawley and might just shoot her the way he would shoot any varmint—groundhog or squirrel or whatever—he found crossing his yard.

"Yet she didn't quake nor tremble, but only kept a steady gait and came up the steps and stood on the porch there, looking down at her husband. His white hat was pulled down so she couldn't see his face and he talked from beneath it, just as calm and cool as springwater. 'Chancy,' he said, 'back in the corner of the closet shelf in the bedroom is an old black felt hat that used to belong to my daddy. I want you to dust it off and brush it up and bring it to me.'

"She didn't say a word, but only obeyed him to the letter, bringing the scrubbed-up hat out to the porch and laying it carefully on top of the rifle in his lap.

"Uncle Dave took it up and turned it over and around in his hands, inspecting it slowly. Then he stood up and tipped back the brim of his white hat and looked straight at her. She was a tall woman and he only overtopped her by an inch or two, so they were looking right into the eyes of each other. He had his thirty-thirty in his left hand and the old black hat in his right hand, and when he spoke, it was in the same calm, cool voice as before.

"'Chancy,' he said, 'I'm going down to Sugar Camp and drink a noggin of whiskey with my brother Bill. Then along about dark I'm going a-hunting alone. I'll be gone the whole night. I expect I'll make my kill, but there ain't no way to be certain. You'll know, though, when you see me come walking up the road there whether I done any good or not. If I've struck my mark, I'll be wearing my daddy's old black hat. If I've made a miss, I'll be wearing my white. If I'm wearing this here white hat, there'll be a matter to discuss between you and me. If I'm wearing the black un, won't be need for any word ever to be said.'

"And that was that. Uncle Dave hitched his rifle stock up under his arm and held that black hat by its rumply crown and down the road he marched through the morning sunlight, with his wife staring after him from the porch and thinking thoughts you and I could never guess at. She stood there a long time after he was gone, looking down the empty road and hearing the robins and redbirds and jays singing. If she decided anything, she must have decided it then."

"Of course, I have to guess about a lot of what went on. The only account I ever got was from Aunt Samantha, and she had to piece the story together bit by little bit from what Aunt Chancy said after her mind had wandered. Who can tell what is true to a disordered mind? It's like trying to figure out the meaning of a dream; some of it seems so clear and straight, you think you know, but then the rest of it is a wild jumble and takes away your confidence about what you thought you understood.

"A few things are for certain.

"Frawley Harper disappeared. No clue to his whereabouts has ever been discovered.

"Uncle Dave Gudger disappeared, too. The only trace of him was that ugly old black felt hat on Aunt Chancy's head.

"The law came to inquire and his brother Bill came around, snorting and making empty threats, but it was too late. Aunt Chancy's mind was gone. She wasn't the same woman as before in any regard. That glory of honey red hair had turned streaky dark and gray. Her clear, bright eyes had gone as muddy as a flooded pond. That wonderful laugh of hers that cheered every heart had changed into a crazy cackle and her singing voice that had lifted up one verse and one verse only of 'Oh Shenandoah' had become a howl that made your very bones ache and burn. *Away . . . away . . . away away away . . .* Her hands that used to be so clever at the cookstove and the quilting frame could only make those eerie sawing motions, not like somebody sawing logs or sewing on a shirtwaist, but more like a butcher hacking at a fresh beef and sawing its bones."

"She killed him," I said. "Aunt Chancy killed her husband."

"Well, that's what everybody thought. But nothing was ever proven. Aunt Chancy couldn't say anything sensible and no evidence was ever brought to light. Officially at least."

"What do you mean, 'officially'?"

"There might have been some evidence if they'd looked in the right places. To tell the truth, though, Uncle Dave Gudger was nobody's favorite, not even his brother Bill's. I think they may not have searched very hard."

"What was the unofficial evidence?"

"It wasn't evidence," she said. "It might have been a clue if anybody had been willing to poke around."

"What was it?"

"Something Aunt Sam told me she wasn't real sure about. She went out one afternoon to make use of Aunt Chancy's outhouse. Happened to glance through the hole down into the pit and thought she saw a hand down there. But it was a deep pit, nine feet at least, and she wasn't certain. The light wasn't real good, she said. She leaned over to look again and saw something she thought might be a man's head with the eyes still staring. But maybe it was just a crumpled-up sheet of newspaper or a page of the Sears and Roebuck catalog. She vowed and declared that she couldn't really tell."

"What did she do?"

"Nothing. . . . Well, she didn't use that jakes. Not then and not for the next five weeks that she stayed with Aunt Chancy. She went up into the pine grove above the house, she told me, and she looked about smartly for copperhead snakes."

"What happened to Aunt Chancy?"

"Her tortured heart came apart to pieces and she died howling. The last word she uttered was from that song 'Oh Shenandoah.' *Away away,* was what she said, but it was just the same as saying the name of Frawley Harper with her last breath."

"Was Aunt Sam there when she died?"

"No. She had to go back home. Aunt Chancy didn't die till a year later when the dogwoods came white again in the moonlight pouring down on Twichell Mountain. Her daughter was there and some other kin. They all said that her last word was *Away.*"

"That's a scary story," I said.

My mother pulled over to the side of the road and stopped. "Get out and I'll show you where," she said. She raised her left arm and pointed. We stood at the dusty, weed-choked ditch, looking north. "You can't see it from here now, but there was a road that ran along that upper ridge and then around to the right and on to the top. Aunt Chancy lived about halfway up, but nobody lives there now. All the land's been sold off as a preserve to a hunting club and they've let the road go bad on purpose. Takes a four-wheel drive to climb that mountain now."

"I'd like to hear her sing it," I said.

"Hear who sing what?"

"Aunt Sam. I'd like to hear her do 'Oh Shenandoah.' "

She looked at me like I was a lunatic descended from the planet Jupiter. "Jess, maybe your teachers are right to make you out such a keen scholar, but you don't have the common sense of a wall-eyed mule. And that's the truth. Do you think

Aunt Samantha would be singing that song after what she went through? If you don't get some good sense to go with all those brains you're supposed to have, you might as well open up your head and feed them to the barn cats."

Most of my mother's suggestions didn't fire my imagination, but that one did. I thought of unlatching the back of my cranium and taking out my brain like taking a pan of corn bread out of the oven and setting it down in front of the half-wild calico cat we called Britches. Then I rejected the fancy. If I did that, I wouldn't have any memory. I'd forget what I'd heard about Aunt Sam and my grandmother and my mother and what I thought I'd learned about the nature of music.

THE SHINING WOMAN

When I asked my grandmother to tell me another story about Aunt Sherlie Howes, she seemed pleased to do so. "I don't know that a lot of boys your age would take such an interest in old folks and past times," she said. I might have replied that I hadn't always been interested; four years ago, when I was only eleven, I cared for no one's goings-on but my own. Now, though, I had a hunger to listen almost as urgent as my hunger to read books. I had begun to feel that Time Past contained secret messages meant for me. In midnight dark I would lie in bed and imagine I heard whispers from Time Past. It wasn't the dead people speaking; that was a dry whispery sound like Uncle Runkin's voice when he spoke so lovingly of graveyards. This voice was a murmur warm but muffled, the syllables flowing together like drops of rain joining in streams on a windowpane. Time Past was as full of story as the Junior Classics Library in its twelve colorful volumes in my brick and board bookcase; the persons my mother and grandmother told me of were as startling as the planet Saturn swimming in space, the way it was pictured in my father's discarded general science textbooks.

"What kind of story did you want to hear about Aunt Sherlie?"

"One where she's smart," I said. "One where she figures out things nobody else could understand."

"She was like that most of the time. . . . I heard tell you used to like ghostly stories. Have you got tired out with them?"

"No, ma'am."

"Well, I don't know whether you believe in hants or not," my grandmother began. "There's a lot to be said both ways. There's ghosts in the Bible, and maybe that ought to settle the whole question. But a lot of people don't believe, thinking it's all old-time superstition and rank foolishness. I won't tell you what I think or what I've seen. Seems to me a ghost you see, if ever you truly see one, will be a deep and personal experience and not one you'd care to share in the broad light of day.

"And that's the way it was with the Lucases. They wouldn't ever have told anybody about this ghost, only it troubled them so much, giving them no sleep and no peace of any sort. Till finally they took their fret and sorrow to Aunt Sherlie Howes in her gray little living room in her little house out on Devlin Road. If anybody could make things clear, she could.

"But you have to consider how mighty desperate they must have been. Old Talbot Lucas: He was a close one in every way. Close with a nickel, close with a smile, close with his words. If the good Lord gives each of us a fortune of words to spend from the day we get born, Talbot Lucas died a dictionary millionaire. And his wife, Little Mary, was the same way. They made a dark and silent pair, those two, and they lived in a dark and silent place. Back in Drovers Holler, where the sun is a stranger almost till Maytime and the hoot owls have all the nights to themselves and the snow lays long and crusty.

"When I name Little Mary, I'm talking about Talbot Lucas's first wife. She was a Simmons by birth, the least and toughest of a brood of four boys and four girls. I reckon she had to be the toughest to make it through, she being the lone straggler by about five years and the others so much bigger than her and as hungry as bears in March. She had to scrabble for what she got. Old Daddy Simmons—that's what everybody called him—fancied himself a right smart feller, but he was as luckless as Job. His bucket didn't have a hole in it; his bucket had no bottom, and that's the truth. If he built a stout-looking haystack, it would mildew and rot in a week; if he planted a hillside of potatoes, there'd come a freeze two foot deep; if he picked up a likely walking stick in the woods, it would turn out to be a copperhead snake. There's some people like that in this world and you have to hope their reward is in the world to come.

"But the other world was no succor to the Simmons children and especially not to Little Mary that hard cuffs and harsh words had taught to be chary and watchful. It must have seemed to her that her fate was sealed; she was always to be wearing threadbare hand-me-downs and being the tail-ender at dinnertime.

"And that's the way it turned out. She was a sallow bitsy thing, not more than five foot five or so; her hair was a mousy brown and she kept it pulled back tight and parted in the middle in the old-timey modest way. Her figure didn't call for notice and her hands were too big for the rest of her. Her face was unremarkable except for the eyes. She had big, dark, steady eyes and sorrow was in them like lamplight that would never go out. When you looked at her eyes—for you wouldn't look *into* them, not for more than a fleeting moment—you felt like you knew her destiny from beginning to end and all the burdens of her spirit. Somewhere in Little Mary there must have been a spark or two of hope, but in her eyes all you saw was that she expected no glory and little pleasure in this life.

"Not every woman needs to be a rose-cheeked, pigeon-chested beauty to capture the fancy of a man. You find a feller clever in his mind and settled in his thoughts and not too wild with the hot blood of youth and he's as likely to choose a plain girl as a pretty one. But she has to attract him with some fetching quality—her wit and humor or her high spirits or a lively step or an agile needle or savorous cookery. She has to show mettle, and Little Mary didn't show much mettle, because her long suit was endurance.

"Let me try to be clear. It was like Little Mary, when she was in the room with other girls her age, was a mule in a stableful of saddle ponies. If anybody peered close, they could tell she was a right good mule, but the men's attention just naturally skipped over her in such situations.

"So when she was chosen, it had to be by somebody who was looking for exactly what she was. It had to be a man who felt he hadn't the advantages of the other beaux of the county, not a high-stepping clog dancer, not handsome of face and limb, not favored by fortune with land or livestock or money in the bank vault. And that was Talbot Lucas. Head to toe he was a dim man. I don't mean he was slow-witted; he could read and cipher about as good as the rest of them, I reckon. It was only that there was no shine to him. Looking upon his tall but stoop-shouldered form, a girl would feel no flutter at her heart, no warmth in her cheek. He was born to plow an inhospitable patch of earth, rocks and briars and steep hillside every step of the way. And a girl had to feel that if Lucas's plow horse happened to die on him, she'd better be ready to step into the traces.

"So they made a good pair, him and Little Mary Simmons. That is to say, they were well suited because they were resigned to each other almost before they ever met. It would be love at first sight in a strange sort of way; it wouldn't be the sudden blossoming of violets and the entwining of leaping flames. It would be a recognition, like when in a houseful of strangers you spot somebody you know must be some kin to you, a second cousin or an aunt by marriage. That's the way they came together and that's the way the story played itself out, as far as anybody could tell.

"They didn't have a lot of visitors back there in Drovers Holler. Talbot Lucas had no close kinfolk and he must've made it clear he didn't cotton to the notion of meeting Little Mary's brothers and sisters too often at his dinner table. The arrangement would have suited Little Mary just as well; she'd always felt put-upon by her brothers and sisters, and the person in the world she was fondest of—her mother—died three months before her daughter wed. About the only visitors they entertained were the necessary ones: the Price boys that came to help Talbot with the spring planting and the fall harvest, the circuit preacher, who made it his certain business to wend back into the holler to call, the occasional peddler or chair caner or tinker, and Doctor Horace, who delivered all three of Little Mary's stillborn babies.

"That's a sad circumstance, but to say the truth, I don't know that children would have made the happiest difference. Talbot and Little Mary were fated to stand on the unsilvered side of the mirror, so to speak. In the waning moon. They had to be some comfort to each other, but that part of their life didn't hardly show. They were devoted to each other pretty much as a matter of duty.

"Still, they endured. They made a way of life where many another couple couldn't have done it, and if they ever looked up from the rooty furrow before them, maybe they could take some pride in just hanging on. When I put myself in the place of Little Mary—and I've done it more times than two, I see myself taking pride in living through, not dead of heartbreak or unending toil or the fearful winters of Drovers Holler.

"But I don't know that Little Mary thought that way. When she came to the wedding of her sister Betty Ann down at the

Bitter Creek Church, she hung back, as always, from the crowd. It was supposed to be a thankful occasion, because Betty Ann had lost her first husband, Ki Melton, in a sawmill accident and nobody had figured on her finding another man at age fifty—at least age fifty. But she'd done it and was just sparkling with joy afterward, surrounded by her lady friends in a circle that her sister Little Mary didn't join, standing by the wall the way she always did and half-turned away. Aunt Delia Thompson made up her mind to go and speak to Little Mary and try to draw her in. She took her hand, which had a man's calluses on palm and fingers, and said, 'Little Mary, won't you give your sister a wedding-day kiss?'

"Little Mary cast her brimming eyes down at her feet. 'I'm shy to step up in front of everybody,' she said. 'Betty Ann knows I wish her a world of happiness.'

" 'It won't do no harm to tell her so right now.'

" 'I'll just wait, thank you, till a later time,' Little Mary said, and no matter how persistent Aunt Delia might press her, it was clear that Little Mary preferred her wallflower place in the room. So they chatted on a while there in the corner and Aunt Delia gathered as much personal information about the Lucases as you can carry breeze in a soup spoon. But her impression was that Little Mary's days were long and wearying but that Talbot was not cruel to his wife, only unbending and cheerless and matter-of-fact.

"Now it's a truth," my grandmother told me, "that life is difficult and man is condemned to earn his bread by the sweat of his brow and we had all better take heed and store up for the hard times a-coming. I've never been one to say a body should spend the livelong day in frolic and foolish merriment. But there's a cast of mind that makes things cheerfuler. You take notice sometime how different women will have their go at a heap of mending to be done. One of them will shake her head and set her mouth in a straight line and begin the chore like she felt that every time a needle pulled a stitch, it went into her skin. But another woman will sort through the clothes, smiling as she thinks about the younguns that wear them, and match the colors of cloth and thread like she was arranging a bouquet of flowers, and make it a contest with herself how straight a row she can sew and how fine she can stitch. Both the women will get the work done proper. But for one of them there's been some joy in it, and it's been my observation that hers will be the tighter, neater work. Tell you what," my grandmother suggested, "you watch the difference between Aunt Caroline and Aunt Frieda sometime, how they do their chores, but don't tell anybody I told you to.

"Anyhow, that was the way of things between Talbot and Little Mary. She didn't say anything specific, but what Aunt Delia was able to gather only confirmed her idea, the same idea we all had. 'I must say this,' Aunt Delia added. 'I don't believe Little Mary is right sound of body.' That was all she could say; it was no more than just a thought she had.

"But her thought came true. It wasn't five years after that when Little Mary was laid in her coffin and had a spare and solemn funeral said over her and was tucked in the gravelly ground on the slope of Siler's Hill where the few Lucas family graves were sited. People had thought that at the funeral Talbot might shed a public tear or two, but he only stood alone, hard and dry, with burning eyes. He couldn't look at any of the mourners, though. He shook their hands and stared above their heads. The stone he erected for Little Mary only said that she was 'A Good and Faithful Wife.' The second word wouldn't seem necessary unless you knew that by *faithful* Talbot meant she was faithful in doing her duty day to day, not that she resisted strange affections of the heart.

"So that was the life of Little Mary. She had got through it, we each of us thought, the way you eat a plate of food when you're not hungry a bit. She was only forty-three when she died. I forget what medical reason the doctor wrote down, but it wasn't the one that counted. The truth was, she wore out. Just wore thin and then wore through, like a shirtsleeve at the elbow."

* * *

"It was the end, too, of Talbot Lucas, we thought, for he could never make it alone on his feeble scratch-ankle holding in that cold, cold holler and he'd never find another female like Little Mary, one that was already beaten down and ready to start turning the heavy millstone without hope and without complaint. But our supposing was way off the track on that one. I have to reckon there's more women been scrubbed threadbare on the washboard than ever we count, for it wasn't a whole year passed till Lucas was able to take him another wife.

"Of course, he had to forage out of Harwood County to find her. The women in these near parts looked upon the fate of Little Mary and decided *that* slope was too steep for them to climb. Even the widow women figured it that way. It's awful hard to be alone and lonesome, but it's worse to be married and lonesome and weary and empty as a churchhouse on a rainy Monday morning. So we expected Talbot to die a bachelor and we expected wrong.

"But it wasn't like he won the heart of Sarah Currie. Talbot Lucas couldn't conceive what it was to do such a thing as that. He must've made an arrangement with Sarah's daddy, the way people used to do in the olden time. Back when you'd see, just like you saw with Sarah and Talbot, a young woman not twenty years old in the yoke with a man in his sixties, if not older. Talbot I'd put in his mid-fifties about this time, but I don't know for sure. He looked old, but when was there ever a day he hadn't looked old?

"So he brought Sarah Currie into Drovers Holler and she settled into place as natural as a door latch slipping into its sleeve. She was even more ready for her fate, it looked like, than Little Mary was. More silent, more obedient, more bowed to the will of her husband. He wasn't a cruel man, given to hard drink and blows. He only just never lifted his eyes from the rocky path to look at the flowers blooming sunny on the hillside.

"I hate to admit this part of the truth, but we all wondered how long it would be before Sarah wore out like Little Mary had. That was an ugly thought, but we couldn't help it coming to us. At least I couldn't. Talbot had found him a woman with even less spirit than the one before. Little Mary showed the soul of herself in those big sad eyes, but Sarah wouldn't even show her eyes. Kept them fixed on the ground or skittering away nervous from the gaze of whoever she'd be talking to. She was a mite taller than Little Mary but slighter in figure and paler. Her hair was reddish and her eyes—if you could catch a glimpse of them—were blue.

"The Lucases now kept to themselves more than before. Talbot hadn't been coming down to Plemmons's Grocery but every two weeks, and now it would be three weeks to a month before you'd see him there, stocking up on staples—flour and sugar and coffee and such like—and nothing else. Sarah, we figured, must have been a thriftier housekeeper than Little Mary, and we wondered how that could be.

"We figured and wondered too much," my grandmother said. "Gossip is a curse on the community. But it's such a refreshment to the spirit, nobody can resist. Well, actually some can. Now and then you'll find one that won't indulge in gossip. And what happens to them? Why, other people talk them down so low, the moles can't sniff them. Ginny Slater—I'll tell you her story sometime maybe. . . . The things we wondered and said out loud about Talbot and Sarah ought to've made a mule blush, but we'd got our teeth into it and the less we knew, the more we rattled on.

"Came a time, though, when I was able to find out some of the truth myself. For I was there, right in the same room, when Talbot and Sarah paid their first call on Aunt Sherlie Howes. I'd been sent to take Aunt Sherlie a syrup cake to pay her back a little for solving a problem my own grandmother Akers had. To this day I don't know what the problem was, only that it was an important one. Syrup cake was a special dish Granny made and she only made it once a year maybe, at Thanksgiving or Christmas.

"I'd presented Aunt Sherlie the cake and she'd marveled at it and we took it back to the kitchen and then she insisted I stay and have a cup of tea with her. There I was, seventeen years old and proud as a princess to be sitting and sipping in Aunt Sherlie's living room, when there came a rap on the door. Well, not a rap—more of a gentle tapping, no more sound than a blind man's cane makes along a rocky road. She motioned for me to answer it and invite the caller in. And when I saw it was the Lucases, I was so struck with surprise that I couldn't speak. Talbot stood there with his old dented brown hat on his head and Sarah half-hid behind him. Aunt Sherlie had to call out, 'Come in, come into the house!' Because, of course, she wasn't a bit surprised, or didn't seem so.

"I stepped back and they passed me by till I shut the door and followed. She asked them to sit in her straight chairs. The other preliminaries were got through in a hurry. Not because the Lucases were unmannerly. They were only tight-lipped and strongly distressed. Aunt Sherlie took their abruptness in good humor and was perfectly willing to skim along to the heart of the matter. But when she asked them point-blank what she could do, all the hurry went out of them and they gave each other uncertain glances and faltered and then fell silent. She didn't try to persuade them, only sat easy and silent in her armchair, turning that well-known silver thimble over and over in her fingers.

"Finally Talbot got it out. 'It's a hant.' he said. 'It's a hant come to vex us in our house.'

"You can just picture how I perked up at that. I leaned forward in my chair and could feel my ears growing as long and twitchy as a hare's in hunting season. A hant!

"But Aunt Sherlie only waited.

" 'It comes ever night almost,' he said. 'We've got to make it go away.'

"Aunt Sherlie spoke as quiet as water filling a spring run, the way she always did. 'It's not so easy to lay ghosts. Of course, I'll do what I can to help.'

" 'We hate to put you out,' Talbot said. 'But it's got to where we have to do something about it.'

" 'Well then,' Aunt Sherlie said, 'tell me about this hant you see. What does it look like?'

" 'It's a woman,' he said. 'All dressed in silver cloth and shining like the moon. Long silvery blond hair she has, that reaches down to her waist.'

" 'Do you see this hant, too, Sarah?'

"The shy woman nodded, not looking up.

" 'Do you see the same one Talbot sees? Because, you know, sometimes with ghosts they will appear different to different people.'

"Now Sarah raised her head and looked Aunt Sherlie full in the face. 'I thought it was an angel. So bright and shining. It's the prettiest thing you ever saw.'

"Aunt Sherlie smiled. 'Well, maybe it *is* an angel. You wouldn't want to drive an angel out of your house.'

"They looked at each other glumly. 'It ain't no angel,' Talbot said. 'We found that out pretty quick.'

" 'How?'

" 'Well, it *dances,*' he said. 'It twirls around in the air and that thin dress of silver floats up all around it and it will keep right on dancing for an hour or better.'

" 'Where does it do this dance?'

" 'In our bedroom,' he said, 'where we're trying to sleep.'

" 'You say it dances. Do you hear any music for it to dance to?'

" 'There ain't no music. Not a sound.'

" 'Does it ever talk to you?'

" 'No.'

"Sarah put in a soft disagreement. 'It don't talk, but it signs to us.'

" 'What kind of signs does it make?'

" 'Signs with its hands,' she answered. 'I don't know what they mean. Sometimes I think it is telling us to follow it to where it is in the world to come.'

" 'Would you like to go there?' Aunt Sherlie asked. 'Would you like to journey to the world to come?'

" 'If I think about it during the daytime when I'm doing my chores,' Sarah said, 'it makes me scared to think of dying. But when I see her—I mean, *it*—a-shining before me in the air, I think it wouldn't be so bad.'

" 'Do you feel like this apparition means either one of you any harm? Does it threaten you?'

" 'It frights me,' Sarah said. 'I am getting a little bit used to it, but it scares me to look.'

" 'How about you, Talbot? Do you think it's harmful?'

" 'I don't know,' he said, 'but I don't want no hants in my house. I want to be shut of it for good and all.'

" 'Does it come ever night?'

" 'No,' he said. 'Just whenever it pleases. But it comes a whole lot.'

" 'Does it always come at the same time of night?'

"They shook their heads. 'Might come just after bedtime, right when it gets dark. Might come just before sunup. No telling when. That's one reason we ain't been able to get used to it.'

" 'I never will get used to it,' said Sarah Lucas, and I saw that Aunt Sherlie took notice of her tone of voice, which was not angry or frightened, but wistful and longing.

" 'You say there's no music to accompany the dance of this spirit,' said Aunt Sherlie, 'but what about smells? Sometimes a ghost will bring an odor into the room with it, a smell that reminds you of something you nearly forgot.'

"Talbot shook his head, but Sarah tugged at his arm. 'Why, Tal,' she said, 'there is a smell. It is the smell of apple blossoms, plain as day.'

" 'I never noticed no smell.'

" 'Well, it's there. As plain as day.' She turned to Aunt Sherlie. 'What does it mean if I can smell apple blossoms and he can't?'

" 'I don't know,' she answered. 'A lot of times a spirit will strike one person one way and somebody else right there in the same room a different way.'

" 'Have you ever heard of any hant like this one?' Talbot asked.

" 'Not exactly. Seems like I heard from Aunt Ora Culpepper something like back when I was pigtail age. Most hants are unrequited spirits. That's been my experience. Mostly they are lovers who never got the man or woman they needed and the waste of their life makes them suffer so they can't rest proper. Some hants are revengeful spirits from days long ago, a way-back ancestor you might never have heard of. They are harmful and mighty powerful sometimes, and the only way to lay them is to find out the awful secret thing they did in their lifetime and open it up to the light of day. But they only visit certain houses and barns and trees and when those are gone, the spirits are gone, too. Now and again, if somebody—a widower or a widow woman—gets married again, there will come a spirit to haunt them out of simple jealousy.'

" 'You mean Little Mary,' Talbot said. 'Sarah and me have talked about that, but she don't have nothing to do with it.'

" 'How do you know?'

" 'If you ever seen this spirit, you would understand exactly. It is a tall and shining woman as bright as silver. It is a woman like she might be made out of moonlight. She is as downy in the air as snowflakes. But she's a natural woman, too.'

" 'What makes you say that?'

"Talbot reddened and swallowed and shook his head and looked out the window into the pleasant springtime weather. Sarah answered for him. 'Because sometimes when she twirls around, her thin gown flies up and you can see.'

" 'Oh my,' Aunt Sherlie said.

" 'But it ain't nothing bad,' Sarah continued. 'It's like she don't notice what has happened, and if she did notice, it wouldn't make no difference. She don't mean any more by it than a four-year-old youngun playing in the yard. It's only natural to her, is all.'

" 'Well, I don't know about that,' Talbot said.

" 'It's the kind of thing a woman will know and a man might not, if you understand what I mean.' The sentence must have darted out of Sarah's mouth before she realized what she had said. Maybe she had contradicted her husband's word before on some dull winter day when they had been in the house too long together. But she'd never done it in public and never imagined that she ever would or could. She glanced at him quickly, but he appeared not to have noticed.

" 'I think I do understand,' Aunt Sherlie said. 'Now, Sarah, I want you to tell me when your birthday is. Just the day—I don't need to know the year.'

" 'June the fifteenth.'

" 'And when was Little Mary's birthday?'

"Talbot thought a good long time before admitting sorrowfully that he disremembered.

" 'That's bad,' Aunt Sherlie said. 'Little Mary's birthday is something you both ought to remember.'

" 'I remembered it when she was alive,' Talbot said. 'But now that Sarah and me are together, it is gone from my mind.'

" 'Are you right certain about that, Talbot Lucas? Mightn't there have been some years you'd forget?'

"He stared at her, reluctant, irritated. 'Maybe,' he said at last. 'Maybe now and then.'

"Aunt Sherlie pondered, turning her silver thimble slower and slower until finally she stopped and rested it on the arm of her chair. 'Perhaps it will be all right anyway. We might not have to hit the exact birthday.'

" 'What are you talking about?' he asked.

"She turned to Sarah. 'Now here's what I'd advise you to do, Sarah, and you should get Annie Barbara to help you out if she's willing to do so.'

"I jumped right in," my grandmother told me, "and said how mighty glad I would be to help them in any way I could. Because I was not going to miss out on any part of this adventure, you could wager to that. And of course I was pleased as punch that Aunt Sherlie felt like she could depend on me. When I got home to tell my mother about this, she would be as proud of me as if I was a prize scholar.

" 'All right, then,' Aunt Sherlie went on, 'this coming Sunday if the weather stays fair, you two must go out and gather a double armful of apple blossoms and take them up on Siler's Hill. When you get there, you must braid some of them into coronets and wreaths and strew the rest on Little Mary's grave. Decorate it real nice and clean up anything around that needs it and just make everything look as pretty as you know how to do.'

" 'Do you want Talbot to go with us? She was Tal's wife.'

" 'That won't be necessary,' Aunt Sherlie advised. 'Not this first time, anyhow.'

" 'Will it work?' he asked. 'Will decorating Little Mary's grave make the hant go away?'

" 'No,' Aunt Sherlie said. 'But it is the first thing that must be done. And the other part ought to be just as simple.' "

"That was an outing I won't forget," my grandmother told me. "It was as pretty a day as you could wish for. Blue sky and sweet breezes. My daddy led us down into what we used to call the Old Broom Orchard and helped us cut all the apple boughs we could carry. We rolled them up like wheat sheaves and wrapped some flour sacks around them and tucked them under our arms. We made some sight, looking like that, because Aunt Sherlie had told us to dress up in good clothes. I didn't wear my very best because I knew Siler's Hill was a steep climb with some briar patches partway around the path. But Sarah wore her best because she had only the one dress-up outfit in pearl gray wool with some broad black edging around the collar. It was light wool, but it was too heavy for a warm day in May and with Siler's Hill before her. The truth is, that was a dress she had for church and for funerals and every other stitch she owned was workday.

"Daddy had hitched Maybelle to the buggy for me and I drove the four miles down to Sanderson Ford and tied her to the yellow maple there by the river. Then Sarah and me got our apple blossoms out and crossed the foot log and started up the mountain.

"That was the day we got to be such good friends, Sarah Lucas and me, and I bless Aunt Sherlie's dear gray head every time I think about it. We did exactly what she said to do and had the grandest time. There was no sadness in it and no jealousy on Sarah's part, and no fear, either. She told me all about how the hant came at night and seemed to be inside the room and out among the stars all at the same time. And how when it first came she'd pull the covers over her head and tremble like the fever had struck. How she had got used to it a little and even admired to see it, though Talbot didn't and never would.

"We sang a verse or two of a hymn before we left, holding hands and looking at the grave site with its coverlid of apple blossoms. Then we came back down the mountain and drove little Maybelle over to Aunt Sherlie's house, where Sarah's husband was waiting to take her home.

"He was sitting in his straight chair with his brown hat on his knee, and they had been talking for some little time, I expect. You could tell from Talbot's face that he'd been provided with plenty of fodder for thought and not all of it easy to chew on. Sarah and I came in and made our manners. Aunt Sherlie questioned us closely about what we'd done and we told her, not leaving out anything. She was pleased, I could see that, but her smile faded a little when Talbot asked in his blunt way if his house was shut of that shameless spirit yet.

" 'No,' said Aunt Sherlie. 'Not yet.'

" 'That's what I thought,' he said, wagging his head like a threatening mastiff. 'That hant ain't got nothing to do with

Little Mary. It don't look like her and it sure don't act like her. It's been nothing but a waste of time to go traipsing up to her grave. Little Mary was a quiet, hardworking woman as dependable as they come. She wont no half-nekkid dancing devil.'

" 'It won't be long till June fifteenth,' Aunt Sherlie said. 'And on that day, Talbot Lucas, you must take your wife, Sarah, down to Plemmons's store and buy her some pretty things—some bright silk ribbons for her hair or some lace she might like the look of, or maybe a little gold locket.'

"He was thunderstruck. 'A gold locket? You must think I'm some sort of railroad millionaire. We've got all we can do already, trying to make ends meet.'

" 'I understand that very well,' Aunt Sherlie told him. 'But we're not talking about spending a fortune. Just a little bit of money once a year to achieve your peace of mind.'

" 'Every year!'

" 'Every time her birthday rolls around, you'll do a little something to put some color and joy into her life. And every year at apple blossom time, you two will climb Siler's Hill together and decorate Little Mary's grave. And if you do these two bidden things, then all will be well in your house. And if you don't, then you had better be pleased to welcome the Shining Woman anytime she appears. Because she will be keeping you close company till you move away or die.'

"He wagged his head again. 'I still don't believe it's got anything to do with Little Mary. If you'd knowed *her* and had seen this hant, you wouldn't believe it, either.'

" 'I did know her—a little bit,' Aunt Sherlie said. 'And I've got a pretty good idea what this ghost looks like. You came to ask what I thought and I've told you that, and anything you decide to do now or not do—well, that's your choice to live with.'

"Sarah spoke up then and said, 'Aunt Sherlie, I don't have no need of ribbons or frilly whatnots. It's a tight fit for us with money. Tal is saying the truth.'

"'I understand you'd never ask for anything like that for yourself,' Aunt Sherlie said. 'Maybe you can think of this little bit of joy on your birthday as a bitter medicine you have to choke down one way or another.'

"'Are you sure about all this?' Talbot asked her. 'Dead certain?'

"'No,' she admitted. 'It's a kind of guesswork. But it's the best guess I've got and the best advice, wrong or right, that you're going to get.'

"Then Talbot rose and touched Sarah's shoulder and she rose too. 'I thank you,' he said, all stiff and formal. 'I thank you for taking the time and trouble. I don't know whether we're going to do what you say or not. I'll have to think about it.' And he clapped that old dented brown hat on his head and the Lucases departed."

My grandmother was silent for such a long space that I got anxious. "That ain't the end of the story, is it?"

"It's the limit of all I know for certain," she replied.

"But what happened? Did the Lucases do the things to make the ghost go away or not?"

"I think they did. I knew Sarah as wife and widow for thirty years after that and she never mentioned the Shining Woman again. But somewhere or other among Tal's things, she'd come across a tiny picture of Little Mary, and she always kept it in that first locket Tal gave her."

"Then it must have been the spirit of Little Mary after all."

She nodded slowly. "I believe that to be the case. Of course, with hants you never know for sure."

"Well, why didn't it look like her? How come Talbot Lucas, her own husband, couldn't recognize her?"

"Because he never had recognized her. . . . I'll tell you what Aunt Sherlie told me when I asked the same question. She said I was a healthy, good-looking seventeen-year-old girl from a free-spirited family and that when I closed my eyes to try to see myself as I wished I could be, it would be just myself

I saw— only at a highfalutin fancy ball or standing in a rose garden or inside a stately house. But Little Mary came from a different way of life and in the secret nighttime she saw herself as tall and blond and lissome as the springtime willow tree and free as the wind. The Shining Woman grew in her little by little every day and when she died, that was the spirit that was set free."

She fell silent then and I could tell a dark thought had crossed her mind. "What else did she say?"

"She said that as I grew older and got along in years, there would be a Shining Woman spirit that would appear in me. It would represent my youth that has gone away, but it would never be powerful in me like it was in Little Mary."

"Did it come true?"

She gave me a swift glance. "Can you see me as a tall blond Spirit Woman dancing in the air and showing her fanny?"

I started giggling, then laughing out loud—maybe too loud. "Yes," I said. "I can see it in my head as plain as anything."

She smiled then what I had decided to call her "naughty smile" and brushed it away with a gesture habitually casual. "You know what I think?" she asked. "I think somebody ought to take a stick to you."

THE FEISTIEST WOMAN

When word came that Ginger Summerell was getting married again, my father said he was happy for her. He added that he was a little surprised, she being the kind of female that prudent men shied from the way a lazy teenager might avoid an algebra test—and with that comparison, he shot me a meaningful glance.

My mother admitted that she, too, was surprised. "I had almost lost faith that there were any stalwart red-blooded men left in the world," she said. "I thought the age of heroes was long past."

"How can you entertain such a grotesque notion with Jess and me sitting right here with you at the breakfast table?" my father asked. "You're looking at two natural-born heroes, handsome and stouthearted. I've been saving up to invest in a pair of white horses and a suit or two of armor." This time his glance my way included a happy wink. "Shining up the armor—that will be your latest extra chore, Jess. I want you to scour those breastplates so bright that your mother can tweeze her eyebrows in the reflection."

"Joe Robert, hush," my mother cautioned. "That's not fit table talk."

"Here we are," my father replied, "just back from the barn chores, where Jess and I waded to our ankles in cow manure. We are sitting at the table chewing smoked hog fat and eating runny scrambled eggs whose origin is too disgusting to recall. Yet the woman of the house claims that talk about eyebrow tweezing is out of the bounds of good taste." He gave a bellowslike put-upon sigh. "I tell you, Jess, the females have an unsteady sense of decorum. They are a vexation and a puzzlement to the masculine race."

"And a source of comfort and never-ending delight," my mother said. "Don't leave out the most important part."

"All right," he said, "never-ending delight, I'll grant you. But comfort and Ginger Summerell have rarely been linked by intention or by accident."

"Who is she?" I asked. "I never heard of her."

"The friend of women and the scourge of men," he declared.

"Why, Joe Robert," my mother exclaimed, "what a thing to say. You know she's one of the dearest persons alive."

"So I've heard at quilting parties," my father said. "But in the hunting cabins it's a different tale entirely."

"Doesn't she like men?" I asked.

"Of course she does," my mother said.

"She's only just mighty hard on them," my father added.

"How is she hard on them?" I asked.

"Just to give you an idea," he replied. "We are calling her Ginger Summerell, even though she was married for ten years or so. She's the feisty kind of woman a marriage name won't stick to any better than a crow feather will attach to a turtle shell. I don't know what caused her husband's demise, but I suspect that he never quite recovered from his courtship with Ginger Summerell."

My mother spoke in her sternest voice: "It was heart failure. I want you to remember that, Jess, and refuse to be taken in by your father's silly rigmarole."

"I'm sure the coroner's report said heart failure," my father countered. "But men of an inquiring and scientific nature will remain skeptical." He rose and lifted the tall blue spatterware pot with its chipped black spout off the hot plate on the kitchen counter. He topped off my mother's cup and filled his own nearly to the brim.

My parents preferred chicory coffee, and when it was brewing, we could smell it in every corner of the house; in winter, with the air clear and brisk, its aroma invaded even the front porch. Sometimes, to save a little money, my father would sweeten his cup with molasses instead of sugar and this produced a smell even more enticing than sugared coffee. But then when I tasted it, the wonderful smell was replaced by a bitterly pungent taste that stung my palate and made my molars ache; it was only one more of the disappointments I had found to be endemic to the pleasures adults adored.

"What has Ginger Summerell got against men?" I asked.

He resettled himself, then leaned back and crossed his legs. He was wearing thick white wool socks; I was wearing blue cotton ones. Our mucky shoes were out on the back porch, lying where we had flung them off when the morning chores at the barns were finished. In winter we changed to street shoes as soon as we came indoors, but the warm summer invited stocking feet. On Sundays, however, my mother insisted that we wear shoes to breakfast and my father teased her about this rule even more persistently than about some of her other mysterious regulations. "I thought Jesus and the apostles went barefoot," he would tell her. "I don't see why I can't come to the table the way Saint Peter did." She explained that as soon as he achieved sainthood he could come to the table in any getup he chose; he could wear a fireman's hat and a blue velvet ballgown, she said, and added that she felt safe in giving him such wide latitude because his canonization did not appear imminent.

He returned to my question. "I don't know all the details," he said. "But the men seem to come out of any intimate situation with Ginger looking all ragged and chewed-up." He began to roll a cigarette, sifting out the delicate tobacco grains, spreading them along the furrow of the fragile paper, then closing the tube with a twirl of his fingers. He licked the edge and smoothed it out and held the cigarette up to admire. It was fat in the middle and wizened at the ends. "It's the truth, Cora, you can't deny that."

"I won't deny that she's got a lot of spirit," my mother said, "and I won't say that she might not be a handful and more for a lot of men. But, Jess, not all the males in the world are as fainthearted as your father seems to be this morning."

"Not fainthearted, never fainthearted—just prudent. Joe Robert Kirkman is noted far and wide for his cautious prudence. Ask around and you'll see. And I judge it more prudent to go over Niagara Falls in a brown paper lunch bag than to marry up with Ginger Summerell. She is the feistiest woman I ever heard of, that I ever heard that anybody else ever heard of."

"What makes her so feisty?" I asked.

"Being of the downtrodden masculine gender, I'm not sure I've got a proper answer," my father said. "Cora, you're going to have to be the one to explain to Jess what we are talking about." He grinned through his blue-gray cigarette smoke, flashing the gold cap of his front tooth at her.

"Oh I am, am I," she said, her tone implying she was not charmed by the proposition, and I figured I'd never hear the story. Then she relented: "Well, maybe I will tell him one of these days. Better for Jess to get it from me than listen to some wild tale you'd dream up."

"Why, Cora," he said, "I'm shocked that you'd say such a thing. Flabbergasted. Wounded. Nonplussed. Amazed, astounded, and astonished. Utterly and completely bumflustered."

"Yes," she said solemnly, "I think I'd better be the one to tell him."

And a week later she did.

"The reason she's that kind of person is where Ginger Summerell came from in the first place," my mother said. "That's *one* of the reasons at least. Marsden County is about a hundred years behind the rest of the world, and Bailey Ridge, where Ginger was born, is a hundred years behind Marsden County. It wasn't long ago that they followed the old ways there. Maybe they still do, but when I was a girl, people talked about that place almost in whispers. You know how folks will go on about how they like old-timey notions and fashions and how the modern-day methods of doing things are hurrying us all to perdition. . . . Well, they didn't say that about Bailey Ridge. It was too close to the way the frontier *really* used to be, I expect. *Backward:* That was the word they used till it became proverbial. You'd hear somebody say of another person, 'Why, she's as backward as Bailey Ridge,' and you'd know what was meant.

"And of course it was a place a lot harder for girls than for boys to grow up in. That's always the case when you're talking *backward.* It wasn't the custom there to court a girl. They never heard of a nosegay or sweet talk or gentle manners. The boys—or older men, most likely—would try to find a girl somewhere alone in the woods or fields and make her pregnant. They called it 'bigging' a woman. If a man could 'big' a woman, then she'd belong to that man as a wife because she would be carrying his child. Those dreadful men took a lot of pride in it, too, just like hunters that bring down a ten-point buck or a fisherman showing off a hefty brown trout. They thought they had done something fine and praiseworthy, but it was nothing but rape, pure and simple."

She paused for a moment and took her hands out of the dishwater and leaned forward, looking with burning eyes into the sunny yard, where Sherlock and Quadrille, our best barn cats, lay, taking up the August heat like they were storing it for a long winter to come.

"I hate that word, to *big* a woman," she said. "It's the ugliest sound in the world. I'm used to the common four-letter words. Children chalk them on the walls at the schoolhouse all the time, just to show their friends they can be naughty. But *big* is different. I'm glad that it has passed from the vocabulary. You probably never even heard it used the old backward way."

I shook my head to say no and finished drying the salad plate I'd been rubbing on, then stacked it with the others on the cabinet top. Aunt Thelma's cousin Hannah had come in from Washington State for a visit and my mother had invited some lady friends in for tea to meet this woman who was reputed to have beautiful hands. She was a model for the movies, in fact, and often flew from Spokane down to Hollywood, where they would costume her and put her in a scene and spend all day filming her hands dealing cards or writing a letter or holding a man's shoulder. Then the next day she would fly back home. This occupation made her seem exotic and important to us. All my mother's friends wanted to meet her and enjoy an interview with her celebrated appendages. So my mother was giving a tea party. There was nothing like a dainty teacup to set off a lady's hands, she told me, and she doubted that she would come by a better opportunity to display her gilt-rim Limoges. Not until that fateful day that I got married anyhow, and I decided that if she mentioned one more time "that cute little Sarah Robinson I was sweet on," I would go out to the woodshed and get the ax and come back and chop her head off.

"But Ginger Summerell was not going to fall prey to that old custom," my mother said. "As soon as she was of an age, she understood that if she got herself bigged, then she'd be for the rest of her life the hand servant—and we might as well say slave and beast of burden—to some old man she would hate from the start. So she determined not to let it happen. And Ginger has the willpower it takes to carry out her plans and the wit to draw them up tight and sound.

"She had the results right before her eyes, you see. You take notice, Jess, the next time we're in Marsden County, how the women over there look. By the time they're twenty-five years old, they look like they're going on forty, and if they reach the ripe old age of forty, they look seventy-five. But it's more likely they'll have been worn out and pitched into stony graves by that time. I know life is hard back in those flint-rock hills and hollers, but it could be a lot easier if the menfolk would only let it be. . . . Of course, that's not their idea about things. They read in the Bible that life is hard, so they set out to make it harder. That's not what my Bible says to do, and I suppose your father might be right on that one little point—that we all read a different Bible."

I remembered my father's saying, but I recalled the rest of it, too, the part she had left out. "All these homemade religionists read a different Bible," he said, "but it makes them all crazy in the same way."

"Anyhow," my mother continued, "Ginger made herself smart and fleet and cunning and fierce and as tough as a pine knot. When she went out into the woods and fields alone, to gather blackberries or pawpaws or to spend an hour in her secret playhouse, she would take no chances. She kept her eyes and ears open and if she glimpsed a suspicious movement or heard a stealthy noise, then she would skitter away like a blue darter. Nobody could catch her, either; not one boy big or small could run as fast as she could run. She would dare any of them to race in the schoolyard and handily leave them behind openmouthed.

"That was another of her stratagems: to let the boys know she could take care of herself and needn't fear them. So she would not only race them; she would fight them, too, wrastle them catch-as-catch-can or rooster-fight or battle them in any way they chose. There, too, she trounced them soundly. She wasn't a big girl, more whippetlike—as lithe as a cane pole and wiry as a bedspring. She could take punishment and dish it out, and the days she didn't come home with a black eye must have been days of gray boredom on her calendar.

"But the way she free-talked and swaggered her shoulders when she walked brought about some cool feelings. The girls admired her, but they were afraid of her, too, though she never offered harm to any of them. The boys, though, were sorely riled and their first thought, after they realized that they could furnish no champion from amongst themselves to defeat Ginger, was to gang up on her. They followed her the best they could, then scoured the woods from the place where she lost them till they located the playhouse.

"It was the custom in that time and place, Jess, for a young girl to find herself a secret hideaway and build a make-believe house. It had to be secret because her brothers or any other passing boy who came across it would destroy it. That was the tradition on both sides, just another instance of being backward, I suppose.

"The girl would gather the prettiest little rocks she could find and smooth out a space on the ground, clearing away the leaves and sticks and toadstools and sweeping the dirt flat with a leafy branch, and then lay out her rocks in straight lines. Those were the walls of her house and she would leave spaces for doors. Then she would place in all her rooms little objects that represented different things. A piece of clear glass would be a window, you see, and a chip of crockery would be a dinner plate. An empty spool might be anything, a settee or a bed or even a harmonium. Outside the walls she might put down a mason-jar rubber and that would be the well for her water or even a neat little pond with goldfish in it. And there, in her own dear house she had designed and built with her own hands, a girl would play at being a mother with a happy family, a kind and loving husband and strong obedient sons and curly-top daughters.

"Whether girls still build playhouses, I don't know, but if they do, it's a sure bet that boys try to find them and tear them up. Still, it wasn't so easy to spy the house that Ginger Summerell made. She had disguised it, you see, in such a clever way that it didn't look like one at first. Instead of rocks laid out in straight lines, she made curvy walls with sticks and different-colored leaves and she made her rooms so big that the stones and isinglass and buckeyes she used to represent furniture looked like they were lying there by the accident of nature. The back of her playhouse butted up against a great huge boulder.

"Even so, the biggest and meanest of the boys found it out. His name was Orlow Jackson and he was a redheaded terror. He had bested all the boys around in wrastling and fisticuffs and so was their leader, only he was the bad kind that would get them into mischief. He had vowed black revenge on Ginger since the time she thrust him into the dirt of the schoolyard and twisted his arm behind his back till he hollered 'calf rope.' He found Ginger's playhouse and laid an ambush for her. I don't know what it was he spotted that gave her away, maybe a scrap of cloth that was a make-believe bedspread or a marble that was an alabaster lamp.

"Anyhow, there were six of them waiting in the bushes one day when Ginger came to play. They had to be as quiet and cunning as Cherokees stalking deer, or she would have seen them. Little good, though, all their sneaking meanness did them. When they rushed out to grab her, she saw them and ran to the shadow of that great boulder and squeezed through a tight crevice there and rolled down a biggish rock to seal it behind her. Then she scampered to the top of the boulder and started showering those mean old boys with stones. Mercy, how she rocked them! It was like a hail of hurting stones out of the clouds of heaven. They couldn't stand much of that. A smooth piece of river rock caught Orlow Jackson on his topknot and caused him to reconsider his erroneous notions of gallantry. Those six big boys left the field to Ginger Summerell. Bruised and swearing and bleeding, they turned tail.

"Because she'd planned it out, you see. She had made a fortress atop that boulder and stocked a forethoughtful arsenal of rocks. As the years went by, she acquired a more serious arsenal: two pistols by Smith & Wesson and some kind of rifle I can't remember and a twelve-gauge shotgun. Her daddy taught her a little and the rest she learned herself and she turned out a crack shot and would have made an admirable hunter of deer and turkey, except she didn't care for hunting. Her weaponry had but a single purpose, as she told one and all—to shoot the dingle-dangles off of any man that might take a mind to come bothering her.

"And none did.

"She always knew what she wanted, had the clearest mind I ever met, man or woman. When her uncle Ferman Ball, who had lived a sad widower for thirty years, died over on Hornet Branch, she moved into his little ramshackle cabin to stay and she dared anybody to roust her out of it. Nobody took that dare, partly because they figured she had as much right to the place as any other of his few scattered kinfolk—and partly because that old house was about ready to fall down anyhow on its little acre of ground that was nothing but ragweed and sawbriar. Then, too, they knew that Ginger's weapons stood ready to her right hand.

"Here, too, she had a plan. She'd kept her eye on that plot as a fitting spot to live if only she could make it so. She could gather a little bit of cash money to buy building materials with because she was good to stay with children and look after them and clever with needle and thread and in a day in the corn patch or hay field would do the work of a man and a half. So everything turned out once again exactly according to her scheme. All the labor she supplied herself, and she changed that ratty old shack into a cabin as neat and sound and comfortable and pleasant as any in the county.

"If we ever get over to Bailey Ridge, I'll drive us by that cabin, Jess. I want you to see how it is as perfect as a picture painted by an artist.

"She tended a generous kitchen garden and a swept dirt yard with a border of marigolds and tall zinnias. She would work for hire when that was needful, and when it wasn't, she would sit on her front porch and maybe take a pipe of tobacco with her daddy when he came to visit or with her older brother Efird.

"Her family was about the only company she ever had, even though her place was as inviting to look at as a fresh-baked strawberry pie. Her schoolmate girls, who had been afraid of her when they were younguns, now were cross-eyed jealous. Because they had never known and never would know the freedom she had won and guarded so carefully. Most of them had been bigged by men who were mostly no better than brutes, if you ask me, and now they were shackled to them for life. The others were the slaves, or worse, of their own fathers. And there sat Ginger Summerell in the notch of the hill above the settlement, as plain to see as a lonesome pine on the edge of a bluff, proud and free and a woman on her own terms such as had never been heard of before in Bailey Ridge. If she was fated to be an old maid whom ignorant people told jokes about, there was many a wife with a baby on each hip and a greasy pot boiling on the cookstove that would look up the mountain to her cabin and wish they could be old maids all their years.

"But they didn't understand Ginger's mind, Jess, for she had another notion entirely. She had never given a serious thought to being an old maid. She sent out word around the settlement that she was a propertied woman in good health with twenty-two years of age on her who was willing to entertain proper suitors.

"Her pattern of a proper suitor was a man who would behave in a civilized manner and was ready to talk calm good sense to a woman and would come calling on her the way sociable folks did who lived in less ignorant places. She had read books and heard tales; she knew how things are supposed to be. None of this rutting in ditches like wild hogs and then a jackleg preacher mumbling at your swollen belly six months later. She knew what she wanted.

"Trouble was, nobody else did. I don't think the menfolk had a glimmer. None of them came to call on her, anyhow. Maybe they were just plain afraid.

"Ginger waited from January till June, finishing up her work by late afternoon, milking her cow, and then setting the table for two in her kitchen. After the table was set and supper was steaming on the stove, she'd go out on her porch and sit till nightfall. Then she would go back in and eat lonesome by lamplight.

"That was the time when people sniggered at her as an old maid, even though the term didn't apply. Ginger was not a woman pining away her prime years, socking and sighing and growing gray and warped as a cow-lot fence."

"Come the warm evenings of June, she was weary of dining alone, so one Friday afternoon she dressed in her usual outfit—which was a man's cotton shirt and a pair of roomy gray corduroy pants and a tall-crowned straw hat—and stuffed a pistol behind her belt buckle and marched down to Bradley's Outpost. That was a little grocery and dry goods establishment hardly as big as her cabin where the single menfolk spent their time playing checkers, spitting tobacco, and swapping lies. Bred-to-the-bone loafers, most of them, and some that were a shame and a sore trial to their mothers and fathers.

"In strode Ginger through the rusty screen door, and when the four lazybones men saw her, the first thing they noticed was that pistol. They fell silent as she swept her gaze over them one by one, top to bottom. When Exum Bradley, behind the cloth counter, asked what he could do for her, she replied, 'I don't see a thing here that I could use. I reckon I'll have to come back later.' And out she strode again, and up the hill to her house to shed her pistol and sit down to a cold supper of buttermilk and string beans and dry corn bread.

"She was as good as her word, of course, and every three or four days she would adorn herself with a revolver, hike down to the Outpost, and survey that day's crop of loafers. Five visits running, she culled them all. There were some women who said she made herself a laughingstock with her straightforward ways, but after five inspections, the joke began to look like it was on the menfolk. Whatever the laughter took up for its subject, it didn't begin till Ginger had legged it up the hill again, well out of earshot.

"The sixth time she pushed into Bradley's, she spotted a tall, big-shouldered, freckle-faced fellow with hair as red as a flame of fire. She peered at him closely for a long minute and then said, 'I believe you to be Orlow Jackson.'

"He colored up and said, 'That's who I am all right.'

" 'You have not been seen around these parts for a while.'

" 'I just got out of the service,' he said. 'I've served in the infantry the past four years.'

" 'I wonder if they cured you in the army of the dirty sneaking ways you used to have.'

"His color rose high again, till it was almost as red as his hair. 'I reckon I don't know what you mean,' he said, holding himself as stiff as the king in a deck of cards.

"She kept looking him over as closely as she might inspect a whiteface heifer on the auction block. 'I believe they might have done you some good,' she said. 'I want you to come along with me outside, Orlow Jackson, where we can have a word or two in private.'

" 'I ain't ready to go anywhere right yet,' he said.

"She answered not a word but withdrew her thirty-two special from her belt, and when he ventured to say he did not expect her to fire, she stretched up on her tiptoes and conked him on the noggin with the barrel, right on the topknot, where she had plunked him with a river rock ten years before. Then while he was staring at her with a sudden new comprehension in his mind, she grasped him by his shirt collar and pulled him out the door of the Outpost and back under a big beech tree by the side of the road.

"Naturally, the other five loafers there in Bradley's rushed to the door to see what would happen next, but a hard glance from Ginger made them hang back, and they couldn't hear what she said to Jackson as she peered straight up into his eyes and talked as low and earnest as a preacher boring in on an unrepentant drunkard. They were dying to ask him, but he didn't come back into the store. When they parted, Ginger commenced to climb her hill again and Orlow Jackson sidled over and got on his roan stallion tethered there and headed in the direction of his own house.

"But she had made a speech that took effect, for the very next evening that same roan horse carried Jackson up the hill to Ginger's cabin, where they sat chatting on the front porch and sharing some sugar biscuit she had baked. And the evening after that, the same thing happened, and the next after that, only this time he had dressed up in creased gray cotton pants and a fresh-ironed shirt buttoned up to the chin. Ginger came out to meet him on her front porch in a blue gingham dress with lace at the collar. I don't know about her shoes, but they couldn't have been those ugly old lace-up boots she affected to wear for everyday's.

"They sat there and whiled away the twilight and then went inside to the kitchen and ate supper by the light of that lonesome kerosene lamp that Ginger had removed from the table and set in a cupboard shelf to cast romantic shadows.

"Have I told you what a marvelous cook she was? Well, she was, one of the best I knew. Maybe only Aunt Pearlie Adams was ever a better. She had dozens of little secrets, you see, for making stewed tomatoes and squash burgoo and okra fried crunchy in cornmeal. And her pies! Her every pie was a wonder, especially her dried-apple pie, where she would soak the slices in hard cider to soften and then pour off the cider and boil it down with brown sugar and cinnamon and nutmeg and maybe the tiniest pinch of mace, if I remember correctly, till it was a thin syrup and pour that over the slices into a crust that was as light as goose down and top it all off with a lattice. She would slide it into the oven and add one more stick of stove wood to the fire pit and then never open the oven door again except to take the pie out when it was the color of a field of ripe oats. She never looked at the clock, either. I suppose she must have judged by the perfume of it when it was done.

"I like the new electrics myself, but there are women who will swear that the old-timey woodstove is the only way to cook. Remind me to tell you sometime about Aunt Pearlie's misfortunes with an electric stove.

"So Mr. Orlow Jackson enjoyed quite a feed on that pleasant evening. I disremember what all Ginger cooked up for him, but I would hope she made him some of her famous lumpless mashed potatoes and those turnip greens that she could make taste fresh and not greasy and some of that chicken she would fry up in a savory batter. . . . Like I say, Ginger was as clever with a wood range as she was with needle and thread and knife and pistol.

"Pretty soon it had got to be serious. Jackson's folks had been complaining how they couldn't get any work out of him on the farm because he was always down at Bradley's Outpost, whittling daylight down to eventide. Now they complained he was always at Ginger's house, but they couldn't say he wasn't working, because he was. Side by side with his sweetheart in her little garden, or up top patching the roof where needful, or helping her to build a milking shed where she could stall that pretty little Jersey she was buying on time from Jerry Jarrett.

"Of course, when Ginger heard of the Jacksons' displeasure, she told Orlow she wanted him to be back helping his mother and daddy on their home place because that's what civil sons and daughters owed to their parents. So he did as she said, plumb crazy about her by now and always a little cowed when she employed that word *civil* on him. But it just about wore him to a frazzle, because when he finished his proper work at home, he would scurry over to Ginger's and put in a good half day's labor there.

"Things just swum right along, slick as a mossy rock in the Cataloochee River, and nobody was surprised when they made the announcement that they were engaged. . . . Well, *they* didn't make it, in fact. Ginger made it herself, and that was what started the next trouble between them.

"Ginger had figured the time was opportune; Orlow was ripe for marriage, she thought. And so he was, only he didn't know it yet. Jackson had turned out a right worthy fellow, nothing like when he was a mean old boy. But he wasn't what you'd call perspicacious and hadn't come to a serious thought as yet about taking the vows. So when he heard from Glenn Harkins that he himself, Mr. Orlow Jackson, was engaged to get married to Ginger Summerell, he bowed his neck against the yoke and set himself down there on the Jackson farm and left off seeing Ginger and wouldn't desert his mind on the point. I believe that Ginger had made a rare miscalculation in this particular matter and had hurt Jackson's feelings. Men like to feel they make the important decisions, you see, and the trick is to let them believe they actually do.

"But if Orlow was a stubborn man, Ginger was a stubborner woman. Weeks fled by that they didn't see each other or send any hint of message. Finally, Ginger did send word by her brother Efird, but it wasn't what you'd call loving. Her reputation had been violated, she said, and she was going to avenge the insult herself. She didn't trust anybody else to repair the good name of an injured maiden girl, not even her daddy or her brother. So, would Mr. Orlow Jackson please make known the weapon or weapons of his choice and meet her this coming Saturday, August second, at three in the afternoon in the bald on top of Bailey Ridge? That was to be their field of honor.

"She coached her brother thoroughly, Efird not being warmly familiar with the term *reputation* or the concept of honor, and when she was satisfied he could say it off clearly—though with a mystified expression on his face—she sent him off to the Jackson farm, where he gave a pretty good account of himself as a messenger. In fact, Efird was so proud of his feat of memorization that he spouted his sister's speech afterward to anybody he met on the road and to the Outpost bunch and to just about everything not rooted to one spot in the ground.

"So when three o'clock Saturday rolled around, there was quite a swarm of people on Bailey Bald, Orlow Jackson tall and gloomy among them. He had not brought any weapons, of course, but he had to show up on the spot or be shamed by the woman who claimed she'd been jilted. And yet he had no more idea what was going on than any of the chance bystanders.

"Finally, Ginger arrived with a big burlap tote sack slung over her shoulder. She asked Orlow if he was armed and ready to defend himself.

" 'Aw, Ginger,' he said, 'you know good and well I'm not. I can't be shooting at you, and I hope to God Almighty you won't be shooting at me.'

" 'My honor must be satisfied,' she replied. 'I will make that clear to you. Nothing else will pacify my mind.'

" 'What are you going to do, then?'

" 'Let's go over yonder to the level place next to that stand of trees,' she said. 'That will give us a firm ground to rest on.' And off she set with those scissor strides, covering ground so fast, he had to trot to keep up.

" 'I ain't going to shoot at you,' he said. 'I didn't even bring a gun.'

" 'I have supplied weapons for us both,' Ginger said. She lowered her tote sack to the grass and began taking things out of it. First object she pulled out was an old twelve-gauge shotgun that had seen better days, but not recently. Then she took out her rifle; I guess it must have been a thirty-thirty; anyhow, it was lever-action. Then out came her two pistols and a hammer and an empty Prince Albert tobacco can. Then she revealed a big hunting knife with a foot-long blade as keen as a copperhead tooth. She reached way down and brought out two little blue milk of magnesia bottles, the kind kids like to play with.

"In fact, all this truck spread out on the grass looked like a trove of children's toys, and the sight of it puzzled Orlow Jackson. He stood there staring at it and rubbing the back of his neck. Nobody else could figure it out, either, and they crowded around to look. There must have been at least twenty people there, not counting the younguns, and some of them must have reckoned Ginger Summerell had totally lost her sanity.

"There they stood, the two of them, with all this silly plunder spread about their feet, and they took careful estimate of each other. Orlow looked as uncomfortable and puzzled and gloomy as a tattooed sailor at a church social and Ginger gazed upon his manly form like he was a side of beef she was fixing to butcher into porterhouse.

" 'Since I am the one offering the challenge, you must choose the weapons we will battle with,' she said.

" 'Ginger,' said he, 'I won't.'

" 'If that's the case, then the choice comes back to me,' Ginger said, 'and I choose that we will duel with shotgun, rifle, pistols, and bowie knife.'

" 'Not me. I don't want to duel with anything,' he said.

" 'What you want doesn't signify,' Ginger declared. 'For as sure as the sun rolls across the sky, there is going to be a duel.' And with that, she picked up the clawhammer and marched over to a big white oak about fifteen paces away. She took a roofing tack out of her pocket and unfolded a scrap of newspaper and nailed it to the tree trunk. She came back to where he stood and dropped the hammer in the grass and repeated her solemn vow: 'There is going to be a duel, Orlow, as sure as the stars shine at nighttime.' "

"Watch out, Jess! You're about to knock over that punchbowl. I don't know what I'd do to you if that bowl got broken. It's been in our family for three generations. And so many of my prettiest things have got chipped and cracked over the years, it looks like I'm going to wind up with nothing but discards. Here, give me that. Maybe I'd better finish up and you go on and do something else."

"No, ma'am," I said. "Not till I hear about that duel. You can't be turning me out now. No, ma'am."

"Well, all right. Go ahead and start polishing on those spoons. But for heaven's sake, be careful. . . . Now, what was I talking about?"

"Oh, yes, the duel.

"Ginger picked up the shotgun from where she had dropped it on the ground so careless and took a shell out of her pocket and broke the gun down and loaded it. That made the onlookers stand uneasy. They edged back from Ginger and Orlow and the women began to look about to see to the safety of their younguns.

"It was hot in the valley, but there was a cool breeze across Bailey Bald. The sun shone bright, with not a cloud in the sky. The birds were singing and the children shouting and chasing butterflies, but when Ginger snapped the breach of that shotgun closed, all the sound died away. Even the cicadas went silent, seemed like.

"She offered the shotgun to Jackson, but he only shook his head and kept his hands in his pockets. 'You say you won't take it? I'm giving you the first go,' she said. 'I'll stand my ground at sixty yards and you can fire at me when ready.'

"But he only gazed down at her with eyes as sad as a beagle's.

" 'All right. That means the first shot is mine,' she said, 'and I'll show you what I might do if the notion was to take me.' She knelt down and plucked that Prince Albert tin off the grass and flung it up in the air and brought the muzzle up and pulled the trigger and blew it to flinders.

"Just like that.

"She laid the shotgun away and said, 'That would be your big stout belly I aimed at there, Orlow.'

"He was like a man in a trance as he considered her sentence. Slowly he took his right hand out of his pocket and tenderly rubbed his stomach. His face was coloring up like the red in a thermometer.

"She offered him the thirty-thirty rifle and he only stood confused. She retrieved the two little blue bottles from the ground and sent them spinning into the air. Bang! She smashed the first one. Then quick as a flash she pumped the lever and fired and smashed the other. Bang!

" 'And then off your head I shot your big old flapping mule ears,' she said.

"His mouth flew open as he took a deep breath and clapped both hands to the sides of his head. Yes, his ears were still there, but only because of the tender mercies of Ginger Summerell.

"Then she held out the two pistols grip-first, but he couldn't move a muscle except to let his hands drop to his sides. She took them back and stuck one in her belt while she searched in the deep pocket of her corduroy trousers and fetched out two Coca-Cola bottle caps. These, too, she tossed way up into the air. With her left hand she shot the nearer one and it disappeared from view. With her right hand she snatched the second pistol out of her belt, cocking as she did so, and fired, and the other bottle cap was gone like it had never been.

" 'Those were your two beady little pig eyes I plinked right out of your skull,' she said.

"He only stared in her direction without seeing her, for it

was obvious he had gone blind for a moment and would have to wait for his sight to be restored. When he could see again, he looked at Ginger and his red face mottled with white patches till it was almost polka-dotted.

"She didn't bother to offer the bowie knife. She just leaned over and grasped it by the blade and threw it as straight as a dart. It pinned dead to the tree trunk that scrap of newspaper that had been fluttering like a kite tail in the breeze.

" 'And that, Orlow Jackson,' she said, 'was your treacherous false heart that I sliced out of your breast.'

"He closed his eyes and swayed on his feet and his face went all white and so did his sweating hands, white as a toadstool in the dampest forest shade. Then he opened his eyes and color came back into his cheeks and he was recovered to life again.

"Ginger dug her fists into her hips and twisted her lips shut and looked into his face with eyes like lightning bolts. She stood as straight and steady as a locust fence post, daring the fellow to do his utter worst.

"The mouths of everyone in the crowd were gaped like bear traps. Men, women, and children let out suddenly the breaths they had been holding and took their gaze from Ginger to turn rapt attention upon Orlow.

"He appeared to study strenuously, like a man considering the finishing touches on his last will and testament. Then he came forward, slowly and gravely approaching Ginger, and there was no telling what decision had come to him, for his face gave nothing away. When he got to where Ginger stood waiting, he knelt down as slowly as sap oozing from a tree cut and picked up the clawhammer. He held the handle toward her.

" 'Here is one last weapon you forgot to use,' he said. 'I believe that if you was to hit me over the head with it, I might come around to better sense.'

"She budged not an inch and moved not muscle one, but only kept him fixed in her electric stare.

" 'Go ahead, Ginger,' he urged her. 'Clonk me a good one.

That will be an earnest of our vows.' He smiled upon her as ingratiating as he could and said again, 'Go ahead. Third time's a charm.'

"Still she scorned him, not accepting the hammer and giving no sign she had even heard his generous offer.

" 'Well, if you won't, you won't,' said he. 'I reckon it's something I must do for myself.' With that he turned the hammer around and brought it up with cool deliberation and smote himself with it right between the eyes. Nor did he go easy with any gentle love tap. It was a blow as stout as you'd please and wrought such handsome effect upon his head that consciousness fled from his brain and he pitched forward face first, plunging like a felled sapling right at the feet of Ginger Summerell.

"She looked down at him, her expression at first like that of a contending prizefighter who has just brought down a favored champion. I suppose she tried to imagine it as her moment of triumph. But I'll tell you, Jess, sometimes the body knows better than the mind what the heart's true feelings are. Ginger looked down at Orlow at her feet, and maybe he'd slain himself for love and maybe he hadn't, but there he lay motionless, with his face in the earth, and so her consciousness gave way, too, and she also keeled over facedown across the body of her beloved, and there the two of them lay on Bailey Bald, making a human-being *X* mark in the grass.

"Of course, the onlookers rushed to where they'd fallen and began tugging them apart and patting and pinching to bring them back to life. It wasn't long before their eyes opened and they stood up and then fell once more, only into each other's arms this time. Now their vows were taken and sealed like bonds of iron and they rekindled their ardent courtship and were married in the harvest moon.

"Everybody who was in that crowd on Bailey Bald said they would never forget the sight of the two lovers passed out on top of each other in the grass. Some of the menfolk said it was about the funniest thing they ever saw, but some of the women said it was the prettiest picture they could ever imagine, a spectacle of passion chaste and pure, but as strong in its current as a waterfall."

"I like that story," I told my mother. "But I thought you were going to tell me about how Orlow Jackson died."

"That's a sad story and I'm not in the mood today to recount sad stories. . . . Tell me, Jess, don't you think the table looks nice?"

I thought it looked splendid. Here were set out the fancy flowered plates and cups and saucers we never used, and there was the big cut-glass bowl she had feared I'd destroy, and there were smaller cut-glass dishes for pickles and preserves. The heavy silver cake platter stood waiting for one of Aunt Jincy's melting pound cakes and the silverware gleamed glorious in the late-morning light. "It looks fine," I said. "I sort of wish I was invited to this ladies' party."

"Why, you are, of course, Jess," my mother said. "You can help me hand around the cake. You just shine up your shoes and put on your nice blue wool suit and you'll make a handsome guest. And that nice red necktie Aunt Holly gave you. She'd like to see you wearing that, and so would I."

I hastened to deflect this line of thought. "No, no, that's all right. Maybe there'll be some table scraps left for me." While we stood there for a moment longer, still admiring, I said, "She must have been an awful good shot."

"Who? . . . Oh, you mean Ginger. Well, she wasn't bad, not bad at all. Of course, I'm a pretty fair hand with a shotgun myself. Did I ever tell you about how I got rid of a pesky red kite that was aggravating my mind? Maybe I'll tell you that story sometime."

"I look forward to it," I said.

THE

HELPINEST

WOMAN

My mother had commandeered me to help string a bushel of green beans. There we sat, all through the amiable summer afternoon, she and my grandmother and I, tugging off stray leaves and vine stems, flicking away the nubbly yellow worms that clung to the hulls and twirling the long runner beans end to end as we unzipped their spines. The open porch smelled like a fresh-turned garden.

Our talk fastened upon religion. My grandmother had a monstrous sweet tooth for sanctified chatter. She had been thinking about the virtues, she explained, and had come to admire charity most particularly. Of course, all the virtues were ace qualities; there was no danger she'd undervalue patience or fortitude, and especially not temperance, but on this bright afternoon it was charity that had captured her affection.

My mother kept her close company. She liked any religious talk that might throw her personal qualities into a flattering light. But she was chary of ungrounded generalizations and insisted upon concrete examples. If there was someone we knew who embodied a salient virtue, we should examine this paragon. But we should pay even closer attention when some unfortunate acquaintance was discovered to be in thrall to a horrid vice; this specimen deserved the most minute examination. My grandmother enjoyed lauding the virtues, my mother delighted in excoriating the vices, and I am convinced that neither of them ever thought that all their palaver about religion provided only a pious excuse for flavorsome gossip.

The conversation took a leisurely turn down memory lane—which for these two was a commodious Appian Way. My grandmother commenced a roll call of folks she had known who were given to deeds of Christian charity and loving-kindness. Some of these names I knew in the flesh, but as she more thoroughly ransacked the past, I fell behind and the names accrued a mist of legend. They turned into names that were no longer popular among the newborn: Gertrude, Emmaline, Dovey, Hepzibah, Flora, and even the blessed title itself—Charity. But all of the latter name-bearers were rejected sorrowfully as having failed the promise of their cognomen.

As I listened to their research, I noted an interesting fact. Not one single example of charity they brought to light sported a masculine name. I thought I might ask why, but then decided—as I often did when in their company—that mousy discretion was a better plan than foolhardy valor.

Then they both lit upon a name at once, like two dragonflies coming to rest on the same touch-me-not. "Angela Newcome," my grandmother murmured, and my mother smiled one of her "Lord have mercy on that poor soul" half smiles and shook her head.

"Who is Angela Newcome?" I asked. "I never heard of her."

"*Was,*" my mother replied. "She has gone on to her reward."

"In heaven," my grandmother said.

"Oh yes, in heaven. . . . She'll be teaching harp lessons, I think."

"And if the streets are paved with gold," my grandmother said, "I feel sorry for the poor angel that has to keep them clean."

"Why?" I asked.

"Because that angel will have a lot of help," my mother said.

"All the help that could ever be needed," my grandmother said.

I asked why again, hoping to unstopper the story jug.

"Well," my mother told me, "it's because Angela Newcome was brimful and overflowing with Christian charity. Folks in the Blue Creek community where she lived called her 'the Helpinest Woman' because she never missed out on a chance to give aid and comfort to whoever she could, kinfolk or neighbors or nodding acquaintances or pure rank strangers. If you had a touch of the flu and needed someone to run an errand for you, Angela was right there. If you needed somebody to mind your younguns while you worked in the fields, she'd stay at your house all day and have a good hot meal on the table when you came to supper. If she was here right now, she'd be helping us string these beans. Then she'd wash them in the sink and sweep this greenery off the floor here and gather it up and take it to the hog lot."

"She'd help us untie our aprons," my grandmother put in.

"And hang them up for us in the hallway," my mother added.

"And offer to wash and iron them."

"And find where they might need any little bit of mending and offer to work her needle after walking five miles to a store to get the exact color thread to match these old shabby workday aprons and inquire if we wouldn't like a little red or green rickrack around the bottoms and to edge the pockets."

"And then help us with the cooking and canning," my grandmother said. "Now you'd think we were talking about a big stout lady, wouldn't you? But Angela Newcome was just a little mite of a body. Wouldn't run up over five foot two or so and wouldn't weigh hardly a hundred. But she just never gave out, never sat down to rest a minute or survey what she'd done already. You know, though, Cora, I can't remember how her face was favored. . . ."

"That's because she was a white blur of speed most of the time," my mother said. "I recall her looks, though, because she fascinated me when I was a girl. Her eyes were the brightest green you ever saw; they shone out at you. And her skin was so fair, you saw her blue veins. And she had blond hair just turning silver when I knew her; it must have been star-bright when she was a bit younger. But the main thing about her, the oddest thing—and everybody who knew her spoke of it—was that her hands never got coarse and rough and hard and red. All her life her hands were as soft and sweet as Spanish leather. Like ivory in color and smelling as delicate as the youngest lily."

"Trouble was," my grandmother said, "she didn't have a family. Her father died when she was real young and her mother not long after, and she had no brothers or sisters and so went to live with her mother's sister and her husband. But Uncle Jake Miller was quite old by then and when he died it wasn't long till Martha took to her grave. Charity begins at home, you know, but Angela didn't have a home, so the gift of all her charitable feelings and helpful goodwill was bestowed upon the community."

"I thought you were going to say *inflicted upon,*" my mother interjected. "Because that was more the way it was. I don't want you to think, Jess, that folks were ungrateful for all the things Angela did for them. They were extremely grateful.

They felt beholden to her—and not just upon occasion but all the time. Suppose somebody was to come along while you were off at a family reunion or some other important do and weeded your garden. You'd think, Well, that was awful neighborly; I expect my friend would enjoy a mess of spinach. Then while you were on your way to her house with the greens, she was already back at yours, dusting the furniture and sweeping the floors. When you can't pay favors back and they keep on piling up, it gets to be a ponderous burden."

"It might make you a little aggravated," said my grandmother.

"To tell the truth," my mother said, "you get to where you dread to see your benefactress coming. You might even get to where you don't really like her."

"You had to like Angela, though."

"Yes, it was duty. Because the only thing she would ever say about you or anybody else was, 'I'm glad to call that lady my friend.' "

"Which made you so ashamed of your vexatious thoughts, you'd hang your head and blush."

"I hope you comprehend what we're saying, Jess," my mother explained. "You do understand that Angela Newcome was a wonderful woman, don't you? And I hope you can understand how she was also a sore trial. Maybe what I'm saying is against the Bible, but sometimes folks can come to believe there's such a thing as too much charity."

"Remember the time Melissa Carter wrenched her back?" my grandmother asked. "Angela moved right into the house with the Carters and took the place of Melissa, keeping the house and washing the clothes and making the meals and tending the garden. Melissa was out of commission for six weeks and Angela took over her every duty."

"Took over a few too many," my mother said. "Because there came a day Melissa heard some uncustomary sounds from the front room and crawled painfully out of bed and crept to the door and cracked it and beheld her husband and

Angela with neither of them hardly a stitch on and just having a high old time on that red corduroy sofa."

"Well, I wouldn't call that *charity,*" my grandmother said.

"But Angela Newcome would and did," my mother replied. "She told Melissa that her husband, Alfred, seemed to be in such straits, him being deprived of home comfort for so long, it only seemed her bounden duty to try to ease his burden. And the thing is, Melissa believed her. She took Angela at her word, though she did bring a swift ending to such activity by saying it distressed her own feelings and she knew Angela would never wish to do that. But she accepted Angela's every syllable when she explained how she considered the whole thing purely in the light of neighborliness and friendly aid. I'd like to see Joe Robert's face if I got myself into such a pickle as that and offered Christian charity as my excuse."

"Now, daughter, you know you'd never cut such a shameless dido."

"No, of course not," my mother proudly averred. "I'm just saying I'd like to see my spouse's face, is all. I'd like to hear what he had to say."

"That would be one thing, anyhow, he wouldn't pass off as a joke."

"Well, he might. You'd be surprised at the things Joe Robert finds funny that everybody else takes serious. What I'd really like to see is how he'd act if Angela Newcome was around and hatched a notion to help him. With all her clothes on, I mean—helping Joe Robert with his chores here and at his furniture store and with all the other new ventures he's trying out."

"Angela did something like that one time," my grandmother said. "I don't know if you heard about her and William McPheeter or not."

"I never did," my mother said.

"McPheeter tumbled off his disk harrow and it rolled over him and mangled his legs so gruesome, they had to cut both of them off. They kept him in the hospital over in Braceboro for most of a year and he came back in a wheelchair. Angela Newcome moved right into his house, him being a bachelor and having no one else to do for him. No scandal ever attached to any of Angela's comings and goings because everybody understood her nature, and in the case of McPheeter there couldn't be any tickle-me. He was chopped up too bad for foolery. She did for that man everything there was to do and maybe saved his life and certainly his sanity, for the accident had turned him into the bitterest angry person you could imagine. Laid the blame for his condition on everything except himself—his team of blaze-face horses, the rocks in the field, the manufacture of his disk harrow that was only three years old. He didn't blame himself, never mind the whiskey jug he kept tucked in the shade of a sassafras bush. I'm not saying that whiskey caused the accident, only that he left that part out when he scattered blame around.

"His mind turned bitter, as I say, and he lost his religion. Became a black atheist and spoke such blasphemy, you might not be surprised to see brimstone smoke pour out of his mouth and ears. A king's golden treasury wouldn't induce me to repeat the things they say he said; lightning might reach down and render me to tallow. Some were amazed it didn't strike him at least once or twice a day.

"Nor was he soothed by Angela's ministrations. He cursed her together with all the other elements of creation, even when she was caring for him in the most particular ways, helping him to use the bedpan and then emptying it and washing it. And bathing him and rubbing him down with alcohol. Not to mention fetching him whiskey anytime he had a thirst, and she no friend to the jug, far from it.

"But all the time she was doing these things unpleasant to do, McPheeter was not thanking her nor showing gratitude in any little way. He was cussing her instead, up one side and down the other, without let or stop. Truth is, he would even lash out to hit now and again, though she never admitted to it. But folks would notice her bruised on occasion, and while she never admitted, she never denied, either.

"My wellspring of charity would have run dry the first week in that house," my grandmother continued, "and while Angela Newcome's supply seemed boundless, it surely must have ebbed a little. But on she kept, living there week after month after year, not complaining, not sassing back, hardly ever resting. She had to do most all the other business, too, shopping and banking and watching after the insurance checks McPheeter received, these being the most cash money he'd seen or hoped to see in his whole life. Enough to keep him in bonded whiskey, except he only drank moon, and plenty to pay Angela a just wage for her services, though she would take but what was required to keep herself fed and decently clothed.

"It was a case of finding out which was most powerful, the red rage and fury of the maimed William McPheeter or the patient sweetness and watchful care of Angela Newcome. Fire and water, that was. There will never be but one fire an ocean can't put out, and I don't think it's coming in my lifetime. Angela was an ocean of charity and little by little she dampened the conflagration that was McPheeter's soul. She did it without thinking to, only going on with her duties, fetching and toting for the lame man and looking to his every need.

"Three years she stayed with him, so it was slow progress, but by and by McPheeter's feelings softened and his temper sweetened and a little ray of sunlight peeked into his dark despair. But Angela's attentions did not slacken; in fact, a whisper of gratitude only made her minister to her charge more thoroughly and more cheerfully until . . . Well, you can guess what happened."

"Yes, but tell Jess about it," my mother said.

"McPheeter changed, after all. Took up his Bible to read just a verse or two every day and softened his ugly behavior toward Angela and began to be a calmer and gentler man. Angela encouraged this new heartening in him, but without saying anything, simply going on as she had done before, laboring in his service. Some might call it slaving, but such a thought was never hers. McPheeter kept sweetening up, requesting Preacher Hardy in once a month and sometimes twice and they would hold little prayer services in the front room or out on the porch if the weather was fine. Angela sat through these with damp eyes and a shining face and splendor in her heart. These would have been the proudest times in her life, not that she took any credit for the change in McPheeter.

"So, to make a long story a little shorter, McPheeter had transformed for the better and began to feel a great debit of gratitude. He thought back on the earlier times, how hard and sour and mean he had been to Angela, and he tried to think in what ways he could make it up to her, but he couldn't conceive of a single course of action. What he had changed into, though he couldn't know it, was a person like everybody else in Blue Creek, a body so heavily obliged to Angela that he was miserable. Every time she laid a meal on the table, every time she cut his hair and gave him a scrub bath, every night when she turned down his bed and helped him lift over into it, he felt like the lowest of the low. Fouler than a hog-pen rat.

"There was no way he could take back the things he had said and done to her. God would forgive him for the blasphemies and curses he had cried out in his pain and anguish. He had Preacher Hardy's word on that. But Angela wouldn't forgive him because she didn't think there was anything to forgive. It had been his fearsome wounds that spoke, she reckoned, and not William McPheeter. So he couldn't ease his soul with clean confession. And anytime he saw her, he felt worse, and he saw her all the time, almost every daylight hour.

"He needed Preacher Hardy's private counsel about this new trouble to his spirit, so now he asked Angela not to attend the prayer sessions that had become so regular. I know how I'd feel," my grandmother said, "if two men, and one of them a minister, started having meetings in my house and shutting me out and talking in whispers about me and giving me sigoggling shamefaced glances. But I can't say how Angela Newcome felt, because I don't have the saintliness of character to imagine that. My best notion is that she accepted this development, took it in her stride, as she did all the rebuffs and injustices that came her way, and went on with her business.

"Whatever advice the preacher gave to McPheeter didn't help much. He got bluer and more long-faced every day. The only thing that would save his peace of mind was if she went away. He couldn't ask her to do that, couldn't stand the thought of saying the words. But no more could he bear to see her around always. It got to where he believed in his heart that if he saw Angela perform one more act of charitable goodness, he would find a way to hang himself, awkward as that must be to manage when you're bound to a wheelchair.

"So she had to go—there was no other choice. Preacher Hardy understood the situation entirely. The two men plotted and conspired together for hours without glimpsing the least gleam of a solution. Preacher Hardy thought long and strong, recognizing that when Angela was asked to leave, he would be the one saddled with that unhappy task. Then one Tuesday afternoon word came that Hamish Twilley, that lived with his wife, Elsie, in Saltlick Holler over on Coleman Mountain, had died at age eighty-five.

"No one on this porch has ever been to Saltlick Holler," my grandmother said, "and none of us is likely to go. It is a far piece now and it was farther then, the roads being what they were. The Twilleys had to be hardy spirits. Difficult to imagine what they found to eat back amidst the rocks and scrub, poorest old hardscrabble clay hills in the world, I reckon, though, as I say, I never viewed the place myself and only heard your grandfather talk about it. They had the old pioneer endurance, the Twilleys, and, like Daniel Boone, were not fond of dwelling within earshot of a neighbor's ax chop. A lot of young fellers dream about living in the old-fashioned way, and some of the young women, too. That's because when you're young you never foresee the day when you'll be old and helpless and feeble and beholden to the goodwill of other folks. Of course, if you've got your children nearby, you might be able to make out, but Hamish and his son, Zebulon, had spoken words and then Zeb left and never returned.

"So with Hamish in the burying ground, Elsie was all alone and friendless at the frosty end of a holler where the whip-poorwills are starved for company. It was a sad situation, but Preacher Hardy saw it as an opportunity. Now there was somebody that needed Angela even more than the legless McPheeter did, and when he told her about Elsie, she nodded her agreement, seeing it on the instant as her born duty to go to Saltlick Holler and be to the sickly widow woman what she had been to so many others. Her only regret was in having to leave McPheeter without her ever-present care, but the preacher assured her he had worked it out for two of the MacCallum girls to take turns with William. Angela nodded and packed up her few belongings.

"But the leave-taking must have been a strange one. Here was McPheeter that Angela by patient service and unwearied devotion had brought back not only from the edge of the grave but from the very brink of perdition to his immortal soul, and he felt toward her more gratitude than he could ever express by word or deed, and yet when she came to bid him good-bye, it was all he could do to choke back a hallelujah of pure joy. There she was, leaning over him in his wheelchair, with her head on his right shoulder and tears trickling on her face like sweat running down the side of an icebox, and so moved by sadness, she could not speak. And there he was with his face turned in the opposite direction and as red as sunrise, his eyes bugging out because he was holding his breath so tight. If he opened his mouth to take a breath, he would have laughed. And if he laughed, he wouldn't be able to stop. And if he couldn't stop laughing, Angela would understand why and that would break her heart. Or if it didn't, if she was already in such a state of blessedness that his laughing wouldn't distress her, then it would surely break McPheeter's heart. They hugged each other close and soundless, their high feelings running exactly contrariwise. Then Angela left with Preacher Hardy.

"Back then, the journey to Saltlick took the better part of two days. Which meant they'd have to stay overnight at somebody's house along the way. The preacher had sent out word that he and Angela would need accommodations but received no welcome reply. There was not one family from Blue Creek to Coleman Mountain that wasn't beholden to Angela Newcome for some charitable favor big or small, and they were all ashamed of the debts they owed her. Finally, Hattie Sawyer sent a message by her oldest boy that she and George would be pleased and honored to take in the pair and feed and bed them royally, only Angela must promise not to do any good deeds in the household or anywhere else on the Sawyer property. In fact, she was not to stir foot nor lift finger while she was there, but only sit where she was told and be entertained. The preacher didn't relay that exact message, of course, but he did assure the messenger that Angela on this one occasion would find it more blessed to receive than to give.

"So in two days the toilsome journey was accomplished. They rode through briar thickets and skirted laurel hells and forded ice-cold creeks. Finally, Preacher Hardy brought Angela to the dirt-floor log cabin where the newly widowed Elsie Twilley dwelt. They were met at the door by Doreen Raxter. She was a girl from the family that lived six miles down the creek, a sullen, dirty thing. All those Raxters are a shaggy bunch, even the ones over in Harwood County. She let them in and departed on the instant, being no hand at caring for the needful, her head full of boys and nothing but. I expect she finally got satisfied on that score, giving birth to three boys herself, and all out of wedlock.

"In they went, and it was no palace that met their gaze. Light shone through the roof shingles, the floor was lumpy because Hamish had never succeeded in getting all the rocks out, and the three windows were not square in the walls and had no frames. I could go on describing it to you as my husband described it to me. Your grandfather was the most skillful of carpenters and had an eye for the way houses were put together. When he told me he wouldn't raise pigs in such a hovel, I told him that was what he said every time about another man's handiwork. He thought again and said he wouldn't raise blacksnakes in this one.

"As soon as Elsie Twilley and Angela Newcome laid eyes on each other, something passed between them. Elsie was eighty-two years old and had been married to Hamish since she was fourteen. Sixty-eight years that couple was wed. Think how awful close they must have grown, with little but gumption to support them in a place like Saltlick Holler. When Hamish died, it must have ripped a hole as big as a cave mouth in Elsie's soul. But with nobody there after the funeral except that Raxter girl, she couldn't give in to her grief. She had to go on, sick and dizzy with sorrow, nobody to talk to, nobody to feel for her. So when she saw Angela, she let go all at once—began to weep softly and her knees buckled and she dropped to the ground with a thump. She recognized that her aid and comfort had been delivered to her, you see, and the sudden uplift within her made her fall in the dirt.

"Angela rushed to her and began stroking and petting and murmuring. Then she pulled her up and walked her to an old busted rocking chair and got the preacher to pray with her while she readied the bed for Elsie to lie in. The bed making required a mighty effort. Everything in that rude cabin was filthy and vermin-infested. But she prepared it the best she could and led Elsie to it and laid her down and loosened her clothes a little and then Elsie's staring eyes closed and she slept for the first time in who knew how long.

"Angela stood above her, gazing down, and Preacher Hardy watched as the change came over her. He could tell by looking that Angela had discovered the strongest calling of her life. All her heart went out to Elsie; caring for her would be her happiest crowning. She turned around and said so. He could only agree; he had seen Angela's face change in a manner that made it seem to glow with strange light.

"He asked what he could do to help. Angela waved her hand to take in the whole situation—the sorrow-broken widow woman, the lonesome surroundings of Saltlick, the shambly cabin. If anything could be done to remedy the situation, Angela herself alone would have to do it. He acquiesced to that and held Angela's hands and prayed with her and then took his way back to Blue Creek, riding his horse and leading the borrowed one. It was nigh dark by then, but he was needed for a funeral as soon as he could get to the burial ground. That was Cousin Ronnie Haskell; they were keeping the body as cool as they could in a springhouse, but you can well comprehend how that was not real satisfactory.

"He left with heavy heart and uncertain mind. If anybody in the world could manage to make things better there, Angela was the one. He couldn't foresee how she'd do it, though; it would be like trying to make a downy feather bed out of a heap of jagged rocks. Preacher Hardy surmised that Angela Newcome might at last have encountered the challenge that was too much for her.

"Of course, nobody knew for the longest time just how the two women were faring. I have pictured them there a thousand times," my grandmother said, "and all I can see is misery and hardship a hundredfold worse than I've ever had to endure.

"Yet they made it somehow. Some willing folks had stocked in food for Elsie after the funeral and that helped them along till Angela could begin to make do. It was late in the season, but she got a little kitchen garden staked by. She cleaned out the spring above the house and found it to be sweet. She started in on the house, repairing where she could and rebuilding where she had to. And all the time she kept a close watch on Elsie and was all the consoling company to her that she could possibly be.

"Elsie gained a little color and her spirits warmed. But her long, hard years and the loss of Hamish had taken heavy toll. From the first moment she saw Angela, she loved her as the daughter she had never borne. Yet even that was not enough; she was only lingering now, observing in pure wonderment the ministering angel that had come to attend her. A miracle, that's what Angela was to Elsie, but not even a miracle could pull her through. Little by little her small light dimmed like the spark of a blown-out candlewick that glows red for a long time but is never going to burst into flame again.

"That's the way I have figured it," my grandmother said. "A thousand times at least I've traced the trail of events in my thought. So have others. Many another woman has puzzled at it just as close as I have, and, as far as I know, we all reached the same conclusion."

"You can't stop now!" I said. "I've got to hear the end of the story."

"Your grandmother doesn't take orders from you, Jess," my mother replied. "You'd be wise not to be telling your elders what they should do."

"I'm sorry. That's not the way I meant it. But I hope you'll tell me the end of the story and not leave me hanging like Daddy would do."

She relented and gave a small smile. "No, we don't want to be copying Joe Robert with our style of storytelling. He must be the most unhandy man with a tale who ever drew breath."

My grandmother spoke gravely. "The trouble is, Jess, that we don't actually know the end of it. Nobody does that is now alive. Preacher Hardy pieced it together the best he could, and he was a right smart man and trustworthy. But he could only make a guess from the way he found things when he returned to Saltlick."

"What did he find?" I asked.

"Well, almost six months passed before he was able to get back, and when he rode up to the cabin there, his heart misgave him. He told us what a dread feeling came over him at the sight. No smoke from the chimney, no movement from inside the dwelling. Everything all around as still as a midnight pond. He observed that a halfhearted small patch of ground had been staked out and scratched up for a garden, but no headway had been made. The earth was shriveled and dry. He was afraid of what he would find inside, but he took a long breath and pushed the door open.

"Still, he was surprised. The two women had passed away, just as he'd reckoned, but everything was different from how he'd pictured.

"Elsie Twilley was lying on her bed with her eyes closed and her arms straight along her sides. Her face was as calm and peaceful as any pleasant dream would make it. The bed was clean and unrumpled; it did Angela proud.

"Angela herself was lying on the floor on a pallet of leaves and pine needles, all still green about her, and with her arms straight along her sides just like Elsie's, and her hands still as white and soft as those of the finest of young ladies.

"They must have been dead a good while, maybe even weeks. Preacher Hardy could tell that much from the shriveled-up garden and the dust on the dishes and chairs and the cobwebs in the corners. Angela would never abide that kind of dirt. . . . But, Jess, no rats or other varmints of any kind had molested them. Nor had corruption overtaken their bodies. They were as fresh and untainted as sleeping children. They had passed away quietly at the same time."

"How could that happen?"

"Nobody knows."

"But what do people think?"

"Some think one thing, some another."

I understood that she was hesitant to say further, but my curiosity spurred me painfully. "All right," I said, "but what do *you* think?"

"I've studied on it," my mother replied, "and my mind has gone round and round about. Finally I saw it happen in just one way. I closed my eyes and watched it play out in my thoughts. Why don't you close your eyes and try if you see it the way I do? Maybe you'll come to a different conception."

"All right." As soon as I closed my eyes, all the sounds about us that I'd been taking for granted made themselves known afresh. I heard the cardinals and jays in the oak grove below the road, the stop-and-go buzzing of a couple of flies on the porch, and the soft breeze in the nearby hickory.

My mother said, "I see the two women alone there in that drear cabin and I hear the wind soughing around its edges and swooping in through the cracks and shivering the two of them by night. I see Angela having to watch as Elsie grew weaker and grayer every hour. I see Elsie lying down to die in spite of anything Angela could do or say. And Angela deciding then that death was going to enter this shambly room and take away a life and that it ought to be her and not the dearest love she'd ever known. I see her making a green pallet on the floor there beside Elsie's bed and laying herself down on it and praying for the doom to be her own and not her friend's."

"You mean she wanted to die instead of Elsie Twilley," I said.

"That's what she wanted. But nobody can go that journey for another. Somebody might try to go with you; it would have to be somebody real special. But they can't go far. . . . Have you got your eyes closed tight?"

"Yes, ma'am."

"Can you see in your mind's eye those two women lying there in that bare-bones cabin?"

"Yessum," I said, but I was fibbing. Behind my eyelids I saw only red streaks and stars and burning rainbows. The tighter I squeezed shut, the more incandescence I saw.

"All right . . . Elsie is lying in her bed watching the roof and the stars through the cracks. Angela is lying in the same posture on her pallet on the floor and watching the stars the same as Elsie. They are waiting to hear one certain sound they have never heard before. They are still and patient and willing to wait a long time. Then finally at last they hear it. . . . Do you hear it?"

"Yes, ma'am," I said. But I heard only the flies and the rustling hickory and the jays quarreling in the grove below.

"This sound means that death is in the room and one of the women must go the long, long journey. But the other woman is there, too, and offering to take the place of her friend. But if it can't be done, if things are fixed so they cannot trade places, then she will keep her friend company every step of the way to the end. . . . Now do you see what happens next?"

"I'm not sure," I said—because now I didn't see anything, not even the sparks and streaks and stars written on my eyelids. And I heard no more the sounds around us, the flies and birds and trees all shut out. I saw nothing but blank dark as a chilly shadow began to creep over all my skin and sweat bathed the roots of my hair. I smelled a breath on my face as cold as frosty glass.

Then I opened my eyelids so fast, they must have clicked. My grandmother and mother were looking at each other, silent and expectant, taking no notice of me.

At last my mother broke the silence. "That story makes me sad," she said. "I don't often care to think about it." She turned her face away and looked out into the daylight, staring at nothing or everything.

"Well, daughter, I have a real different feeling. Whenever I remember the story of Angela and Elsie, I feel comforted," said my grandmother.

That was a great distinction between them. My grandmother had not the slightest fear of death and would speak of it with warm familiarity. But my mother couldn't abide the thought. Whenever a hint of death brushed her attention, she frowned and made an annoyed gesture with her left hand, as if someone in her presence had made a joke of dubious taste.

THE REMEMBERING WOMEN

This is the tale with four tellers. My grandmother told it to me a number of times and at other times my mother gave the account in very different terms. Sometimes they would talk about it simultaneously, shooting each other puzzled or affirming glances as they ranged from point to point. Most importantly, it is a story told in the words and thoughts of a famous man named Holme Barcroft. And now I set it down on paper for my sister, Mitzi, to read at her leisure someday and maybe pass on to her children.

It is a strange story of the most ordinary happenings and it might be difficult to understand why my mother and grandmother returned to it so often, sometimes touching it only lightly but at other times piercing it deeply, like hummingbirds at the blossoms of a trumpet vine. I think its attraction for them lay in the figure of Barcroft, the celebrated musicologist and folklorist. He was striking and romantic, and I believe he captivated their hearts, although my mother was only eight years old at the time and my grandmother a proud matron in her fortieth year with two children living and one dead.

I also think they liked to tell it because it showed the kind of people we were in our mountains, the way we would like for others to know us, and because it was a story that celebrated their friends the Laffertys, a family I knew only by reputation. Perhaps there were other reasons, too. Stories have a hundred motives and a thousand sources, some as recognizable as tiger lilies, some as hidden as secret mountaintop springs.

At any rate, I hear it in my own memory as a kind of music, its themes rendered in the measured tones of my grandmother—like a viola singing—and accompanied by the clear pipings of my mother, remembering herself as an awestruck child—the warbling of clarinet arpeggios. Dr. Holme Barcroft's story is present as a grave cello ostinato that in the end takes the dominant melody. It is this music I would like to render here, as if I put supporting chords to stave paper. The fourth voice is my own as I try to harmonize the sounds in my head. Together we are a quartet: soprano, alto, tenor, baritone.

We were appointed by the superintendent of county schools (my grandmother might say) to serve Dr. Holme Barcroft as a guide around our region as he searched for songs and tales and sayings. These things he would put into books so that all the world could read and know us the way we lived in the coves and on the sides of the hazy hills. They would learn from his books that we were people like other people, wise and foolish, brave and frightened, saintly and unholy and ordinary. The only thing we mountain folk lacked was riches, and it may be that our poverty only displayed our other qualities in a sharper light.

Of course, there are degrees of poverty, just as there are degrees of wealth. No one had ever called the Laffertys poor. It's doubtful that they heaped great stores of money in bank vaults, but then, they never owed a dime, either—and that was a situation hard to avoid in the hungry years. It would be mistaken to imagine that money or the lack of it would make much difference to them; this was a family that brimmed over with happiness come drought or flood, come frost or fire. They had a talent for happiness the way some folks have a talent for fine embroidery or for putting up strawberry preserves that shine in the jar with the light of rubies.

The father and mother were named Quigley and Qualley (my mother might say) and there were nine or ten or maybe an even dozen children. "Whippets" was what their parents called them, and it was impossible to get an accurate count because they wouldn't stay put long enough, swarming here and yonder like ants streaming out of a hill someone had poured boiling water into. And how would you ever sort them out from their cousins and friends who flocked to the Lafferty farm like it was a candy store? There didn't seem to be much need for an exact count anyhow; the younguns could look well enough after themselves and after one another. Each of them had a sense of where all the others were at any time and what they would be doing.

Even their mother hardly fretted about them. Truth was, it seemed that as soon as Qualley could get one of her whippets weaned she'd just set it on the floor and off it would toddle like a windup toy. Then every now and then she'd have a look to see if all its teeth were coming in straight or if its eyes were crossed or if it was putting off till December snows the wearing of shoes. As for keeping them scrubbed and brushed and polished—well, she'd trained the oldest girl and oldest boy and she didn't expect to be birthing any whippets too dull-witted to learn from their siblings. Once a year Quigley would drive over to Braceboro and come back with a tub of clothes as big as a cotton bale—all sizes and genders mixed together. He dumped it out on the wide front porch of the house and let them divide among themselves. It was a puzzle and a scramble and to watch the spectacle left Quigley laughing till his eyes teared.

The accepted wisdom is that if a man has got a pretty fair amount of farmland—the Laffertys laid claim to about seven hundred acres, counting the wooded hillsides and ridge tops—then he needs a good-sized family to till and harvest. But it may be that what Quigley and Qualley were after was their own square dance troupe. Because that was the one and only sure way to get most of the Laffertys in one place: strike up with the fiddle and the banjo and throw a handful of cornmeal on the polished floor so that the tall and limber Lafferty girls could glide across it like muskrats in a twilit pond going from bank to weedy bank.

Square dancing was the Lafferty passion; any of them would rather clog than hunt or fish or eat or go courting. After they achieved a certain age the whippets were called whippets no longer; the boys were titled "buck-os" and the girls "ladymisses," and as they climbed into their later teens the ladymisses were as spry and nimble as weasels when they danced and the buck-os' clogging was as thunderous as a turkey shoot. It gave Quigley such pleasure to see them in their turns that you feared he might roll out of his skin. "Look at her go, look at her go!" he would cry out. "Ain't she the proudest beauty? Look at her chin raised high and her shoulders rared back. Oh me oh my, what a heartacher. She'll make the preachers bust the Commandments." He'd be talking about a whippet not more than five years old and not much taller than the knee of the brother she was dancing with.

Because all the Lafferty younguns turned out tall and blond and lissom and strong. That was a wonder nigh unnatural because both Quigley and Qualley were short. Somebody once called them "the Button Couple" because they both had smooth bodies with button faces and in the faces small shiny eyes like shirt-cuff buttons. And Quigley had a nose like the red button the miller mashes to stop his grain crusher. Here were the mother and daddy short and squat and their children tall around them; it looked like a couple of toadstools had spawned a crop of mullein. Those younguns had just the kind of build that square dancing requires, lean and smooth and limber as willow withes.

Quigley was a caller, acknowledged to be the best in Hardison County, which means the best in the whole wide world, and he played the fiddle. He wasn't the best fiddle in the county because there was never anything but dancing in his head and whenever someone asked him to play a slow and mournful ballad like "The Triplett Tragedy" or "Down in the Valley," he might not get half through a second chorus before he would begin picking up the measure, and what had started out as a doleful, sad song ended up as "Billy in the Lowlands."

Just to give you an idea how strong the current of his passion ran (my grandmother and mother might say): One time they lost their closest neighbor and Qualley's bosom friend, Aunt Una Mae Stanton, who got blood poisoning from a pigsty nail and suffered to death. Qualley had stayed by her every minute and Quigley had done what little a man can do in the circumstances, but when she passed on, he was at a complete loss. He broached it to Preacher Sam Gwynn that since they were going to have the funeral and there would be a big crowd anyway, mightn't they honor the memory of the dear departed with a square dance?

But they wouldn't let him hold that dance and it is doubtful that Quigley ever understood why. It would seem as natural to him as weeping at a funeral. More natural, perhaps, given his character and the way he knew Aunt Una Mae.

Well, anyhow . . .

Holme Barcroft had heard about Quigley and the fashion in which he called a dance and that was exactly the kind of thing he took pains to write up in his books, so we were sent to fetch him down to the Lafferty place. Dr. Barcroft drove down in an old Model T he had borrowed from the school superintendent and pulled it underneath the big turkey oak in the front yard. We sat beside him in the front seat to show him the way. The family knew who was coming, of course, and we didn't get the truck doors open before whippets and ladymisses and buck-os sprang out from every corner of the farm and mobbed us over.

As soon as Holme Barcroft stepped off the running board, the tallest Lafferty boy strode into his light and said, "Dr. Barcroft, we are proud to have you here, but we have heard that Scotchmen all wore skirts. We were looking forward to seeing you in the female getup."

In that voice that was as clear and crisp as the blue of his eyes, Holme Barcroft said, "Young man, a Scotsman never wears a skirt. He may well wear a kilt, but it's nothing like a skirt."

"What exactly is the difference?"

"The difference is one that some fine, handsome laddie buck will break you a nose or a tooth for failing to understand." Then he reached over and squeezed the Lafferty bicep and said, "But I don't believe you'd run away from a tussle, would you?"

The buck-o grinned and blushed and retreated.

One of the whippets said, "You don't talk like I thought you would. You sound more like an Englishman than a Scotchman."

"Have you met and talked to an Englishman?" Dr. Barcroft asked.

"No, sir," she said. "But I saw a Negro one time. Me and Toodie both did. He was dark all over, except his hands were white."

"Perhaps he was an Englishman. There are many Englishmen of color. Did you talk to him?"

But shyness had overcome her and Birdie Lafferty giggled and reddened and ran to hide behind a sister's gingham skirt.

There looked to be no end of these encounters and the three of us had not yet traveled six feet from the Model T. We could see Quigley and Qualley waiting for us up on the porch, grinning as proud as trophy fishermen, but how would we ever wade through this thicket of offspring to get there? Finally one of the ladymisses parted a way for us and we passed through a line of whippets who plucked at Dr. Barcroft's woolen trousers.

On the porch we got a warm reception and then Quigley made a grave and formal introduction of Dr. Barcroft. The younguns looked him up and down, and there was a lot of looking because the Scot stood six foot six in his black rubber boots. With his hair gone bright silver now and his bushy eyebrows frosty, he was truly distinguished-looking, and in his ruddy face those cool blue eyes were cold fire asparkle. A man meeting Dr. Barcroft for the first time would square his shoulders and draw himself up to his full height, and Quigley did so now, but maybe only Qualley would notice he'd become taller by a fraction of a cubit.

"Well, sir, Dr. Barcroft," he said. "We're mighty pleased to have you here. We've never met anybody that came across the seas. When you were in our parts before, you didn't stop in with us, and that was a disappointment."

"Mr. Lafferty, it has been two decades since I was last here. Wouldn't you have been rather young?"

"I meant my daddy, Dr. Barcroft. He was a man proud of his dancing and calling and his fiddle and his table. He wanted mighty bad to show off to a person from a foreign land."

"I regret the missed opportunity," the Scotsman replied. "I learned last time that there is such a wealth of folkways here in your beautiful hills that it would require an army of scholars many years to record even the smallest amount."

It was not apparent that Quigley understood the gist of this speech, but he had a ready answer for almost every conundrum. "Let's go in and set and have a cup of coffee and a piece of Qualley's vinegar pie. Dinner ain't quite ready yet, but maybe that'll hold us through the hour."

Dr. Barcroft showed some surprise at this suggestion, the hour being only 10:30 in the morning. But he graciously acquiesced and we went inside. Three whippets stood watching us from the porch, excited faces pressed against the door screens.

It was a fresh May morning and all the doors and windows were open, yet the house was full of kitchen smells. Qualley was never one to let down her side and she kept as toothsome and plenteous a table as had any Lafferty spouse of past generations. Ordinarily she would not have cooked a full meal at noontime. It was the custom for only one or two fresh dishes to be offered at that hour. The table was always filled with bowls and platters: Stewed corn and tomatoes, boiled greens of various sorts, cold country ham, green beans, pickled beets, and other viands waited under the shroud of a clean white tablecloth for a hungering whippet to come by and take a spoonful or a handful or a plateful. Busy at so many tasks in so many different corners of the farm, the Laffertys could not easily dine together at midday, so each came by the table to graze at convenience, stopping by the kitchen for a cup of sweet coffee as thick as asphalt and maybe bringing in a plate to chat there with Qualley and an industrious ladymiss or two as they were preparing supper. Supper was the major meal of the day and quite a bounteous affair.

But today they were entertaining a foreigner. Dr. Barcroft wasn't really a stranger—Laffertys never met strangers—but they wanted to put on for him the best they knew how. So the diminutive farmer and the towering professor strolled through the kitchen, each gathering a slab of vinegar pie and a cup of coffee, then went out onto the back porch, leaving the womenfolk behind to stir at the wood range and clatter at the counters. There they ate their pie in silence and leaned back in the rocking chairs to sip from the tinware mugs. Quigley produced a cold briar pipe to suck on.

He was considering his first question with all the care of a man judging the worth of a salable heifer. Yet it was simple enough when he uttered it at last: "How many younguns do you have, Dr. Barcroft?"

"I've always lived a bachelor, Mr. Lafferty, and I do desire you to call me by my first name, Holme."

"You never have been married? How old might you be, I wonder."

"I have looked upon this earth for sixty-five summers, Mr. Lafferty."

"Sixty-five years and never been married." This information plunged Quigley into such a thoughtful long silence, his organs of speech seemed to have been affected. "Now what manner of life is that like, if you don't mind my asking? I know a number of widowers, but the only other bachelors I know are kind of runty and sour. You don't appear to be of the bachelor make, if you take my meaning, Dr. Barcroft."

"It is my lot in life to travel extensively, Mr. Lafferty. In eastern and middle Europe, in the loneliest corners of Wales and Ireland, across the Rocky Mountains of your own great nation. I was never able to see how I could keep a family together under the circumstances or how I could expect a woman to share such hardships and dangers. I do wish you would call me Holme, though, as all my friends do."

"It's hard for me to think how a man might live that way. I've got so used to being fenced around with kinfolks, I'd feel undressed without them."

"My life is sometimes a lonely one, but I made up my mind to it a long time ago. When I return to Glasgow, I do enjoy the company of my nieces and nephews. My sister has two boys and two girls."

"That's good," Quigley said, but it was clear that he considered this arrangement makeshift and that he began to see some disadvantages in being a foreigner. "How is it you come to know Annie Barbara Sorrells in our part of the world?"

"One of her teachers many years ago recommended her to me as someone who came from mountain stock and knew the old ways and those families who still lived in the old style. But I needed someone with enough formal education to help me take notes and keep records. She was an excellent choice."

"And you're interested in writing down on paper the old ways and styles?"

"Yes, sir, I am. Everywhere I go."

"I'm afraid you'll find us an ignorant crowd, Dr. Barcroft. All we mostly know around here is what we learned from our elders or on our own. But everybody of age in the Lafferty family can read and write and cipher. I hope you'll set that down in your book."

Not the richest bribe would ever get the name Holme out of Quigley's mouth; he took too fine a pleasure in calling his friend Dr. It was such a source of pride to him that he sucked at his pipe stem a little more sharply and rocked a little harder each time he spoke the title.

"I'll certainly write it down," the Scotsman said.

Quigley questioned the professor about his travels and we were then gratified by descriptions of the Urals and the Andes, the wheaten plains of Canada, the sweltering jungles of the Yucatán, the bustle of London, and the drolleries of Paris. We heard about people who made music with wire prongs and the bones of jackals and by slapping their cheeks and chests and thighs. We learned that Dr. Barcroft had eaten locusts, snakes, monkey brains, green lizards, and fish eggs, yet hungered for nothing so keenly as for oatmeal and liver boiled up together in the intestines of a fat sheep. We listened to accounts of travel by llama, yak, Arabian pony, dogsled, burro, steamboat, raft, airplane, and balloon and gave our entranced attention to tales of peril from Mongols, Arabs, Tartars, thuggees, Jivaro, cutthroats and thieves, renegade soldiers, and jealous husbands. He had escaped death and usually injury from pistol, knife, machete, the noose and the branding iron, the injured tiger and the untamable bronco, snakebite, malaria, blood infection, and unsanitary whiskey. Dr. Barcroft had met the great of the world and the obscure, the prized and the despised; he had dined with satraps and with peasants, with scientists and poets and drunkards, had eaten off silver and gold and tortoiseshell and banana leaf. He had heard and recorded on paper or wax cylinder or magnetic wire or simply in his memory, which was as indelible as cut granite, the songs of coal miners, flatboat men, railroad firemen and switchboard operators, furnace stokers and cattle drovers, hoboes and hangmen, housewives and hackabouts, scullery maids, roughnecks, banjo pickers, zither players, Jew's harp masters, fiddlers, sawyers, coopers, roofers, tailors, bootleggers, jailbirds, murderers, constables, sheriffs, Negroes, painters, well diggers, priests and preachers of every denomination, of every religion and condition, narrow and sober as coffins in aspect or with painted faces and trailing scarlet feathers.

Our eyes began to glaze, not from boredom but because after an hour of talk our minds were foundering like horses fed too much grain. It was like a dam had given way and all the world we'd barely heard of and all its history we didn't know had flooded in upon us. There was no way to take in so much of it at once and finally we sat dazed, Dr. Barcroft's stories buzzing in our ears like a swarm of midges on an August afternoon.

We were roused from our trance when Teensy Lafferty stepped out onto the porch and started clanging an iron bar that hung above the porch railing. She kept at it for three vigorous minutes and when she laid down the horseshoe that served as a beater and when the ringing of our ears had subsided, we heard shouts and giggles and whispers. Then younguns of every size, gender, and demeanor poured onto the porch, bustling, jostling, and tussling as they crowded to the washstand with its four tin basins and three buckets of cold water and six bars of yellow soap. There were towels enough, but the boys wiped their wet hands on their pants legs or ran them through their hair. Dogs accompanied the younguns onto the porch and had to be shoved off lest they sneak into the house. A tiny black-and-white fice overturned one of Dr. Barcroft's rubber boots—he had taken them off to sit in his leather slippers—and burrowed as if it had found a groundhog's lair. It was all chatter and chaff, furtive punches and pinches, blushes and fleeting tears—and then as quickly as the space had filled with youth, it emptied and the three of us made our way to the washstand. As we were finishing, Dolly Lafferty came out with two fresh towels and then nipped back inside again.

At the long table, the younguns were already seated, watching in keen expectation as we entered together. Quigley stood at his customary position at table head while Dr. Barcroft commanded the other end.

"Whippets," said Quigley, "this here is Dr. Barcroft, who comes to visit us from Scotland, across the seas. I want you all to take notice of him as an important man who has been around the world. Now Dr. Barcroft will ask our blessing for us."

The Scotsman nodded and, taking note of the eager appetites on every side, responded with the shortest table prayer ever heard in the Lafferty household. Then the father sat, we all sat, and the destruction began. Platters of biscuits and corn bread were passed and pitchers of cold fresh milk made the round. Yellow butter from wheat-sheaf molds was hacked into lumps. And then the food began to arrive from the kitchen.

Qualley reserved for herself the honor of serving the first dish to Dr. Barcroft and she chose the one that was her particular pride, those sausage patties that she ground from lean pork shoulder and seasoned with sage and savory and a pretty long list of other herbs, including a shaving or two of sassafras root.

"Oh, I was never supposed to tell that," my grandmother said. "That was her special secret I was not to give away."

"But it was so long ago," my mother said. "She's dead now, of course. Sometimes it seems all the really good people are gone."

Then the rest of the food was brought in, great steaming heaps of it. Everything was devoured, but not in reverent silence. Quigley asked the professor to tell of his sojourn in Haiti, and so he did, omitting from the account given earlier on the porch only the detail of an agreeable cinnamon-colored lass with a captivating dimple.

"Now tell 'em about those cowboys you trailed with, Dr. Barcroft," Quigley said, and as the professor told of journeying from the plains of West Texas to the railroad in central Kansas, his listeners foraged through green beans and baked onions, stewed chicken and trout fried in cornmeal, boiled potatoes and salad greens, pickled beets and applesauce. We went through those victuals like we were famine itself.

When the desserts appeared, four pies as well as a plate of fresh biscuits and several jars of preserves, the younguns began unpacking their questions again and Dr. Barcroft was rather put to his mettle in explaining how it was possible for Eskimos to build houses out of nothing but snow, why Mexicans confect human skulls of sugar for children to gnaw, and who made up the first song that was ever sung. When they asked him about his native land, he told the dear story of the poet Burns and ended his legend by reciting some lines:

"As fair art thou, my bonny love,
So deep in love am I;
And I will love thee still, my dear,
Till a' the seas gang dry.

"Till a' the seas gang dry, my dear,
And the rocks melt wi' the sun:
O I will love thee still, my dear,
While the sands o' life shall run."

"Well then," said his host, "that's well spoken. I believe that's a good old song we already know, don't we, Marilee Lafferty?" He spoke to a whippet of nine years or so who blushed and hung her head at being so fondly singled out. "Why don't you sing it for us? Don't be bashful. We'll all be proud to hear it."

She would not disfavor her father's request. Marilee rose and sang in a voice as pure and silver as a spring that spouts from a ferny stone:

"And fare thee well, my only love,
And fare thee well awhile.
And I will come again, my love,
Though it be ten thousand mile."

The silence that fell upon us was brief but laden. We all recognized a benediction when we heard it, and we rose to carry our soiled tableware to the kitchen, where Qualley and four kitchen-duty ladymisses would scrub all up before they sat themselves down to take a bite or two in peace and talk over the things they'd heard Dr. Barcroft tell about.

After that the table had to be cleared and the dishes washed and the room swept and dusted, for everything was to commence all over again in preparation for the dance that evening in the house. The ladymisses would be mighty busy and would brook no mischievous or lazy buck-os underfoot. Four of the latter prevailed upon Dr. Barcroft to go for a horseback ride up the mountain. There was a white mare just right for him, they said, strong and tall and silver.

So off they cantered for the long, sweet afternoon, and what they did on Baldpate Ridge is a mystery, though it is likely that the professor regaled the boys with spicier tales of tribes and islands than ever the ladymisses would hear.

"But we stayed behind to help in the house and the kitchen, didn't we, daughter?"

"Yes, we did. There was plenty enough work to keep us all busy."

" 'Little hands help bigger hands and all whip up together.' That was one of Qualley's sayings. Do you remember?"

"Yes I do," my mother replied.

* * *

Dr. Barcroft and his crew of buck-os returned when the hill shadow was long and cool. After milking time, people began to show up for the square dance held in honor of the professor. By twilight there were new faces all about. Men stood talking in small groups and two impromptu string trios had formed there in the yard; a number of visitors had brought their own banjos, fiddles, guitars, and mandolins. The Lafferty barn supplied a couple of holey washtubs for basses and these were given to aspiring whippets to thump. And there were plenty of stone jugs to aid in keeping rhythm, and there were Jew's harps and harmonicas.

Females were mostly inside the house, in the clamoring kitchen, but some were out on the porches, arranging the long tables. These had been covered with yellow oilcloth, and to them dishes and tinware and cutlery had been brought. Guests were to wander to the porches to eat and drink at their convenience. There was no place to feed inside, for the dining room had been emptied, the furniture of the living room had been pushed against the walls, and the two downstairs bedrooms had been cleared as much as possible—all to make room for dancing. The floors were swept and polished, the gleam of them bright as brass. This farmhouse had been recently wired for electricity, but the Laffertys put small trust in the newer inventions of mankind and so also kept kerosene lamps burning in their old accustomed places.

In the backyard, whippets were turbulent. Some of the small boys were practicing clog styles while girls looked on or practiced making figures among themselves. Others jumped rope or played hand-clapping games. Some, excited by the crowd, by the onset of twilight, by the prospect of the dance, only ran hither and yon in a state of fevered bewilderment.

It was difficult to say when the dance actually took shape. One quartet of musicians came together in the dining room and started toying with a reel, "White Cockade" it might have been, or "Miss Brown." A few buck-os and ladymisses gathered round and shuffled through maneuvers casually, gossiping and laughing as they joined in for a turn or two and then wandered off as if having lost interest. On the side porch a brother and sister from Sugar Camp had struck up with mandolin and guitar and were singing "The Old Oaken Bucket." They drew a circle of pleased elders and a changeable minnow school of curious whippets who gave ear to a few bars and then scurried off.

As more and more guests arrived, more and more Laffertys came in from the fields and from evening chores at the barns and stock lots. The volume of sound from house and yard increased in loudness and excitement until there occurred a certain moment of the light.

In the valleys after the sun rolls behind the hills, and just before the sky turns gray and the little brown birds seek their bushes, there is a period of violet light eerie in its effects. The jonquil's yellow and the dogwood's whiteness become almost vocal in the intensities of their colors and the sides of hills and buildings lose definition of surface and become softer in aspect. You feel that if you put your hand against the ground or against an outside wall, you would touch not hardness but cloudiness; it would be as if you had discovered the world as it underwent change, all things shaping differently as they readied themselves to receive the nighttime.

"That's what he said," my grandmother mused. "Dr. Barcroft often made observations like that. He was a long-thoughted man."

"I don't understand *exactly* what he meant," my mother replied, "but I've seen twilights like that sometimes. I just never knew how to talk about them."

The light had assumed that certain strange mood as the professor came up from the barn, having left his borrowed mount, Sophie, to the care of Bingo Lafferty. And as the light took on its eerie aspect, a silence fell upon the valley. Everyone had stopped talking at the same time, even the whippets, and from the kitchen came no clink and clatter and from the barns no sounds of cow and horse. The dogs had fallen silent, including the fices.

Then a single note sounded on a fiddle, the tuning A, and Dr. Barcroft recognized it at once as Quigley Lafferty's tone: pure, clear, confident, easy, and lyric, but full of calm strength. He had never heard Quigley play, but the authority he recognized in that single note was unmistakable. He knew immediately why his host was reckoned the best square dance fiddle in the county and he felt he also knew why the life of the man and his family and his acres seemed so happy and complete.

By the time the professor reached the great turkey oak in the yard, Quigley's fiddle had been joined by a rhythm guitar, a mandolin, and a banjo, and a tune was in progress: not a hell-for-leather breakdown but an easygoing stately quadrille, the rhythm well marked but not faster than a steady allegro, and the phrasing melodic rather than driving. The tune was "Prince of Good Fellows" and the quartet played four choruses without embellishment before Quigley called the simplest of figures.

"On your heel and on your toe
All join hands and round you go
Other way back you're going along
Listen to the music of the old-time song."

The rhythm of the dancing, too, was subdued; the clogging sounded like a far-off drum and the girls' sliding steps like the whisper of wind. We could not see the dancers, but we could tell that they were slipping along smoothly, not breaking a sweat and not grinning, but smiling gravely at one another. The crowd parted for Dr. Barcroft as he went up the steps and looked through the window into the living room. Dignity was the character of this first old-fashioned quadrille, and we were surprised. Quigley's reputation was for lightning figures and diabolical tempo.

"Dos a do your corners all
Do the same with your own best doll."

The musicians were ranged on the stairway and the dancers swept round on the living room floor, twirling in the bright light, their motion soft and dreamlike. Quigley stood above the other musicians, halfway up the stairs, and he looked down at the dancers—there were only twelve of them at this point—with an expression of dazed benevolence. Sometimes when he called, he kept playing through, sometimes he simply held his fiddle and swayed slightly to the melody the banjo or guitar had picked up when he passed it on to them.

"Right hands to your partners all
Right and left around the hall
When you meet her pass her by
Kiss the next one on the sly."

As the dancers formed their squares and took them apart and went round and round to re-form them, they stirred a pleasant breeze that Dr. Barcroft felt on his face through the open window. The girls' gingham skirts swept by slowly and kept the air lively.

Now Quigley began to play more softly and the other players followed suit; his calls became softer, too. A diminuendo was unique, Dr. Barcroft told us later, as the music and the call and the sound of dancing sank to a mutter, a murmur, and finally to a silken susurrus, tender and almost regretful in its close.

"Bring on home the one that's odd
Bring her back and promenade
All stand where you used to do
Bow to your partners and so adieu."

The final figure was this formal leave-taking. After the bow, the squares came apart like snowflakes melting and in the brief silence that followed there was a feeling of both completion and expectancy, and then the first rustle of night wind was heard in the trees in the yard and the long glass curtains in all the downstairs windows began to waft in and out like the skirts of lady dancers a long time gone in a valley barely remembered.

Dr. Barcroft straightened from his stand at the window and went around and through into the living room, where Quigley hailed him. "There you are," he said. "There you are, Dr. Barcroft. We were wondering where you'd got to. Grab you a ladymiss for the next number. I expect they're all mighty anxious to dance a step with you."

"If you don't mind," he replied, "I'd rather look on. That way, I can see a little better what I need to be seeing."

"Then come up the steps and take your place on the landing. There you'll have a better look-see. We're about to kick her off again, ain't we, Claudie?"

The banjo player, his face expressionless as a bedsheet, nodded agreement.

So they began "Darling Nellie Gray," taking it much faster than the first quadrille, but now a good two dozen dancers were on the living room floor and Dr. Barcroft could see through the doors and windows that impromptu squares had formed on the porch and in the other rooms. The figures Qualley called were a little more complicated this time, the first couple coming down the center to cast off six, all balancing then, and allemande and grand, and down the center again to cast off four, allemande left till the break of day and swing your darling Nellie Gray, when the blackbird flies to his home in the west ladies to the right and gents to the left.

The professor was charmed by the fluid power of the dance; the lines knotted and untied as smoothly as if the dancers did nothing but rehearse day long and night long for months on end. He saw the kaleidoscope patterns they made as evidence of strength in reserve and he was reminded—because of this seeming effortlessness—of the symmetries and geometries that nature takes: the sharp constellations of stars in wintertime, ice crystals on the edge of a spring, a stalk of fern with its leaves opposed, the inward whorl of the snail's shell, the circles that spread on a pool when a dewdrop falls from an alder leaf, the echoes in a narrow cove when an outcry rings from rock to rock.

Dr. Barcroft had the impression—and not for the first time that evening—that he was involved with a place and a people, with a time and circumstance, that was not only human in all its affections and interests but linked also with nonhuman nature, with sky and stream and mountain, in its reverences. He felt that he was standing near the origins of a strength that helped to animate the world, a power that joined all things together in a pattern that lay just barely beyond the edge of comprehension. He felt that an individual personality would feel itself conformably and joyfully a part of this pattern simply by giving in to the current of the dance, this small current being but a streamlet of the larger current that poured through the world and everything that was in the world and beyond it.

"Jess, I don't know what he was talking about, but these were the things he told us as we drove back home over the mountain," my grandmother said. "He was a highly learned man. He knew Latin and Greek and French and I don't know how many other languages. He had traveled everywhere. So when he talked about what he felt and thought, I paid attention. You can learn things, you know, that you don't completely understand. I was just thrilled he opened his mind. How many men like Dr. Barcroft, known around the world for his books and adventures, would talk so freely to a mother and her daughter like he expected the both of us to keep up with him step for step? Mostly in that day and time women weren't acknowledged to have an interest in such things."

"Did he write down what he told you in any of his books?" I asked.

"I don't know if he ever put these same thoughts on paper or not. I'll have to admit I've never read any of Dr. Barcroft's books and I'm a little ashamed of myself for not. . . . Well, it's a disgrace to my name, isn't it? But it's so hard to find time to read."

The next dance was familiar to Dr. Barcroft; "Lady Walpole's Reel" was traditional in his homeland. He was interested to note that these Carolina mountain folk omitted the boisterous kissing the Scots insisted upon, although the custom was remembered in Quigley's call.

"Ladies to the right and gents by their side
Balance off now and kiss the bride."

The music had achieved a sparkling pace and Quigley was adding pert furbelows and lacy flourishes to the melody line. The other instruments kept up with him bar for bar and the rhythm guitar began to rush, standing on the front edge of the beat, urging Quigley on and pushing the dancers a little harder, ever a little harder.

After this reel there was the briefest of pauses and Dr. Barcroft, feeling a need for refreshment, squeezed down the steps behind the musicians and went out on the porch to investigate the feast on the cluttered tables. As he had expected, there was a cornucopia of food and drink almost forbidding in its plenitude: cold meats of all sorts and corn bread and wheat bread and butters and cheeses and canned vegetables and preserves and jellies and jams and comfits and candies and crisp hand pies and amber pies of dried apples latticed like fishermen's nets, ciders hard and sweet, and cool perry and sweet cherry wine. He took up a hand pie of veal and potato and stood in a corner, where a squint-eyed farmer passed him a jug and he tilted it to taste the first American corn whiskey he'd drunk in twenty years. It was as oily and sugar-edged and heated as he recalled and it brought back memories in a sudden freshet, memories he pushed to the back of his mind to sort and savor at a later hour.

Distance seemed not to lessen the volume of the music. It was as distinct and driving out here in the cottony dark as it had been inside on the stairwell, and Dr. Barcroft heard the sound of whippets dancing in the grass. He could hear, too, he thought, the sounds of buck-os and ladymisses beginning to spark and fondle yonder in the farther dark and the merry whispers and giggles of whippets looking on, discovering how life and love were performed, how couples came together and apart. The ladymisses' hair was tumbled on their off-the-shoulder ruffles and their eyes were bright with happy desires and their mouths warm with kisses fleeting or fervid.

It seemed to the professor that he floated more than walked, that he drifted down the steps, past the couples holding hands and the wide-eyed whippets shuffling their feet and the farmers in rolled white shirtsleeves smoking slow roll-your-owns, and into the yard. There he felt about him a pulsing of desire so strong, the treetops seemed to bend with it, but then he realized it was the Maytime night breeze growing in force. Yet in the air, desire was as easy and affable and palpable as the wind, and when now someone turned off the electric lights in the house and left only the glow of the oil lamps to illuminate both inside and outside, he heard around him breaths caught back, sighs and whispers and whimpers, and saw, it seemed, only pieces of young bodies, a finger caressing the peach-flesh cheek of a girl, arms around necks and shoulders, the flash of ankle, knee, and thigh, and he thought of the springtime rituals of tribes and nations perched on every prominence and snugged in every pocket of the globe. The lamplit dancers inside the house spun dizzily past the windows like the fantasy angels of carousels and their eyes seemed as fixed as those painted eyes. The music was "Old Joe Clark." Grab your partner and promenade, someday we'll dance at the throne of God.

Dr. Barcroft stepped out into the center of the yard, retreating from the spell of the shadow of the great oak tree, and became aware of a strange powdery light sprinkled on the tops of the mountains on every side. The sound of Quigley's fiddle was in the air all around; it seemed to swoop and climb like black moths in the dark, a note here and there glowing like a firefly, glissando figures sizzling past like shooting stars. Something was about to happen—he could feel it on his skin—something large was preparing to take place.

The sky kept growing lighter, the starlight was washing away; the moon, he thought, must be coming up.

> *"Gents go forward to a left-hand star*
> *And think upon whose sons you are*
> *Turn that star the other way*
> *Until you've said your final say."*

The light was grainy, dusty; it looked like the Milky Way had spread from the top of the sky all down the west, and the tented shapes of the mountains were huge and satin black against it, and the ridgeline trees made a filigree of onyx. The wind had increased but had not cooled; the promise of full summer was in it. And when Dr. Barcroft turned from the west to look again at the house, he was hardly surprised to see that it had begun to turn like a wheel upon a vertical axle as the silhouettes of the dancers raced past window after window. It was as if their dancing, the female slide and shuffle, the masculine drum and thunder, propelled the house behind them; it had become a merry-go-round, turning steadily and stately as the music went just a little bit faster, just a little more, and he could tell there were furies in it, whirlwinds and cyclones and hurricanes that Quigley's fiddle barely held in check, that his calling could barely control. When a woman holds a man's heart fast, will he stay with her until the last: Swing your corner and come around a man only needs six foot of ground. He thought he saw the left-hand corner of the house heave into sight and was waiting to see the back porch turn frontwise toward him, knowing there would be dancing and sparking and feasting on that side of the house, too, when quite suddenly the thing that had been going to take place did so.

The moon: The moon rose all at once, as if it had escaped the mountains, as if there had been a force in those hilltops that held it back, restrained it until it bounded away from them and rose like a hot-air balloon, as silent as that and as awing, and it was the hugest moon this doctor of music had ever seen or imagined, so huge and close, it seemed to spread a perfume in the air, the scent of frost on new-mown grass, the smell of the cold, rough linen sheets you crawled into on a deep winter night with the moonlight pouring onto the bed, a smell almost odorless, like the smell of porcelain plates taken from the dark cupboard shelf. Leave your partner but come back soon there'll be love in the springtime moon swing the ladymiss on your right there'll be moon till the sky goes white.

"Lord have mercy," my mother said. "I don't remember he told us all that. Of course, I was only eight and wouldn't understand. But I'm grown up now and I still don't understand."

"I can't tell it the way he did," my grandmother said. "All his thought and all his feelings were far beyond me. I have tried to remember the best I could. He got all excited in talking, you know, and almost drove us off the road up there at Betsey's Gap. I could just picture us tumbling to death down the mountainside."

"I don't remember that, either," my mother said.

"He had a way of talking that was full of strange words and lilts and sometimes he made you feel you were inside his head and could see and feel things the way he did. He would have made a grand preacher but had no calling, as he once told me with some sadness."

"There was something magic about that night, though," my mother said. "Do you remember how I told you the music had called ghosts out of their graves? They came to dance, strange silent people of long ago."

"I remember how you thought so."

"And you said—"

"I told you it was the family that liked to come to dance parties in old-time clothes, of which they had a great store. It was just their way to do so. Maybe they honored their departed that way, I don't know. Dillards, that's who they were."

"It was strange to me, but I wasn't frightened."

"No. You were always a brave one. . . . And then it started to get light with morning coming on."

It was only a hint of sun, the east going platinum gray just above the apple orchard with its greening leaves, but it was enough for the music to start to mute, for the moon to lose some of the lightning hue of its silver, to become a listener rather than a dancer and to recede from the valley, slowly diminishing in size till it found its way, now small and secondary, back to its usual orbit.

Dr. Barcroft stopped spinning, too, and steadied himself and looked, to see that the house was motionless as any stone and Quigley and the boys had subsided into a waltz, "The Silver Lake Waltz," taken at a dreamy slow tempo. It was full of the sweet and sad.

Ladies go in and gents outside for you're going home with your own dear bride. Go out to the porch for one last drink for now is always later than you think.

He shook his head, the tall professor, and suddenly felt himself as sober as a bucket of well water as he watched the guests pack up and make ready to depart. He would go in now and talk to dancers and musicians and make notes in his neat little black leather notebook. He would drink coffee and perform his manners to Qualley and Quigley and get all fixed to drive with Annie Barbara and Cora Sorrells back over the mountain through Betsey's Gap. Yet he found it hard to let go so easily the dance and the music and the moonlight and he asked himself, as he had asked before in a score of nations and after a thousand feasts and ceremonies, What exactly happened here and how did it all go away so quickly?

"Well, I'll say again, I didn't understand and still don't," my grandmother said.

"I don't either," my mother said. "A man like Dr. Barcroft, how could we understand? But we were proud of his notice and wanted to be in the books he wrote. You have to realize, Jess, that a lot of people looked down on us, saying we were ignorant hillbillies and other things they ought to be ashamed of saying. Fancy people that lived in expensive places. So if our works and days got written up in his books that were read and admired all over the world—well, why shouldn't we take a mite of pride?"

"I believe us to be as upright as anyone in the nation," my grandmother said. "Only we hold to some of the old ways."

"Not all of us," my mother said. "My husband likes the new ways. But you know what? There was one thing about Dr. Barcroft that reminds me of Joe Robert. It's the way he talked about the moon, like it was as dear to him as someplace he might have lived. What is it about men that they can't keep their hands off the moon? Joe Robert told me he thinks men will travel to the moon someday."

"I think so, too," I said.

They looked at me for a long, strange moment and then my grandmother said, "Well, if you and your daddy are going to the moon, you had better take plenty to eat. It looks to me like slim pickings up there."

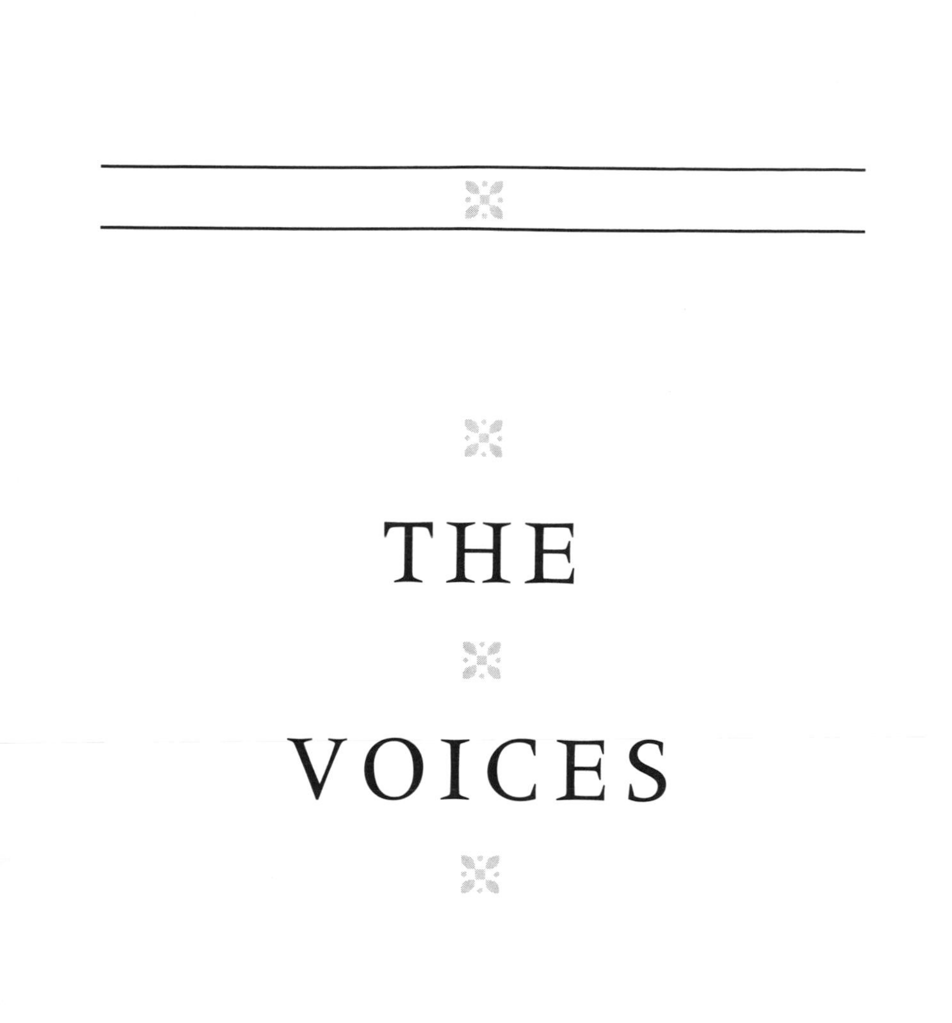

THE VOICES

10:17 4:44 8:20 1:28

The clocks were as crazy as ever, yet there we sat, my father and I, patient before that cold wood heater, watching the wild hands as if they might point to the true time if only we mustered the courage to wait them out. But the wind was too mischievous in their works. The minutes and seconds got lost among the years and dropped away to wander eternity.

Outside this too-large house, the wind would rise to a fury and then subside, no more predictable than the times the clocks were telling. To the window behind our chairs it brought weathers of every sort—drought and tempest, spring rain and early snow, Sahara-like sunshine and melancholy fog. This old house had always stood steady before, but now the time this wind had so distressed was rocking the structure with dread power. We could feel the foundations clinging to the ground with desperate fingertips.

"All right," I said. "Now I'm scared. Pretty much scared, I'll tell you."

"I can't blame you, Jess," my father said. "I'm scared pretty tight myself. It's a good thing we let your sister sleep over at the Williams place tonight. We didn't think she should be here, your mother and I. Mitzi's too young to understand."

"I don't understand, either."

"Neither do I," he said. "I know that the way time and space and matter are built together makes death inevitable. But I don't understand."

"Maybe they're built wrong," I said. "Maybe it was a bad plan to begin with."

"Maybe so. Have you got a better one?"

"It's too hard on Mother."

"Yes," he said.

"It is just too hard. I can tell. I can hear them talking together or thinking together all the way from the bedroom."

"Yes. So can I."

I hung my head and closed my eyes to hear.

And so farewell I'm bound to leave you, All away you rolling river, I'll be gone when dawn is breaking.

O Mama, don't say so. Not this dawn or the next or the next. It is too soon for you to go.

I wish that song would quit me. I am trying to think of Jesus, but that old song is in the way. I do not wish to think of Frawley Harper in this fateful hour. I must think of Jesus or of Frank, my husband. I have been mostly good with my thoughts, but now I can't.

You mustn't blame yourself, Mama. Thoughts come and go—you can't help that.

I need to be steadier in mind. If I am steady, Jesus will come to me.

O Mama.

"Now they are thinking or saying the same thing," I told my father. "Sometimes they split off from one another like a little creek up high in the mountains that will divide around a big rock and then come back to meet itself."

"Yes," he said.

"I don't understand how we can hear them all the way down that dark hall with the doors shut."

"We can't hear them," he said. "We only know what they are thinking or saying. We are not hearing with our ears."

"How, then?"

"It is the way of families," he said. "But only at special times."

"What kind of special?"

"Hard, mostly," he said.

"I still don't understand."

"Be quiet and I will tell you something," he said. "Not long from now there will come an icy cold into this room. There will be a darkness like we were trapped inside a vein of coal. I want you to be brave and show me what you are made of, and I will try to be brave, too. Then it will pass off like a slow and painful eclipse of the sun and moon and stars. It will be terrible. But we must overmaster it. So hang on tight, Jess. It is coming soon."

"It is already here," I said. "It is in the hallway, making the darkness darker. And it is already cold in here and getting colder. It is just outside the door, ready to come in. Don't you feel how close it is?"

"Yes," he said.

Then the shadow was upon us and within us and was as bad as he said it would be. I don't know how many eternities we suffered there, my father and I, but they were motionless with despair. Yet the shadow lightened a little at last; the windows went quiet with predawn light. We knew that the final thing my grandmother said or thought was, Farewell, daughter, it is Jesus at last, and that the final thing my mother said or thought was, Don't leave me alone in this world without you. And then there was light enough in our front room to read the clocks. My grandfather's watch in its case read 12:12 and the other three said 5:11. Time had started up again, but I could tell my father was right: It would be a different kind of time we had to live in now; it would not be steady in the least and the winds would be cold in our faces against us all the way.

"Cora is trying to come down the hallway," my father said. "But it is dark and she can't find the switch and she is frightened. If you and I don't go to meet her halfway, she may not make it back to us. Are you ready to go with me into that dark hallway and bring your mother back here into the light?"

"No, I am not ready," I said. "But I'll go with you anyhow."

"Good," he said. "She's going to need us."

"We're going to need her, too," I said.